SOPHIE
JONAS-HILL
NEMESISTER

RBANE
Publications

urbanepublications.com

First published in Great Britain in 2017
by Urbane Publications Ltd
Suite 3, Brown Europe House, 33/34 Gleaming Wood Drive,
Chatham, Kent ME5 8RZ
Copyright © Sophie Jonas-Hill, 2017

The moral right of Sophie Jonas-Hill to be identified as the author of this work has
been asserted in accordance with the Copyright, Designs and Patents Act of 1988.

All rights reserved. No part of this publication may be reproduced, stored
in a retrieval system, or transmitted in any form or by any means, electronic,
mechanical, photocopying, recording or otherwise, without the prior
permission of both the copyright owner and the above publisher of this book.
All characters in this book are fictitious, and any resemblance to actual
persons living or dead is purely coincidental.

A CIP catalogue record for this book is available
from the British Library.

ISBN 978-1-911129-30-1
MOBI 978-1-911129-32-5
EPUB 978-1-911129-31-8

Design and Typeset by Michelle Morgan

Cover by The Author Design Studio

Printed and bound by CPI Group (UK) Ltd, Croydon, CR0 4YY

urbanepublications.com

For my husband, Andy, my brother Ben and my
friend Martin, for their unswerving support and belief.

NEMESISTER

CHAPTER 1

THE HOUSE HAD something American Gothic about it, though nothing it was minded to share. Wreathed in bougainvillea, it regarded me with the air of one recognizing an unwelcome visitor. There should have been a rocker on the porch or an old dog with greying muzzle, but they were missing.

I stumbled forward, focusing on my feet in their worn canvas sneakers with the impression of toes ground into the pink fabric. Everything hurt and my head pounded like something inside wanted out. The shadow of the house brought the scent of the blooms and the sighs of a swamp; the first step creaked, the second moaned, then my hand secured the wooden pillar at the top of the stairs. I paused, then pulled myself up. I looked behind me, but there was only the road, a line drawn in the dust against an endless, ochre expanse.

I faced a pair of cobweb-covered boots lolling by the door, and heaved myself in past them, plunging from bright into dark. The boots made no obvious objection.

The room I entered was soaked through with the heat of the day and heavy with the stink of damp canvas. There was no source of light save for the open door, and at first the space was a blur of camouflage colours and indistinct, lumbering shapes rendered anonymous by my sun–blind eyes. I made the middle of the room, walking as if on hot coals and became aware of a chair-huddled table, something that might have been a couch and something that probably wasn't.

Panic gripped me, thundered in my head, as I groped in the dark of both room and subconscious. I knew everything but understood nothing from the giddying procession of images in my mind: red boots crossing a winter road, a hand on a steering wheel, the view from under a bed across a savannah of green carpet, pearl buttons on blue velvet, a brown dog barking.

I willed breath into my lungs and, as stars cleared from my vision, the room snuck into focus.

'Whoa, hey!' The man silhouetted against the yellow-white rectangle of the open door froze as I whipped round to face him.

'Keep back,' I demanded as the world spun out of focus again.

'Okay … whatever you say …' he said as his shadowed form sharpened into detail. 'Let's not be hasty now.' He made no move toward me but remained in the doorway.

I swallowed, my tongue swollen to a stone in my mouth. 'Okay, you stay … stay back.'

'I'm staying back,' he said. 'It's okay, I ain't gonna hurt you … no need to fret none.' He eased himself a step further into the room.

'I mean it, stop right there!'

'Okay … all right, darlin.' To my surprise he obeyed and raised his hands, gently patting the air between us. 'But you sure you wanna…'

As I stepped back, pain spiked through my side and the shock of it had me panting. I blinked as a black, glittering tide threatened to engulf my vision.

'I ain't comin' near you, all right?' The man moved slowly, purposefully; took two steps to his left and reached for one of the wooden chairs by the table. 'I'm just gonna take a pew here...' He sat down and brushed at his knees before he settled back. Tears burned down my cheeks but my vision cleared and his taut, hard features converged into a face. He ran his hand through his hair, a little of which sprang up at his temples.

'So ... what we gonna do now?'

'What's your name?' I asked, risking a step to my left and paying for it.

'You wanna ask me that, now?' he said, then smiled. 'Them that knows me ...' He coughed into his fist. 'Them that knows me, they call me Red. You know, you don't look so good.'

'Shut up.'

He raised his eyebrow. 'Maybe you wanna calm down a little here?'

I stepped backwards and my foot found the end of the couch. I pressed my shins against it, praying it would help me stand just a little longer.

'You sure you know how to use that thing?' I saw his eyes flick down. A gun – I was holding a gun, and had been for so long that it seemed fused to my hand, my fingers knotted round it. As I stared down, my arm began shaking treacherously; I gripped my left hand over my right, my pulse hammering in my head.

'You wanna find out?' I asked, staring at him but seeing only the gun.

'I'm happy to take your word on it, only...' He leaned a little to his right. 'Only looks to me as if you've been shot already, so I'm not convinced that you do.'

'Shut up, I mean it, shut ...' My breath was coming faster, harder, lungs heaving. Trying to keep the gun trained on him, I risked a glance at my side. In the second I looked, Red lunged forward.

He'd grabbed my wrists and yanked my arms up above my head

before I'd even thought about screaming. He ripped the gun from my hand, turned me about and clamped his arms round me. Pain lit me up, blazed through my ribs and punched the breath from my body. I went limp and dropped to the floor but he went with me and broke my fall. I heard the gun impact seconds before I did.

'Get the fuck off me,' I said, trying to twist from under him.

'Just you hold on.' He had me on my back and twisted my hands together, pinning them above my head. 'You need to hold still,' he demanded, his face inches from mine, knees either side of me. 'You come in here wavin' that gun, what d'you expect? Jesus, darlin', you gotta remember who's you shootin' at.'

'Who the hell's that?' I asked.

He huffed a dry laugh. 'You're a piece of work and no mistake. Now look …' He shifted position. 'I'm gonna let you go now, so take it easy.' He grinned. 'You look fit to faint anyhow –you's in a mess, girl.'

He let go. I struggled to get a grip on the floor, my hands scrabbling against damp boards for purchase, but pushing against the floor hurt like hell.

'Get away from me!' I managed to get up on my elbows, dragging, willing myself away from him. He grabbed at me and I flinched sideways but he let me go at once.

'Just hold on … look – we don't need this shit, now–' He snatched up my gun, and when he was sure I'd seen he was holding the barrel between thumb and forefinger, he clicked open the chamber. His face registered surprise. 'Goddamn it, you were bluffing all along!' He laughed, then with deft movements he disassembled the weapon and tossed it aside. 'Whatever, see, I ain't aiming to hurt you none, okay? Let's just calm down now, shall we?'

I propped myself up, the last dregs of my adrenaline burning through my limbs and stealing sensation from my fingers.

'What is this place?' I asked and swallowed hard.

'This? Just a fishing lodge.'

'Is it your place?'

He shrugged. 'Sure, it's mine.'

'It is?'

He bent over me again. 'Look, you gotta let me take a look at you. What in the hell you done to your face?'

'Don't touch me!' I jerked right, and the throbbing in my head turned vindictive in revenge for the sudden movement. I slumped back against the floor, screwed my eyes shut and forced my mouth to bite back a scream.

'Hey!' I felt him move closer, felt him get hold of me and turn my face to his. 'Hey, you still with me?' I looked once I had the scream under control, pressing my back against the floor and pushing against the pain. 'Don't you pass out on me here.' He adjusted position to look into my eyes. Desperate not to meet his gaze, I clamped my jaw shut again and tried to thrash free of his grasp. The effort overwhelmed me; my head fell back into his hands and I let my eyes roll shut.

'Hey, you ain't checking out on me, not yet. Focus, ya hear, focus. Now, tell me your name, come on, say your name, say your name!' I laughed, the sound breaking free involuntarily. Anything, he could have asked me anything, but the last thing I could have told him was my name.

'My name ...' My mouth stretched into a grin despite everything, my lips dragging on my teeth. Barking dog, under the bed, little pearl buttons.

'Your name ... shit, count for me ... count for me!'

'One, two, three, that do you?'

'Good, so what's your name ... what the hell's your name?'

'I don't know my name!'

'Mercy ...' he said as the darkness seeped back into my vision. 'What on God's green earth ... you expect me to believe that?' He tilted his head, one eyebrow arched as he frowned. 'What you saying ... you got no memory of your name?'

'No name, no rank, no number, sir!' I laughed and he let my head fall gently back to the floor. We looked at each other, and for one, desperate, joyful moment, I really thought he might tell me who I was.

'How ... unfortunate.' He shook his head. 'Well, darlin', whatever the hell's you about ...' He chuckled, but the sound fractured before it reached me. He seemed to be moving away, taking the world right along with him. 'That must have been one hell of a bump on your head.'

'Please,' I said, my hands flinching against the floor. I tried to sit up again, but I could barely lift my head. It seemed I'd nothing left but to rely on the kindness of strangers. 'I've got to get out, I've got ... I've got to go, please!' Dark brown and heavy, fatigue slunk through my limbs as my strength bled out from my fingers into the swamp, sucking and snatching at me from beneath the floorboards. When Red spoke again, his voice was indistinct, no more than the murmur of the dank earth below.

'You ain't going nowhere. Seems to me you oughta close up them pretty eyes now, get yourself some sleep.' But I'd already closed my eyes, pretty or otherwise. As a sucking, glittering blackness pulled me into the quicksand of the day, I tried one last time to surface, but my mouth filled with dust-dry words which choked me.

'You just lie back there, I'll look out for you. Seein' he never did."

Before I could ask, unconsciousness embraced me and his voice spiralled into darkness.

I had to get to ... Paris. Paris? I had to get to ... Paris?

CHAPTER 2

I RAN.

Dry grass whipped and snatched at my legs, my breath came hard and fast, rattling in my lungs. The sky was a glass blue expanse above me, then I was hit and it tumbled down around me. I was Chicken Licken and the sky was falling in. I struggled to wake, straining against a dream that would not leave me; aware I was calling out through layers of heavy sleep. I fought as if it were a cocoon that smothered me, clawing and tearing at the stuff clogging my mouth, my eyes. I thought I broke free, but my memory unravelled before I could reach it and slipped through my fingers into darkness. I tasted cinnamon and sandalwood; generations of perfume on an old fur coat which wrinkled my nose in recognition. I was billowed, buffeted and spun as translucent as silk, then I heard a voice.

'Some men must do evil,' it said. 'But not all become evil. Those that do, may still chance on good. Be sure as not to let the devil know your name, ma Cherie.'

Then, the strand broke.

The weight of the dream rolled off me and I sat up and scanned the room, aware of my breath in my lungs. The air was heavy with heat, and a dirty yellow light. I was on the couch, in the room, in the house, in the swamp, light pouring through the open door in front of me, and through a naked window blinking by its side.

I'd been covered with a blanket. I threw it off and relief flooded over me when I discovered I was still fully dressed. However pretty he'd thought my eyes, he'd kept his hands to himself. Or bothered to dress me afterwards.

Next to me I saw a side table, its missing drawer leaving a slot grinning up at me. On it was a glass of water, with the dismembered revolver placed ostentatiously by its side, a peace offering? I snatched up the glass and drank; it was glorious, but the shock of it jolted me and I gasped and spluttered.

'Good morning.' The laconic voice came from over my shoulder. I flinched round, grimacing at the movement's pain. 'You wanna take that a little easy now, give yourself time to swallow.' He smiled. 'I hope I didn't wake you, when I came in just now?'

'I was awake already,' I said and cleared my throat.

'You slept most like the dead,' he said. He was holding a wrench with a rag wrapped round it. 'Insensible.'

'I should get going.' I swung my feet onto the ground but they burned as they touched the wood, cool though it was.

'Going?' He frowned, working the rag over the wrench. 'I suppose it ain't that early, though I've always been an early riser. My mama said it's the southern climate, makes one rise with the dawn and take something of a siesta in the heat of the day. An army life behooves a man not to be a slug-a-bed.' He stopped moving the rag. 'I been up the morning already, seein' to the engine. We're getting well on for noon.'

My head wasn't pounding but it hadn't forgiven me yet. 'I need to get going, been here too long, I should …'

'Now just you hold on.' He took a step toward me. 'What sort of gentleman would I be, sending a lady off with no breakfast? Hell, I'd not treat my ex-wife so, and she did plenty more in the way of imposition.'

'Really, it's fine …' The word 'breakfast' had my stomach growling. 'You got a car?'

'Sure do.' He tilted the wrench in his hand. 'My old truck. Shame to say though, she was makin' a terrible fuss on the way over yesterday. I been under the hood a while, seems as she ain't prepared to play ball just yet.'

'No car?'

He grinned. 'Give me an hour or so more, sure that's all I need. As we find ourselves some forty miles from anything one might call …' he tilted his head to the side '… civilization, you best stop a while. Seein' as you're …' he pointed the wrench at me. 'Recuperating 'n' all.'

My fingers found the wound on my side, now swathed in gauze and Band-Aid. 'Did you touch me?' I demanded, backing away from him along the couch.

'Now just you hold on,' he said, holding out one oil-blackened hand.

'Did you touch me?'

'You were bleedin',' he said and jabbed his finger at me. 'You wanna ease up on me a little?'

I looked at my hand where it gripped the wad of bandage. It was grimed with dirt and sweat, my wrist swollen and ringed in filth. Beneath my fingers I saw the red-brown bloom of blood on my t-shirt.

'It's just a graze, not as deep as I feared,' Red said. 'Seems it just passed you over, much like the spirit of the Lord. Not that I reckon he were after you.' He grinned. 'He never misses.'

'So, what, you some kind of doctor?'

'Well, sorta. You're gonna have to forgive me for layin' hands on you, but it was that or let you bleed.' He took a step towards me. 'I don't claim to be no surgeon, but I seen my fair share of bullet wounds serving Uncle Sam, and done my turn with a field dressing. They say it's not what you know ... but what you remember that counts.'

'You call 911?' I asked, edging further down the couch.

'Oh, there ain't no phone here, darlin', that's why I like it. Man needs a space where he can think things out, once in a while.'

'I need to get going,' I said.

'You might wanna take another drink first.' He nodded toward the glass on the side table. I looked at the water and, glancing up at him, shifted back towards it and picked it up. 'You got no memory still?' He came a little closer. 'No idea what fate befell you down that dirt track?' He ran the cloth over the wrench again, as if he hoped to summon a genie.

'No,' I said. From his expression, this was not the genie he'd hoped for.

'Such a queer thing.' He held out his hand. Though it was dirty, I figured mine was worse.

'I'm sorry,' I said, relenting enough for a brief handshake as I drank.

'No need to apologize, sure I'll forgive you.' He walked back to the kitchenette and slung the wrench onto the sink. He ran water and began washing his hands, whistling through his teeth. The water and the noise of washing sounded like heaven; my skin, choked with dirt and raw with sweat, crawled under my clothes. I drained my glass and set it down.

'Seems to me,' he said, turning back towards me as he dried his hands. 'Seems to me as you're the victim of some sorta incident.' My God, I thought, he spoke like he'd been baptized in the bayou and raised on syrup and sunshine. 'Perhaps the victim of a carjacking, as the modern parlance has it, judging by the mess of them shoes and your lack of transportation.' He smiled. I took him to be in his late thirties, perhaps early forties. Time had scored vertical lines down each cheek of his sun-worn face, but he looked well used rather than aged.

'You've been real kind, but I need to...' but where did I need to go? Paris? As I stared past him to the side exit, I couldn't shake the impression that I'd already arrived. 'Do you have a cell?' He reached into his back pocket and held one out.

'Dead, I'm afraid. I was aiming to charge it up in my truck but...' I looked at the phone in his hand but did not take it. 'Suppose you must'a mislaid yours ...' He licked his lips. 'Along with your memory. Still, once I get the truck goin' you can call whoever.' He put the phone away again. His eyes were pale, almost animal in their intensity. 'This place here's something of a weekend retreat. A bolt-hole, if you will, for fishing and suchlike. Normally, its very isolation is a ... a boon to me, but it has its limitations.'

'So, we're kind of stuck here,' I said, glancing toward the open door again.

'Just a few hours, that's all.' He scratched his nose. 'Listen, I'm gonna fix us some food, call it breakfast if you like. I'm hungry even if you ain't. You could even get a shower, if you want?' he asked. 'The facilities are basic, but this place has runnin' water. It's cold, but in this climate that don't matter. One thing we have in these parts, is an abundance of heat.'

A shower sounded like the nearest thing to heaven this side of the grave.

'I can wait, thanks.'

'As you like darlin',' he purred. 'But if you change your mind, I can lend you something to put on. I haven't much in the way as would suit you, but I can let you have an undershirt and pants, seein' as you ain't a whole lot shorter than I. Anyway, seems ladies do dress in a most masculine style these days.'

'I'll bear that in mind.'

He shrugged his shoulders and looked away from me, as if self-consciously breaking his gaze. 'There's a mirror upstairs. You might care to take a look at that …' He indicated his forehead with spidery brown fingers. 'Substantial blow to your head.'

I raised my hand and encountered swelling and pain. 'Yeah, no shit.' It hurt to frown. It hurt more to remember; I concentrated on a whole kaleidoscope of nothing, while he went back into the kitchen.

'You'd care for coffee? It's only instant, 'fraid my supplies are limited. I was not …' He opened a cupboard above the stove and closed it again. 'Not expecting to entertain.' I flexed my feet tentatively as I watched him locate a kettle, a jar of coffee, a large skillet and mugs. He'd decided I was staying for breakfast, and the pain in my feet made it difficult to argue with him.

'You got my shoes?' I asked.

'Shoes … what's left of them's by the door here.' He drummed a teaspoon on the lid of the jar. 'No milk, I'm sorry to say, but I like mine black.'

I got up, moving cautiously, testing the extent of my injuries and walking on the sides of my feet. The place seemed smaller than yesterday; the kitchen little more than an offshoot of the main room, balanced by the wooden staircase.

'That's fine, I take mine black too,' I said. Red looked up from the stove with a crocodilian smile.

'I dare say as you do.' He licked his lips and turned away, so he didn't see the smile that tweaked at my lips.

I bent and cautiously retrieved my shoes. His assessment of

them was generous; they were little more than laces and holes, the soles walked clean away. It seemed I really was on my uppers. I returned what remained of them to the corner of the kitchen and leant against the doorframe. I watched him work, trying to glimpse what was concealed in the kitchen drawers.

'I don't claim to be much in the way of a chef …' A halo of blue fire erupted under the kettle at his touch. 'My mother was the real cook in our family, when she was minded to send the maids to bed.' He paused by a plastic cool box. 'It surprises you to hear we had maids when I was a boy?'

'Oh, no, it doesn't …' I was only half listening to his words; the sound of them was enough. I could have eaten that voice off a spoon.

He smiled. 'I'm not always as you see me here. This place is something of a refuge for me. A place of …' He took out bacon and eggs. 'A place of discovery.' He flicked the gas on under the skillet and added bacon, its fat moistening the iron surface. My stomach howled and gnawed in protest, hunger making me giddy.

Focus.

'We learned a thing or two, when we was serving Uncle Sam. How to cook eggs on the hood of a truck, that sort of amusement.' He turned the bacon and picked up an egg. 'I cooked this for my wife – I was married once, you understand, but serving the flag is not kind to the state of marriage.'

'I'm sorry.' I watched as he cracked the egg.

'Still nothin' you got to be sorry about, not that anyhow.' The egg turned from glass to porcelain as it hit the pan. I shook my head. 'By your accent, I'm guessing you're a long way from home.' He flipped the bacon and turned toward me. 'I'm accustomed to calling a lady Ma'am and it don't bother me none, but perhaps I might offer you a temporary name, until you're … re-acquainted with yours?'

'I guess,' I said, a chill warning prickling down my spine as he came closer. I had the unnerving sensation that he meant to touch me, or take hold of my hand, and I was not sure what I would do if he did, or if I would find it wholly repulsive.

'I had an aunt once, you bring her to mind, not that she was as well formed as you ...' He chuckled. 'But when I knew her she had no memory also, so maybe that's why I light on her ...Margarita?' His gaze flickered intently over my face.

'Sorry?'

'Margarita, her name was Margarita, as in the drink. She were partial to one or two, in her day.' He watched me as if trying to tell the time from an unfamiliar clock. 'I like 'em easy,' he said.

'Easy?' I swallowed, the smell of cooking flooding my mouth. I could see the pulse in his neck; the hard, spare muscle of his chest under his tight grey shirt. 'I've always preferred them easy, my eggs. How d'you take them ... Margarita?'

I inhaled the scent of him, made glorious mixed with the smell of breakfast. I met his gaze and released my smile.

'Hard. I like mine hard.'

'Hard?' His eyes flinched at the word.

I met his gaze, stared him full in the face. 'Real good and firm.'

He looked down, something lazy and eager playing over his lips, pulling them into a grin. 'I best go see to the pan.' He turned on his heel and flipped a kitchen cloth over his shoulder in the manner of a short-order cook. 'Go sit at the table.' He got out two plates. 'Be ready in a moment.' He smiled his crocodile's smile.

When he set the food down, I found I was so hungry I'd eaten half before I looked up. I swilled a mouthful of coffee.

'Good to see a lady enjoying her ham and egg,' he said.

'Thank you ...' I swallowed more bacon. 'For the food. I'll get out of your hair soon as I can.'

'About that.' He smiled over his coffee. 'Seems I've done a little more to my old truck than I'd intended.'

'What's the problem?' I set my fork down.

'Nothin' one could name. Be another hour or so, I hope.' He shrugged. 'Can't always tell with these things, and I don't have all the tools a man might want.'

'I could walk,' I said, though I doubted I could do so for more than a mile. He raised an eyebrow and tilted his head.

'On those poor little shoes? You've walked them through to the sole, Margarita, thin as prison gruel.'

'Well …'

'But don't you fret none,' he said brightly. 'I'll get right back to it. Maybe you'll assist me, turn her over for me? Can't claim to be much of a mechanic, but I can claim to be mighty persistent.' Red stood up and carried his plate and mine into the kitchen and I watched him tip the cutlery into the sink. Sure, I'd give him a hand. I wanted to see what was out there.

The ground out back was dry and desiccated and with the skin on my feet as sensitive as a newly peeled blister, I moved with geisha's steps, feeling faintly ridiculous as my hesitant, ladylike progress had me sweating. Though it was dry above, I had the strong impression this was just a deceptive crust, and that if I were to dig only a little deeper, wet, black mud would boil up from under my feet

'Best find yourself somewhere cool,' Red advised as he began considering his eviscerated truck. 'I've got a few things to do 'afore I need you, and you don't wanna catch no sun, not with that bump on your head.'

Shading my eyes I glared around, as if the world I knew was hiding from me just out of spite. The only barrier in the landscape was the curved edge of the river. The back of the house was much the same as the front: grey-green boards and blinded windows. I saw that the main room where we'd eaten could have opened out this way, but what once might have been French windows had been covered over with clapboard in place of glass, making the side door the only other exit – improvements designed to make your average redneck cannibal feel right at home.

I turned my back on the house and inched towards the river, where the ground softened nearer the water. There was a single, tangled tree at the side of a boathouse, its roots exposed to air thick with the whine of insects. Only our side of the river was defined; the other bled into marsh fused with wiry grass and shrub.

The tree gave scant shade and the sun pounded almost spitefully on my head, so I made my way tentatively to the boathouse. It had no door, its entrance a black rectangle opening in the sun-dried wood. I saw a walkway no more than eight feet long, water lapping either side. It was invitingly cool.

The thin film of moisture that clung to the jetty was kind to my feet as gloom embraced me, the caress of the shade almost indecent. There were three wooden posts along one side of the walkway, but I ignored them and raised my arms as if on a tightrope. I inched forwards on the sides of my feet, enjoying the shiver of cold air from the water.

When I got to the end, I curled my toes over the edge of the last plank before I looked down. The river was a gelatinous black. I watched my reflection materialize in its depths and become a phantom, no longer anchored by memory or comprehension. I yearned to walk across the inky surface and have it kiss my feet better, my crawling, filthy skin aching to be clean. As I stared, my feet seemed to slip away, as if already descending on their chosen path. The world closed down until it was nothing but a beautiful black jewel of water. I smiled, my heart rate slowed as my body exhaled at last and the drip-drip of my fear dissipated. The world dissolved into cinnamon darkness.

'I'm not playing.'

'Why d'you always have to spoil everything, why must you be so difficult?'

I saw cards, counters on a board and her screwed-up little face under blond curls before she sent all of it tumbling over, furious, tempestuous with tears, stamping feet, everything falling, scattering, rolling away.

Then the jetty collapsed from under me.

CHAPTER 3

I THREW MYSELF BACKWARDS, heels striking wood as I ran in mid-air. Before I went down, the sodden planks of wood hit the water and great gouts of it sprayed over me. I screamed; my arm caught the post at the end which, made of stronger stuff than the jetty, remained firmly rooted in place. I slithered downwards, collecting slime and splinters.

Something grabbed me, caught me fast and held me between the devil and the deep blue sea. I gasped as my head rushed and whirled away from me and the light on the water danced and fractured into stars.

I cried out and sucked air into my lungs. A face was inches from mine, nothing but a black-eyed shadow mask against the light, a thing from a nightmare holding me above the water. Holding me, or pushing me under? A scream stuck in the back of my throat. I thrashed my legs until I got a foothold in the mud of the bank under the jetty, panic beating through me. With my free arm I grasped the jetty and pulled, my hip then my thigh snagging on the edge. As soon as I was able, I jerked my arm free, tasting nothing but brackish water and the metallic burn of adrenaline.

'Hey, what the—?' but I couldn't make sense of who or what spoke as the roar of the water bellowed in my ears. I yanked myself up to standing and hit out at the shadow, my feet in agony as they slid on the wooden floor. The rectangle of the doorway burned light and bright in front of me, then the shadow tried to get hold of me again.

'Get off!' I blurted, turned to face it, and saw it was Red.

'You want me to throw you back?' he said, hands up in surrender.

'I'm sorry, I …' A wave of embarrassment flushed over me, my skin prickling with heat against the chill of my sodden clothes. 'I didn't realize it was you,' was all I could manage, which sounded utterly ridiculous.

'Come on,' he said, and not demanding just who the hell I'd thought he was, put his hand on my shoulder to encourage me outside. 'This place ain't safe.'

'Oh Christ,' I said, looking back at the chaos I'd achieved. The last three planks were gone, leaving the end pillar in splendid isolation. Red dragged me out, our feet stumbling on the rough grass into the heat of the sun. I dropped to my knees and Red threw himself down beside me.

He waited for our breathing to calm, before he glanced sideways and asked, 'Shit, what was you doin' messing about near the water like that?'

'Fuck, I don't know …' I laughed. 'How the hell did … I'm sorry.'

'Don't sweat it.' Red lay on his back, shielding his eyes with his hand. There was now a grimy slick down the side of his pants where he must have hit the deck to rescue me. 'You gave me a hell of a turn there. Shit, you gotta be so careful round water. I never meant you to go swimmin' or nothing!' He laughed, shaking his head.

'I was just looking for some shade. Oh fuck … look at the state of me.'

'Lucky I saw you go in, I ain't much of a swimmer.' He sat up again, rubbing his arms. 'You sure got a knack of finding trouble.'

'How's the truck?' I asked, scuttling away from my humiliation.

'I could do with your help turning it over, if you ain't forgotten how?' He smirked. 'Or maybe you'd rather get that shower now?'

'I'll help you with the truck first,' I said, though my legs were now mired with black mud and I was soaked through with river water, just to complement the sweat, blood and tears.

'Are you sure? Seein' as what you just did to the boathouse, not sure I should let you near my truck.'

I stood up. 'Yeah,' I waved over my shoulder toward the boathouse. 'You'll have to let me know what I owe you for the damage, when we get back into town.'

Red's smile faded. 'All right.' He sniffed.

I climbed into the driver's seat of Red's flatbed truck, noting the film of dust over the windows. I drew my finger through it and glanced into the back. There was a tool bag, a spare tyre but no fishing poles. Red popped the hood and disappeared from view inside the mouth of the truck.

'Just give me a sec …' While he was out of sight, I peered into the glovebox and the door compartment, but there was nothing much to see other than the familiar detritus one might expect: an empty water bottle, sweet wrappers and an ancient workshop manual. I glanced through the passenger side window and something flashed in my vision, a square of mirror on the grass catching the light. It looked like a wing mirror. I glanced side-to-side to check, but the truck still had both mirrors in place.

'Okay,' Red said from inside the truck. 'Give her a go.' I turned the key and pressed the gas; the truck spluttered and whined but did not start. 'Again!' Nothing. After a third attempt, Red slammed the hood and came to lean on the edge of the door in the manner of a high school sweetheart.

'Fraid to say, my truck? She's still sulking for attention.' He turned his head and spat. 'You best wait inside, I've got some more tricks I can try.'

'Look, I … I better try and bandage my feet or something and walk it, I can't …'

Red shook his head. 'Forgive me, but I ain't keen on letting you go anywhere alone right now, not with you as you are.'

'Red, look, this has been real nice of you, but I need to get to a …'

'Well just you hold on.' Red's smile eased across his face. 'Did I not tell you my brother was due to stop by?'

'No,' I said levelly, watching him.

'Sure, just for a weekend's fishing and chewin' over the fat?'

'You didn't mention you had a brother.'

'No?' He smiled. 'Got an uncle in Kansas also. But my brother's due tomorrow with his vehicle and fresh supplies.' He sniffed. 'Now I've aired out the place a little. Sure he won't mind none taking you into town.'

'Your brother – he's coming tomorrow?'

Red shrugged. 'That's why I'm here. Spend a little time with my big brother. We don't see much of each other, so once in a while we hook up for a little bonding.' He jerked his head in the direction of the house. 'Kind of what this place is for, getting re-acquainted.'

I pressed my hands against the steering wheel, thumbs prickling. 'So, have I crashed your vacation then?'

'I suppose so, but don't you fret none. We try and get together when we can, don't get together much seein' as … darlin' … you okay?'

Have I crashed your … have I crashed?

'Sorry, it's nothing …'

'What?' He frowned.

Crash.

The sound of tyres on grey dirt, of velocity interrupted.

'What you doing, you crazy bitch?'

'Crashed,' I said, gripping the wheel. 'I remember a car, maybe ...' I closed my eyes and caught a whiff of something hot and metallic. 'A car, a crash, a ... a road accident?'

Red looked at me and nodded slowly. 'It's a possibility. I'd be surprised if there's been a road crew out this way in a good while, bound to be a few potholes.'

'Did you see a car?' I asked.

'When?'

'Coming here, you must have come here down the road, did ... did you see anything like a crash?'

'Well now ...'

'How long have you been here? It must have happened nearby for me to have walked.'

'I came up yesterday,' he said, glancing over to the boathouse and the tree. 'I don't recall anything ...' he straightened up. 'Anything unexpected.'

'You saw nothing?' I asked, but he was silent. In the space between us the marsh clicked and sighed under the ochre sky and the wind rattled the grass.

'Sure as I see you here.' Red sniffed. 'Ain't nothing down that road but a whole heap of empty. My wheels are the only ones for miles.'

'Until your brother gets here.'

He smiled. 'S'right. Or, unless I get her going.' He patted the hood of the truck.

'But,' I said and his smile dimmed. 'If I did crash ... what if it was the other way, I mean, further on past this place?'

Red considered what I'd said, his expression that of a man wondering how best to kill a wasp. 'I suppose so. Seein' as I came in from one way, guess I never checked t'other.'

'It could be that way then,' I said. 'I could go see?'

'You will not,' Red said and clapped his hands together, brushing dust off them. 'You, darlin', is still half asleep and all beat up with a bullet wound in your side. You's gonna stay right here.'

'No, really, I should go, if my car's there, maybe ...'

Red pulled a hurt face. 'Spending time with me is such a trial for you?'

'No, I didn't mean ...'

'Sure you didn't.' He ran his fingers through his hair and shrugged on his smile. 'Look, you go get a shower, and when you're done, if my truck ain't ready, we'll strap up your feet and go see, if you really got to.'

I got down from the truck. 'Yeah, I think I should, get out the way, you know? I'll go wash up,' I said and hobbled toward the kitchen door.

'You best close up the front,' Red said after me. When I glanced round at him, he shrugged. 'Not sure if this has occurred to you in all your considerations, even if you had cause to crash your vehicle all by yourself, someone else had cause to shoot you.' He grinned. 'Whoever it were, they might not be done with you yet. Wouldn't want some ungentlemanly type slippin' in while you're takin' a bath.'

I made it to the kitchen and stood in the gloom by the sink. I ran water into a glass, watching to see what Red did. The smell of river mud was an assertive undercurrent to my now-familiar perfume of sweat and blood, the whole concoction rising up around me as I lurked in the darkness. Red disappeared from my line of sight and then reappeared, picking at an engine part. I pulled the door to until it was standing half open and gave me a little cover. All I found as I opened cupboards and pulled out drawers was an old lamp, a couple of buckets and a mismatched collection of cutlery and plates, the dog ends of other kitchens. There were blades, but nothing grander than a butter knife. If my unknown shooter chose to disable Red, or if the man himself turned nasty, a dented potato masher would not be much use. I put my empty glass down by the sink. No matter how much I tried to fit him into the puzzle, I couldn't make Red into my shooter, though that didn't mean I'd trust him with a potato masher.

I closed up the main door as he'd instructed. There was a hasp and ring on both sides, and a large padlock hooked through the ring on the inside. I eased it out so I could flip the hasp over but then paused, padlock in hand. I didn't have the key, so although I fitted the arm of the padlock back into the ring, I didn't close it up. I felt safer not locking myself in right now.

I stood in the main room and let my gaze wander over its greying walls with their tidemark of rising damp, and the cancerous swelling of ceiling plaster in the corners. I felt as though I was trying to remember something in a world where everything had been long forgotten.

The staircase creaked on my way up to the landing. The first door was locked, though I gave it a push just to make sure it meant it. Its round, ceramic doorknob refused to budge. The door at the end stood open to reveal a mildewed bathroom, and a glance confirmed the other as a small bedroom where Red had, hopefully, spent the night.

I'd forgotten I'd no idea what I looked like, until I met the stranger in the bathroom mirror. Red was right, something had made an almighty mess of my forehead. Distracted by the geometric quality of the swelling, I almost forgot to check the bathroom door for a lock. There was one – though I doubted it would hold under a sustained attack.

The mirror doubled as the door to a shallow cabinet, which I opened to postpone facing my reflection again. It revealed two white shelves spotted with black mould, their paint peeling and coming off in flakes. There was an ancient tube of something curled up on the lower one, and next to it a medicine bottle. It was empty, but had once held a prescription for the relief of angina. The name on the label was almost gone, but I made out what could have been a Mr D-something. So Red had a heart condition? I wasn't convinced, even in the face of the medical evidence. Nothing for it then, but to look.

I closed the door. I was not a stranger, though I was unfamiliar. I saw my reflection as if I were both the observer and observed, like one does in a dream. I already knew my hair was short and dark, but I saw then that my roots were that sort of in-between brown and blond colour, dyed to blue-black at the tips. God, but my forehead really was a mess, the swelling at my hair line purple and angry looking, with a starburst of dried blood. I moved as if to touch it, but faltered as I looked into my eyes. They were brown, the sort people call hazel, and though I knew they would be, and that of course they were mine, there was something other about them; a sense that the face in the mirror, the gaze that met mine, was watching me as much as I watched it. I smiled, and my reflection smiled too, as if she knew something I didn't, as if she'd seen me across a room quite unexpectedly, and was amused to see I'd been invited to the same party. The light from the square of window was bright in the corner, and cast the space behind me into shadow. The longer I looked, the more the sensation grew that there was someone else there only in the mirror world, someone looking at me as he sat in the tub, arms up behind his head, long shadow-made limbs.

'Pop, pop, pop, firecracker! You's all fourth o' July.'

The words came to me with a rush of emotion. A smile grinned from my memory and sent me reeling back from the glass. I spun round, so sure he was there, only he wasn't. I was alone with the echo of those words trickling.

'Pop, pop, pop – firecracker!' And that smile, that smile; black, warm, all for me. It curled its way deep into my spine, and left me cold and shaking.

I strained for the words again, but they were gone and I couldn't remember who'd said them, me or my reflection. Paris … why did I have to get to Paris? I wasn't just a library with no autobiography section; the travel guides were also missing. I rubbed my face and looked down.

I was wearing track pants, which when new might have been pale blue with white piping along the seams, but were now unspeakable. They were not a style of garment that could take a lot of pocket stuffing, but when I stepped out of them, I ran my hands over the seat for the sake of argument. The left pocket crackled. I pulled out a folded piece of paper. It was a flyer for a bar, printed on black shiny stuff that was sufficiently water-repellent to have survived its soaking. It was printed with the image of a dancing girl sat in a martini glass, and written above in neon pink was the single word, PARIS.

I exhaled.

This was the PARIS, my Paris? A place labelled 'drinking, dancing and entertainment'? I frowned, disappointed. So, what? Was this just the last place I'd gotten drunk before driving out here to crash? There was an address, so if Red ever got his old truck running again, we could head out that way. Perhaps I'd left my purse, if I'd ever had such a thing. I re-folded the paper and put it on the edge of the basin, feeling none the wiser. Then I picked it up and put it back in my pants pocket, deciding against leaving it around.

I remembered Red's offer of jeans and an undershirt, but there was no sign of them on the rail beside the two utilitarian towels. If this was his idea of a weekend getaway, he was Spartan in nature; no four-ply double plush luxury for old Red. Then, seeing as he was a military man, maybe this was the charm for him, like going back to basic training?

I checked the lock again before I turned on the shower, then kicked my despoiled track pants hard against the bottom of the door. When I was sure it was jammed as tight as I could manage, I ripped off my bloodied, sweat-stained t-shirt and surrendered to the shower. The water was the simplest, most innocent pleasure I could have imagined, memory loss or not. I was convinced I could even hear steam rising from my feet as the water embraced them.

I was careful of the bandage Red had applied. Stained dark though it was, it was still tight to my skin and I didn't want to see what lay beneath just yet. I angled myself so that it was free of the water, and tried to wash around it. There was a Lilliputian bottle of shower gel on the side. I squeezed out what was left into my hands and worked it over my body, taking a perverse glee in the brackish sludge that washed down the plughole.

Crazy as it sounds, it was only looking down as I washed myself, one hand over the bandage, that I saw my hands for the first time, I mean, kind of really took in what they looked like. My nails were pink, bubble-gum pink, set with rhinestones and sharpened into talons. Now the filth that had encrusted them since I'd woken was gone, they looked startlingly bright against the bathroom tiles. Hooker's claws – a couple missing on my right hand and my real nails raw and stubby underneath, like shelled prawns.

The memory of them flashed behind my eyes, of me getting them done. I caught the echo of a smell, hot acrylic dust, plastic and acetone, and the whir of the pendant drill as it sharpened their points. I knew they were for a special occasion, because they really weren't my usual sort of thing. I could remember how it felt to watch my hands change, like slipping on the wrong gloves, and how I'd been talking all the time to the girl who sat opposite me, a white dust mask over her nose and mouth. She'd been nodding, and I'd talked, loud and fast, as if I was trying out a new voice, a rehearsal. I'd watched the girl as she worked and I talked, to see if she realized I was acting, sneaking a glance when she looked down at her tools, trying to gauge the impression I made on her. Then I made her laugh, a joke, something filthy – she laughed, mouth hidden behind her mask, eyes crinkling at their corners, dark eyes, make-up moist.

I shivered, and the vision receded, or became a memory again, a single picture fluttering alone in my darkness. I wiped the water from my eyes and looked down at my body as if it was someone else's, laid out for inspection against the slab of the wall. My bikini line was stripped bare, deforested. That wasn't me either, I was sure, not a wax job that severe, that punishing. I ran my fingers over the mound of my flesh, hardly a trace of stubble. And I'd applied fake tan too, and I knew I'd done it, or rather, it wasn't a professional job, because there were streaks at the top of my thighs, and its tobacco tone darkened clumsily over my knees.

I squeezed the last of the shower gel into my hand and gave my thighs a final scrub. An ounce of it might have gone a long way, but couldn't get my sort of dirty clean. I dropped it into the tub, closed my eyes and let the water run over my face. Had I been a girl in a glass, like some cocktail olive, served up skewered on a pole?

I became aware of a dry, musty smell: curled cinnamon and sandalwood. At first I thought it was the scent of the soap, but the perfume grew stronger and the hissing of the water seemed to recede.

'Be careful, little fish,' a voice whispered to me. 'Ya swim with a fisherman ...'

Laughter buzzed in my ears, rich and purple-gold and sweet, like a curl of honey from the pot. An image came to me: my hand holding a gun.

'What the hell you doin', you gonna shoot me now?'

It wasn't in the shack but somewhere else, somewhere bright and loud, music pulsing through my feet. I screwed up my eyes and pressed my head against the tiles, desperate not to force it,.

'What you doin' you crazy bitch?'

But the voice wound down the plughole with the dirty water, until it was nothing more than the gurgle and splash. In frustration, I gripped my hands together, screwed up my face.

'Not all men who do evil, become evil.'

I stepped out of the bath and wrapped myself in the towels, hugging them close as the floor seemed to lurch under my feet. I let my legs give way and knelt down, one hand on the floor to steady myself. My other hand spasmed, jumped, as if it meant to clutch at something, or as if I'd dropped something I'd be desperate to hold onto. Not the gun, though, a soft thing, a precious thing – pearl buttons on blue velvet? Then the ghost of the sensation melted into the cracked linoleum. I crouched, listening to my breathing come back under my control. The movement of the room subsided, then the fall of water from the shower grew loud enough to mask the rest of the world again. Whatever had come to me, had gone. I opened my eyes, and stood up.

The bathroom's single window was above and a little to the left of the toilet. From where I was, it showed me nothing but sky through the grimy glass, but I figured it might give me a new perspective on the world outside, if I got a little closer. I put one foot on the can, then stood up on it to grip the windowsill and peer out. I could see the side of the house and a whole lot of green, undulating swamp, bisected by the thin, grey road, running like a scratch across a marble tabletop. Directly below me, I saw Red's truck, hood still yawning open, then he came up for air from below it, wiping his hands on his jeans. He stood for a moment, absorbed with his work, while sunlight caught on a wing mirror on the ground and reflected off the windshield.

Had Red shot me? Paris, Paris, Paris – the word buzzed around my head like it was trying to find a way out, a fly caught against glass. The light made my eyes hurt. There seemed to be as little out there to help me remember, as there was in here, so I got down. Red was busy with his truck. He'd promised to take me into town when it was fixed, and I didn't want to interrupt the fixing, so decided to get the clothes myself, leaving the water running in the hope that the noise would cover my movements.

The house was never silent, but I had the feeling it was holding its breath as I stepped out onto the landing, oozing disapproval along with the damp from the walls. My spine tingled; how many hurricane seasons and rainstorms had this place lived through, how many more before it would give way to the inching, creeping wetness?

'I'll outlive you, whatever,' I promised it. The floorboard under my foot creaked as I moved forwards, as if it was sniggering behind my back.

The compact bedroom was sparsely furnished, the iron bedstead and skinny mattress spread with a thin sleeping bag. I looked over the banisters, checked the towels were as tight around me as I could make them, then went in.

There was a small case on a chair under the window and a narrow wardrobe with a grey suit hanging on its door. I read the label, not bad. I might not have remembered my name but I remembered this one. There were shoes by the suit, well-polished and well-heeled.

'I am not always as you see me here.'

I inhaled and the fabric smelled of aftershave and cigarettes. When I poked my fingers into his case, I found neatly folded clothes, shirts and pants. I deliberated for three whole seconds before I pulled out a pair of jeans and a white tank. Red could get angry with me, but I'd rather he did so when I wasn't naked.

Once dressed, I was going to leave, then I remembered the shoes and picked one up. They'd be big, but if it came to it, maybe I could stagger a few feet further down the road if I padded out my feet with his socks. They were nice quality, very well-heeled indeed, much too smart for a fishing trip.

I put the shoe down and pulled the mouth of the case open again. Where were the plaid shirts and cargo pants your regular weekend fisherman would wear? Sure, a fisherman would have some 501's and a couple of plain t-shirts in his bag, but what fisherman bothers to pack a suit? Did he intend dressing for dinner?

I patted the case into shape, stepped back to make sure it wasn't obvious that I'd searched it, and saw a pile of small change and a matchbook on the bedside cabinet, just like in every good detective story.

'Well, of course,' I said and picked up the matchbook. It was black and glossy, and when I turned it over, had a word printed on it, in neon pink script.

PARIS.

I snatched up the towels and made the bathroom in three strides, locking the door behind me. I leant against it, the noise of the shower roaring in my ears.

If Red wanted me dead, I would be. He could have pressed a pillow over my face while I lay on the couch and dumped my body in the swamp out back. If he knew me, if he knew who I was, he had a reason for not finishing me off and for not refreshing my memory. If he thought I still remembered nothing at all, maybe I'd buy myself time, until I actually did remember what the hell it was he wasn't telling me.

I needed a plan, I needed something - fuck, I needed to stop my heart racing and my stomach doing an adrenaline-powered three-sixty. I needed to get a grip. I looked up at the bathroom window, blinking at the bright, blue white square of it on the wall.

It exploded.

CHAPTER 4

I HIT THE FLOOR as the noise ricocheted through the bathroom, eyes closed as the shower of glass rained down around me. For an instant the world seemed stunned, then Red started shouting from downstairs.

'Margarita?' There was a second volley of shots, muffled and chaotic, then nothing. I got onto all fours, straining to hear something, anything, but everything was quiet save the hiss of the shower. My God, had they shot him?

Heart thudding in my throat, still on my hands and knees I inched the bathroom door open. The space beyond was dark, the only light falling from the open bedroom door onto the landing. Keeping low, I slipped out, hanging back from the banister railing. Shit, I cursed under my breath, I should have locked the front door, and where was Red, what was happening?

'Maybe they ain't done with you yet?'

I heard something, a crack against the background noise of shower and swamp. I listened against the dank heat, crouched at the top of the stairs, panic beating inside my chest. Nothing. I inched forward and peered through the banisters. Heart beating in the darkness, I felt the weight of my injuries drag on me, felt the spin and ache at the back of my eyes. Sweat prickled over my forehead and stuck strands of hair to my face; the house crackled around me, counting, waiting.

Then it came again – crack. Was that a footstep? Red would have called out, surely, or I'd have seen him by now? I gripped the banister; a child alone in a house that knew more than she did. Where the hell was Red?

Tick – snap – tick – it was nothing, it was the house, fidgeting over the swamp like it had ants in its pants, like it had a bee in its … a bee in its bonnet? A sound juddered through the space below and fear washed over me, had me white and sweating and clamping my hand over my mouth, to muffle my fear.

'Count to ten, count to ten, then he'll go away again. Make it through to twenty-one and you'll live to see the sun.'

Crack.

'You okay up there, darlin'?' Red's triangular face appeared below, framed in the space between the banister's uprights.

Relief flooded over me. 'Jesus, what's going on?' He motioned me to be quiet and come down. Christ, I thought, had he been there all along, moving through the space with hardly a sound, hardly a ripple?

Keeping my head bent, I scrambled to my feet and creaked down the stairs to where he was crouching. When I was close, he took hold of my arm and pulled me down onto the floor next to him, our backs to the wall a few feet from the front door. Peering over, I saw the kitchen door was shut.

'Okay?' he asked.

'What's going on?'

'Not sure yet.' He waved me to silence, finger up, his eyes scanning the gloom as we listened. All I could hear was our breathing and the house. Red started, his head snapped round and

I looked, but saw nothing.

'What?'

He shook his head. 'What happened up there, they took out the window?'

I nodded. 'Who is it?'

Red shrugged. 'Didn't hang around to ask. If someone's shootin' at you, they ain't usually much bothered 'bout introducing themselves.

'What happened?'

We inched a little further along the wall, both of us moving as if past a pack of sleeping dogs.

'I was just fixing myself a glass of water in the kitchen,' he said. 'You lock the front door?' I nodded. 'Heard the window get shot, just about to stick my head out when the damn windshield went out too. Like I said, when someone's shootin' at you, you get hid an' don't ask why.'

'Did you see anyone?'

Red raised his finger, then got slowly to his feet. Back to the door he paused, risked a glance through the window, then ducked down beside me again.

'Nothin' out front.' He looked sideways at me. 'I was wrong, you ain't good at findin' trouble, trouble's good at finding you.'

'You think they're after me?'

'Damned if I know.' Red got up and moved toward the couch, head down. He took hold of one end. 'Hate to impose, but if you don't mind?' It was surprisingly heavy but between us we got it against the front door.

'Three possibilities,' Red said, keeping his voice low. 'They've gone, or they're waiting.'

'You said three?'

Red grinned. 'Or they're 'bout to walk in.'

He didn't need to ask twice. Together we blocked the kitchen door with the table; then Red dragged the kitchen cupboard across it, spilling out its dented ephemera as he dragged it in place.

We stood and listened again, my spine bowstring taut. The light from the window Red had uncovered in more optimistic times bore through the gloom and burned a square on the floor behind me. Then I saw Red was looking at the staircase.

'What's that noise?'

'Shower … oh!'

'Shit darlin'!' I realized why he'd bolted, and followed him to the foot of the stairs. He banged into the bathroom, re-emerging a moment later.

'Ain't no more than a trickle.'

'Shit, I'm sorry.'

'Never mind that now. Maybe it ain't all gone …' halfway down the stairs he paused, squinting through the window, then he raised his hand to shade his eyes and frowned.

'What?'

'Light caught something out there, moving on the road. Car?' He looked down at me. 'You ain't got another gun, do you, tucked away in your purse'?'

'No.'

He came back down the stairs. 'Shame, ain't much here if it comes to it. Might still be nothing, though.'

'Someone's out there,' I said. Red nodded. 'But they haven't tried to get in yet?'

'No, they ain't.' He walked over to me, his shoulders hunched, moving with little noise despite the uneven floor.

'So what, they've gone or …' He sat down on the couch.

'Or they're waiting.' Well, two out of three left then, I guessed.

We waited too, side by side, Red twitching his head from time to time, a dog with his ears pricked up. With the doors closed, the heat had built up in the house, and Red's t-shirt was stained with sweat, a dark line spreading down his chest.

'You think they've gone now?' I asked, unable to bear the whole minutes-passing-like-hours thing.

'Depends who they are. You wanna poke your head out the door and see?' He sniffed.

'You think they're after me?' I said, watching his face as he stared at the floor. He drew breath through his teeth, and stretched his lips back into a grin before he looked at me.

'Don't forget, there are two of us here.' He grimaced. 'Might just be a car full of drunk kids. This place is in the middle of a whole heap of nothin' now called a wildlife preserve or some such, and there ain't many as comes this way for much but birdwatching. Even so, you'll always get kids looking for space to misbehave, let off steam.'

'With guns?'

'You are from back east after all,' he said and smiled. 'Welcome to the South, darlin'.'

'If it was just a car full of drunk kids, then they're probably gone by now, right?' But Red didn't look convinced by this. 'You don't think it was a car full of drunk kids, do you?'

'I'm open to suggestions.' He glanced down at my side, raised his eyebrow. 'You've been shot, someone shoots up my truck. We know someone don't like you, or me.' He met my gaze. 'Or us both.' He looked at his watch. 'Okay.' He got up. 'Let's go see how the land lies shall we?'

'You think?'

'Gettin' bored sitting on my thumbs,' he said, and stood up on the couch, his profile black against the light. Looking up at him, I could see the arc of his spine, the talons of ribs beneath his shirt.

He looked compact, I thought, the way a greyhound looks sleek under the velvet of its fur – all that power just waiting for the crack of a starting pistol.

'So …' he said and I jumped, then pretended I'd been lost in thought. 'Why don't we shift that table? Take a look what's out there. You wanna stick your head out, or shall I?'

'I dunno, you still think they're shooting at me?'

'You think they care?' He got down again. 'I might just be gettin' paranoid here; I was inside when they started shootin', so it's possible they just saw an old shack and an old truck and took a shot, didn't bother to stick around and see what they hit.'

'I guess.'

'Well, if they're after you, then I reckon they won't be so keen to take a shot at my grizzly old mug. And if they're after me, well … won't make no difference.'

'Why?'

He didn't answer at first but walked over to the kitchen and took hold of the cupboard, waiting for me to join him. When I did, he said, 'Well, 'cause if they're after me, I'm already dead.'

'Who the hell's after you?' I asked, and leaned against the cupboard. Together we eased it back then moved the table, ploughing it through the drift of spoons. Red straightened up and looked at me.

'Later …' he muttered. Then he crouched down by the door, back to the wall. 'You're gonna stand behind the door, then you're gonna ease it open slow, and stay right behind it, okay?'

'Fine by me.' I got hold of the hasp and swung the door inwards, keeping behind it as Red advised. As the door opened, a line of light ran between the hinges, a gold thread in the dark. Red took a moment to check his cover, then slipped out. I moved to watch him, my eye to the hinge crack.

He kept low, moved like he knew what he was doing. His truck was a few feet away, but having only the crack of the hinge to look through, I couldn't see what state it was in. I saw Red make its shadow before he too was obscured from my view, and as far as I could tell, nobody shot at him, no black-clad assassins wrestled him to the ground. I closed my eyes and listened, fatigue washing over me as I struggled not to ask what the hell was going on yet again. I opened my eyes as the line of light flickered; Red was back inside and he closed the door, softly pulling it from my fingers. He was carrying a plastic water bottle, scant reward for his bravery.

'You're alive then,' I smiled.

'Seems so.' He leant against the door. Now it was closed we were in near darkness; what light there was licked over the whites of his eyes. 'Truck's fucked,' he said. 'Shot out the tyre along with the windshield.' He twisted the cap off the bottle and drank. I was close enough to see the water pulse down his throat, and watch a drop trace a line down his neck as it escaped his mouth. I slunk back and leant on the edge of the kitchen sink. Red lowered the bottle and wiped his mouth. 'Forgive me, but after all that, I'm none too keen on changing the tyre in full view of the road.' He held the bottle out to me.

I put my hand over my eyes. I felt sick, heavy and was aware my hands were trembling. Somehow I'd enough energy left to take the bottle from Red and limp from the kitchen to throw myself on the couch, back to the door. I swilled water into my mouth and tilted my head back, holding the liquid in my mouth as I closed my eyes.

I heard Red move into the room, then heard a chair scrape across the wooden floor as he pulled it out and sat down.

'If it makes you feel any better, reckon they've gone for now.'

I swallowed the water but did not look at him. I heard him sniff.

'Maybe they were just tryin' to see if this place was empty or not, looking to see if we'd run? Kids with an ants' nest.'

'I'm sick of not knowing,' I said under my breath.

'Well.' I heard his chair creak. 'I'll give you a moment, I need to freshen up a little.' I heard him walk away, then opened my eyes to watch him go. I breathed deeply and took another swig of water as he ascended the stairs and disappeared into the bathroom. I thought of his reaction to the shot-out window, imagined him throwing himself down beside the truck for cover, and that made me think of the shot-out windshield. If, of course, it really was shot-out. I focused on the kitchen door and the mess of scattered debris. He'd rather insisted he go out there, hadn't he? Maybe that wasn't just his gentlemanly concern for my wellbeing.

I got up and slipped across the room to the kitchen door. Outside, the light burned my eyes as I blinked them clear. The sky above was blue, but the day was turning toward the evening; something in the light had a sense of gathering in. There was the truck, and just as Red had said, its windshield was shattered, the spiderweb of glass somehow still clinging to its frame. A second step outside, and I felt dangerously exposed, my clean shirt a bright, white target. I glanced back at the truck, which even if I could magically start it, was now missing a tyre, according to Red. Then I shaded my eyes and scanned the horizon, the boathouse, the road, the alien landscape that was my world, seeing nothing, imagining everything.

For all that I wanted to run, for all I was sure I had to leave, something stronger was nagging at me, telling me that I was meant to be here. Like the 'PARIS' matchbook in Red's room, like the fear that someone was out here, waiting, watching; like the half-remembered snatches of voices that seemed to come, if only I could be quiet, if only I could stop trying to make them. I looked up at the house, its broken window the blinded eye of a Cyclops. It knew, I was sure of it. It knew why I was here and who I was, and it mutely challenged me to find out. I looked at the road one last time, hoping against the gathering dusk that I'd see a car, but there was nothing save for a flock of white birds scratching across the sky, heading home to roost.

'All right,' I told the house, squinting up at it again. 'Let's see what you got for me.'

When I re-entered, Red was on the landing. He was stripped to the waist, an undershirt thrown over his shoulder and his sleeping bag rolled up, tucked under his arm. He sauntered down the stairs and paused at the bottom, dropping the bag on the floor.

'You see anything?' he asked. 'Anything that alarms or ... appals you?'

'No, it's just like you said.' I closed the door, snuffing out the light behind me. 'Looks like we're not going anywhere today.'

Red took a few steps closer and stopped to pull his shirt on over his head, then paused with it halfway down his body. 'The kitchen padlock's there, might be wise for you to lock up. Just in case we're wrong.'

'Wrong?'

Red grinned. 'If they do intend on coming back, don't wanna let them in without a struggle, do we?' Then he pulled down his shirt.

The padlock was on the edge of the sink. I reached for it and felt its weight in my hand. I brushed the key jammed into its lock, then fitted it into the hasp on the door and clicked it shut. I withdrew the key and set it down on the kitchen counter. I kept my forefinger on it a moment longer, trapping it against the pitted wooden surface as if it might scamper away. There I was, all locked in, and I'd done it all by myself.

'Best make ourselves comfortable,' Red said as he came toward me. He glanced down at the counter where I'd placed the key. 'All right with you, darlin'?'

I pressed my finger harder against the key and slid it a few inches forward. 'Sure.' I smiled at him. 'I'm fine,' I lied and took my hand away.

CHAPTER 5

'WELL, ALL'S NOT LOST,' Red said. 'All we gotta do is wait for the mornin' and my little brother.' He took the water bottle from me.

'Isn't he older than you?' I said as he unscrewed the top, though I honestly could not remember what he'd said.

'Sure, but he's a head shorter.' He grinned. 'Really riles him up when I call him that.'

'What's his name again?'

Red sipped the water. 'Robert.' He ran his tongue over his teeth.

'Red and Robert. I gotta say, your Daddy sure liked his 'r's.'

'Reckon he did.' Red tapped the bottle on the edge of the sink. 'Best make this last; there ain't much in the tank and I doubt it's all that clean anyhow. I'm gonna take the weight off. Care to join me, shoot the breeze?'

'I guess, while we're waiting for Robert.'

'Don't you fret, he ain't one to be tardy. Now, I might just be misremembering this, but I'm sure I read somewhere ...' Red turned on his heel and opened the cupboard I'd placed the key on. 'That if a person's trying to recall what's been forgot, then it's best just to keep on talking.' He crouched before the cupboard and peered inside. 'They do say that if one gives the conscious mind something to bother itself with, what's lost ...' He closed the door without producing anything. 'What it's lost just kinda bobs up.' He frowned and then tapped the side of his nose twice with his finger. 'Maybe if we were to talk awhile, it might bring that something to mind?' He reached up, opened the high cupboard opposite the stove and took out a bottle and two stumpy shot glasses. 'Ha, knew I'd seen it earlier.' He grinned. 'May have myself a little, seein' as we ain't in a hurry. Join me?'

I inhaled. 'Not sure I should, seein' I'm so messed up.'

'Good for what ails you.' He shrugged. 'Besides, we ain't overburdened with supplies, might have to be a frugal supper.' He reached in again and held out a bag of chips. 'Touch of whiskey might oil the wheels, as it were.'

'Sure, why not?' I dug my hands into the pockets of the jeans I'd taken from Red's case, and walked into the main room.

Red gave me the couch, though I wasn't sure if he was deliberately putting himself between me and the kitchen door, or being a Southern gentleman. He settled back on his sleeping bag, leaned against the seat of the couch and popped the chips.

'This seems to be it as far as supper goes,' he said, crunching a mouthful. 'Can't say as I care that much for chips, but hell, it's not the food but the company as makes a meal.'

'So what, you ain't gonna catch us a catfish?' I said and stretched out my legs until my feet were behind his head.

'Ahh well, 'bout that.' He kicked off his boots. 'I must 'fess up here, I ain't really all that for fishing and the like, that's kind of my brother's ... my brother's amusement.'

'So what, this is his place then?'

Red set the bottle down on the floor and unscrewed the lid slowly.

'Nope, nope, though I ain't had it long. There's quite a story to that, seein' as I sort of won it in a poker game, but perhaps that's for another time.'

'You won this place?' The sunlight square had receded across the boards towards the back wall, picking out the French windows fossilized in clapboard. 'What the hell did you put up?'

'Oh don't be like that, I kind of like it.' He set the cap next to the bottle. 'Sometimes a man needs a place where the phone don't ring and the walls don't stream twenty-four hour news, somewhere he don't got to be ...' he poured a golden thread into the shot glasses. '... he don't got to be found, if he don't wanna be.'

He held out one of the glasses to me, and against all my better judgment, I took it. Hell, nothing I'd done so far struck me as a good idea, not what I could remember nor what I couldn't.

'Bottoms up,' he said and we drank. I let the liquid moisten my lips and it crept hot and smoky into my mouth.

Red drank his and shifted a little, arranging the sleeping bag so he could look up at me.

'Course, one don't need no pole to catch a fish.' The gloom of the hot wet room softened his face nearly to a silhouette. He laid back, left hand behind his head as he leant against the couch.

'No?'

'Nope. Sure I've seen a man stretch out on the bank of the river, and dip his arm in, hardly makin' a ripple. Then he lies there for a while, lettin' the river kinda get used to him.' Red closed his eyes. 'He just waits, bides his time. Catfish are wary things, but with him just sittin' there ...' He looked at me again. 'After a while, they kinda forget. Some get so used to his hand, they just snuggle right up to it.'

'Snuggle?' I pursed my lips.

'Sure thing, fish snuggle, they snuggle right up once they got used to you ...' He drew his knee up and rested the hand that held his glass on it. 'They get real comfy, if you take your time with them.' I leant against the arm of the couch, gingerly stretching my side as far as I could before angering my wound.

'What about your brother?'

'My brother?' Red sipped his whiskey.

'Yeah, your brother, that's how he catches fish?'

Red grinned. 'My brother – no, he ain't so cunning. He just uses fishing poles, darlin'.' The grin melted into the darkness of his face. 'He don't have the touch.' I sipped the whiskey, wondering which one of us was the fish.

'What 'bout you?' Red leant forward to open the bottle again. 'You reckon as you have a family? Someone missing you?' I inhaled, feeling the torpor of the warmth and the whiskey settle into my limbs. It wasn't that I couldn't remember them, more like they were in another room, sunlit and far away. It was as if I pressed my ear to a keyhole and tried to recreate my history from a snatch of laughter or the sound of feet running on a wooden floor.

'I'm not sure. I mean, I know I must have, I guess?' Something was forming in my mind, moving like it might have woken but then fell back into a dream. 'I think I can see things, but like they're far away, down the wrong end of a telescope, you know?'

'You do have a way with words,' he said, but I wasn't listening.

'I'm sure I had sisters, and a brother ... one brother, older? And a ... a sister, two sisters, hell, maybe more. No one sister, I'm sure, only—' I laughed, and then my laugh died away. 'One ... one I remember ... perhaps?' The room around me faded to monochrome, I could barely see Red's face as it waited in darkness, just a slice of light on the edge of his cheek, then that too faded.

'She had ... a name. I mean, I know she must have a name, but there was a name we called her. Not me though, I never liked it ... buzz.' I focused on him again. 'That was it, they used to go buzz at her, make buzzing sounds because, because Mom used to say she'd get a bee in her bonnet, and then she'd get angry because they were laughing at her. All of them, buzz, buzz, that's what they'd do when she wanted to say something, make a point. I'd hear them say it, buzz, buzz, buzz, and I hated it, I hated that they would say that to her.'

He leant a little toward me. 'I guess all families are a law unto themselves, with all their own peculiarities,' he said.

'I'm sorry, this is …' I rubbed my eyes, the ghost of the memory lingering inside my eyelids.

'Why hell no, we're conversing with the hope of making … making sense out of your darkness as it were.'

'I'm telling you memories, and I'm not even sure whose they are.'

He tilted his head toward me. 'All conversation … all conversation is just layin' out a memory for another, but half the time you don't know if it's true, or just what you thought was true. Amnesia or …' He tapped the whiskey bottle. 'No amnesia, Margarita.'

'I can see things, things from the past but I can't make sense of them, and I can't remember anything from three days ago even, nothing. It's so stupid!'

'Hell, the aunt I told you of, Amarita.' He laughed 'Why she, she'd remember the war and the men going off to fight, but she couldn't remember when her eyeglasses were sat on her head…'

'Amarita? I thought you said she was called Margarita?'

'No,' he said, raising his head as my question jerked him out of his reverie. 'No, she liked the margaritas, so that was my name for her; that was all I meant.'

'Oh, my mistake.'

'Suits you better too, you don't look nothin' like an Amarita anyhow.' He moved again, adjusted his back rest. 'Another one?'

He extended the bottle towards me.

'I'm good, thanks.'

'Are you now?' He smirked.

'You tell me … how many good people get shot?'

Red laughed and settled back again.

'Darlin', I shot a great many people in my time, I ain't ever bothered with finding out if they were good or bad. Seems as a bullet wound says more about them that made it, than received it.'

'You shot people, when you were in the army?' I asked.

'Mostly.' Red winked. 'I shot people wherever Uncle Sam had cause to send me.'

I straightened up and tried to make it a casual enquiry.

'Red, you ever been to Paris?' He frowned at me.

'Now how come you had cause to ask me that?' Red turned the glass in his hand, peering through it before he looked up at me. 'You mean Paris, France?'

'I guess I do.' I smiled. 'Sorry, all sorts of things rattling round my head.' Red raised his glass and took a sip.

'Whatever, no, I ain't never been to Europe, I'm sorry to say. Been to the French quarter, not sure I need get any closer. Sure, half the white folks round hereabouts claim to be French, hell, my aunt was real hot on the idea, though I took to playin' it down in the Gulf. Truth be told, my mother had more claim to be French than she ever did.' He coughed.

'Do you remember your mother?' I asked, though I wasn't aware of how the question sounded until the words were hanging in the air between us. I bit my lip, straightened up. The bottle chinked on the mouth of his glass.

'You say that as if she were departed.' He watched me as he lowered the bottle again.

'I'm sorry, I'm not sure why, I just …'

'She is dead,' he said.

I touched my hand to my mouth.

He shook his head gently. 'That was ungallant of me, you're not to know.' He sipped from his glass. 'She died, when I was seventeen, I think. She was a little like you …' He looked at me. 'Dark I mean, she had long dark hair. I must confess that I'm old-fashioned, in that I like a woman to have long hair, though I mean nothing by that you understand. I'm a man of my time.'

'You aren't that old,' I said, which he took for flattery.

'I am older than you. I'd surmise you ain't a tick over twenty-five, sure as I'm forty.'

'Your guess is as good as mine,' I said, but he was watching the whiskey in his glass, swirling a vortex in the amber liquid.

'There is a large and ornamental lake at the rear of our property; we have a great and dignified house. It is quite renowned in the county. She was in the lake, which I now fear is left rather to its own devices.'

'I'm really sorry,' I said in the way you do, when you know there's nothing else you can say.

'There's nothing you have to be sorry for,' he said as he focused on me. 'In this instance, I was merely …' He waved his hand. 'Merely remembering.'

I sipped the last of my whiskey. 'What do you remember of her?' It sounded a lot more impolite than saying I was sorry, but Red didn't seem to mind.

'She was in the water.' He tilted his glass again, squinted through it. 'In a white dress, which had risen up to cover her face …'

'You saw her?' The coldness of the realization sliced through the evening. I'd meant her cooking or the way she dressed, not how she'd died.

His eyes flicked to mine. 'I was the one who discovered her.

And that is not what a young man needs to see, when he's at an impressionable age.' He reached forward and seemed to draw the edge of something over my face.

'You saw her,' I said softly.

'She was beautiful.'

'When she was alive?'

'She was beautiful ...' His hand paused in the air between us. 'But hell,' he said, his voice suddenly bright and businesslike as he slumped back against his pillows. 'I don't mean to dwell on such unfortunate events now. What's done is done.' He closed his eyes.

We lay silent for a while, the room fogging with the smell of grey water and clapboard. The house moaned and cracked as it cooled, twisting against the wet earth as if it were caught in a bear trap and the water in the lake seemed to rise up within me, casting white silk across my face.

'White silk, ma Cherie – spreadin' out over the dark water, runnin' deep...'

Red sat up and the whisper was lost. He ruffled his hair, leaving a little of it standing up at his temples.

'Ain't much in the way of light,' he said, stretching his shoulders. 'But there's a lamp in the kitchen.' I nodded, remembering that I'd seen one in the cupboard under the sink when I'd searched earlier. Red clicked his neck, stood up and sauntered off.

When I heard a click from the kitchen, I looked up. Red had nudged the padlock on the back door – such a small thing – checking it was closed against the night. I could have looked away but something stopped me. I saw him slip the key from where I'd left it into his pants pocket.

Trying to give no visible hint that I'd seen him, I mentally checked my exits. The front door was barricaded and locked, the windows on the ground floor were boarded up and the ones by the door were glazed in safety glass embedded with a grid of wire. Through them I could see a line of dead fire bruising the sky as the sun set. I swallowed against the unease that trickled over me. The only way out without making a lot of noise would have been through the kitchen door, until Red had slipped that key into his pocket. If I wanted to get it without him knowing, I was going to have to get a lot closer to Red.

He put the lantern on the side table with its wide-mouthed grin, and adjusted a lever at its foot. When the warm pool of light expanded, I realized how dark it had grown and how quickly, and how loud the whine and throb of cicadas now was.

'Guess we're in for a long night,' Red said and kicked the sleeping bag into shape before sitting down. I glanced back at the door, the lock, the only way out. The way to a man's heart might be through his stomach, but through what was the route to his back pocket? Animals gnaw through their own feet to get out of a trap, I thought. Just how desperate was I? I glanced around the room. Desperate enough.

I swung my feet round to the floor, let myself slip from the couch and pressed my back against it, stretching my arms above my head and arching my spine.

Not if he was the last man in the world …?

'Sorry,' I said. 'I'm stiff as hell after sleeping on that couch, and everything.' I nodded toward the bottle. 'Can I get another?'

Red slid a grin across his face, the lamplight glinting off his teeth.

'Sure thing, darlin', be my pleasure.' He passed me the bottle by its neck. 'Do the honours?'

I filled the glasses and set the bottle down by my feet. We drank and I let the liquid seep into my mouth. When he turned to reach a handful of chips, I let most of the whiskey back into the glass then tipped it away under the couch.

'This is so crazy,' I said, hooking my elbow on to the seat. 'We're sitting here and I don't even know my own name, let alone if any of this is real.'

'You think I ain't real?' Red leaned forward, resting his arms on his knees and glancing back at me. 'Maybe this is the only thing that is real; maybe we's the two last livin' souls on the planet, you and me, Margarita?'

'That really would be scary.' I smiled. Maybe he was the last man on Earth after all?

'Really?'

'Sure ...' I was aware of the proximity of our feet, our shoulders inches apart. 'I don't even know who I am, let alone who you are.'

'Do I ... cause you concern?' Red asked slowly. 'Do I make you uneasy?'

'No,' I lied. 'But you have killed people.'

'Line of duty.' Red shrugged, but his grin lingered over his teeth.

'Following orders?' Something cracked in the darkness behind me. I shivered. The sound of the tortured house was like hearing a stranger's pain in the bed next to mine.

'I always do,' Red said. 'I always did,' he added.

The darkness curled about us as we sat on the floor, as the house shuddered and the heat of the day bled out into the swamp. The lamp threw shadow spectres on the walls as the beat of the night slowed in time with the sound of Red's breathing, the key in his back pocket, out of reach.

'How long were you in the army?' I asked.

'Hmm?' Red squinted at me. 'Too long.' He emptied his glass. 'Guess it just suited me, never having much in the way of family.' He coughed. 'Army's like that, it's your brother, father, mother, everything. Makes a man of you, but it makes you its own sometimes. Like a wife, kicks you when you're down.' Humidity and whiskey fought to glue my tongue to the roof of my mouth. Out of the two, the whiskey was winning. I stretched my arm out under the couch and ran my hand over the underneath of its seat absently. Red leant forward, glass in hand. 'It gives you life, but it can take yours. Hell, that's a whole other story, someone else's war. Been out two years now, all done and dusted.'

I looked at him from under my lashes. 'Tell me about it,' I murmured, and lolled my head back against the seat.

Red clicked his shoulders and rolled his head before reaching over me for the bottle. The wings of a moth beat and fluttered against the lamplight, the dusty 'tink-tink' of the tiny, frustrated impacts audible in the descending calm.

'Listen, ma Cherie …'

I heard it, somewhere among the sighs and suffering of the house, the voice from my dream, from my memory, perhaps? The world was dragged down with whiskey as I watched Red's hand reach for the bottle. It slowed, the air seemed to solidify as his strong, knotted fingers opened, as they became trapped in the air, like insects in amber. The tink of the moth's wings became a thud-thud, the sweep of its movements encompassing the whole world. I blinked, but I alone seemed to be flickering, bright – a splatter of paint against a dull canvas.

'Listen to him now, ma Cherie, with the ears I give you.'

If I'd had a memory, it would have told me I did not believe, and I would not have heard her. I would not have watched unperturbed as the tick-tock of the universe wound down to the beat of her voice, a smile playing on my lips as time stopped around me.

'Listen what de water's tellin' you, ma Cherie …'

I became translucent, made of cinnamon and silk and the scent of a thousand years on an old fur coat. The house became a film stretched over a reality I was not beholden to.

'Unpick what him have woven, ma Cherie.'

I saw him.

On the floor of the house as the night noises thrilled and crept around him, and the space between us became infinite and fragile.

I saw him.

Walking down a corridor with the thrill of the power and the heat of pain walking with him.

My edge fractured and shimmered into another time and another place.

'Tell me about it,' I said to Red, as he sat on the floor beside me and the scent of him breathed over my skin.

'Tell me about it,' I said to Red as his feet beat hard, hard, hard on the wet concrete floor of a fetid place more miserable even than the twisted house in the backwoods.

'Is this real?'

'Do it matter, ma Cherie?'

'But the key … I need to get out, I …'

'Listen to what him not tell you now, ma Cherie. Listen to what you already know.'

Red passed boxes and cages, each with a hooded, trembling figure bound and pinned in corner. He was their overlord, he would not be denied; his feet beat quick-march on concrete washed with fear and darkness.

His brothers were there also, the brothers the army had made for him, formed from the dust and blood of a different land. They yapped and barked as they waited for him, but he was not victorious; he had a clock hanging over his head, marking out its own time behind his stride and it showed him no mercy.

'It was to save a boy with a good heart, a boy in a man's body; that is why the clock was so heavy on his back, ma Cherie. What would you do, to save a boy who loved you, a boy you loved?'

The woman was with his brothers. He did not know what to make of her, because she wanted to run with the brothers but was not one. He'd seen her before; she'd made herself known to them, knew the one who was lost. She was eager, dirty; she was ugly. She was so desperate to become a brother he knew she would do anything, everything he asked of her. He knew he could have had her if he wanted, but he found her repulsive; besides, she was more use to him in other ways.

'Good men may do evil; not all as do evil, become evil ...'

He had no idea and no care which one he chose, that did not matter, what mattered was that there were witnesses. Not for justice, because he was not there for justice, but for fear, so that his fear would be spread among them.

He saw the face under the head made of hessian and spit, the brown face crying and snivelling. The brothers took the one he'd chosen and the woman yapped at their heels so eager, so excited to be one of them.

'How could she?'

'Why, ma Cherie, there's no evil men do that women do not.'

'You're gonna tell me what I want to know,' Red told the face inside the bag. 'And you will not lie to me.'

The face jabbered and pleaded with him, stretched out against the board like a butterfly waiting for the needle.

'Please sir, please.' There was an older man also, another man released from a hessian hood because he could speak English, and because of that, his face was not bleeding. Red made him kneel next to the man on the board. There were two more behind him, there so that they could see, dumb witness, dumb jury, dumb luck.

'What you want?' Red demanded of the old man who spoke English.

'He does not understand you sir,' the translator said. 'Please, he does not know.'

Red took hold of the translator's neck as if he was drawing him close over a thousand miles. Like a giant's hand, Red's white hand stretched out and caught the brown man's throat.

In the dark, wet house in the backwoods, Red's hand reached for the neck of the bottle as the wallpaper blistered from the wall, as the moth beat against the heat of the lamp and arced to the floor in a blaze of light. Slowed to a snail's pace, the universe began to entropy, fraying at the edges, bleeding to sepia.

'I don't care what fool language he speaks, I don't even care what he knows,' Red's voice oozed into the house in the swamp as if it seeped in with the damp.

'He's just a boy ...' the translator said but Red was furious, angry, driven by the yelping of the brothers and the clock on his back, the clock only he could hear.

'You will not tell me 'bout right and wrong, when I have seen your children with their arms and legs torn off by your mines, and your women with their fingernails torn off because they had the temerity to wear nail polish. He was never a child – he was born a bastard with a gun. If he does not know where my boy is, then he will suffer so as the next one of you knows you do not lie to me, and you do not take my boys.'

In the dark, wet house Red's fingers closed but he missed his mark and the bottle rolled away from his grasp. Slowly, inevitably, the bottle swung on its axis as if falling through water, the sound of it rolling like a blade on a whetstone.

In the concrete prison, watched by the old man who spoke English, they stretched a wet cloth over the face of the boy on the board and the woman hid her eyes in the dark when she thought they could not see. They brought water and one of them drowned him in the air like a fish; like a fish with a hook in his mouth he drowned in the air, with the woman in the dark and the man who spoke English crying for him, and Red not seeing what they did because he was blinded by the tick of the clock.

'Be wary, little fish, you swim with a fisherman.'

Red was not haunted by the wet slip of the boy's body as they cut it free and it washed up newly baptized on the floor. Red was not haunted by the whisper of concern and fear in the faces of his brothers and the woman, or the tears of the old man who spoke English as he held the boy's head in his lap. He was not haunted because he feared he had gone too far, but because he did not go far enough. Haunted that despite this night and all the other nights, he could not save the lost boy with the good heart but was forced to watch him beheaded on a flickering screen a week later, his brothers and the woman watching silent and heartsick beside him.

After that, he could not even try and save his brothers travelling on other roads any more, all his brothers who might step on bear traps. He couldn't fight any more, because of the wet boy drowned in the air of a dark room. He couldn't fight any more, because of what the man who spoke English said, when somebody thought to ask him.

'Keys only unlock the door for which they were made, ma Cherie.'

In the deep, soft, dirty heat where I sat with Red and his dreams, my hand brushed against the side of the couch. My fingers found something, and the familiarity of the shape dragged me back through yellow layers of illusion. Red's soul hardened and became opaque but his energy lingered, coursing over my skin as if a storm were coming. There was so much power in him, and so much of it was dark.

Under the couch, I found a small piece of duct tape, and as my fingers explored it, it came loose. Inside it, was a key, which had been stuck to the underside of the frame, waiting for me to find it.

CHAPTER 6

THE BOTTLE SLIPPED from Red's grasp and hit the floor. As it thumped down the universe snapped back into place, with a rush that made me gasp.

'Damn it!' He scrambled for the bottle, then righted as I got the key free from under the sofa. 'Least it ain't broke. You okay?'

The red clay lips laughed a dry whisper in my ears.

'I was just getting' comfortable, you know, with my side an' all?' I curled my fist around the key and, when he glanced down at the bottle again, slipped it into the pocket of my jeans.

'So … you comfortable now?' he asked.

'Not really,' I said, shifting away from him a fraction. 'Can't get used to the idea that someone shot me, someone I can't remember.'

'Hell darlin', I wouldn't hold it against them. One never knows what one might do when it comes to it. You might have cause to shoot a man y'self, someday.' His words sent a shiver tracing up my back.

To cover it, I said, 'What, you scared of me now?' sure that he wasn't.

'Oh, I ain't scared of you,' he shrugged, pulling his mouth into a grimace, 'well … maybe just a little. Scared of what you make me think of?'

'What's that?' I said, biting my lip. Red leaned forward and filled both our glasses again. He'd seen me bite my lip and he looked as if it had made him hungry. Instead of sitting back on his pillows, he brought his feet up and crouched next to me. He didn't touch me, but his arm snaked along the seat behind.

'After you,' he said, tipping his glass to me. 'Then, maybe I'll tell you.'

We drank, and I knew that being this close to him, I'd have to drink it all. I swallowed, and he watched closely. It burned, and hit me right between the eyes.

'Alright,' I said, 'what do I make you think of?'

Red smirked. 'That there must be someone out there who's lookin' for you.' He moved his head to gaze off somewhere behind me, moving his mouth closer to my ear. I breathed the scent of him, of sweat and whiskey and hot skin.

'Maybe not,' I said, 'maybe there's nobody lookin' for me?' and when I said it, I had the odd sensation that there really wasn't, not anyone in the whole world. If there still was a world out there.

His chuckle rattled deep inside his chest. 'I can't believe that.' He ran his tongue over his teeth, as if checking how deep his smile went. 'Can't see no reason as to why something as pretty as you would have been thrown out on the wayside.' He risked a glance sideways. 'Be a terrible waste.' He turned toward me, tilted his glass, so we drank. I'd taken his nightmare from him, without knowing how I did or wanting to do it. I'd lingered behind his eyes, or imagined what it might be like to be there, and perhaps that had given me a dangerous sense of familiarity?

Lips tingling, I asked, 'Why you care if there's someone lookin' for me?'

'Cause it might matter what the nature of that search is … mother seeking her daughter … daddy seekin' his little girl …'

Daddy. I didn't like him saying that, not in the way he did. I got an odd sense of memory then, a scent perhaps, old leather and Sunday heat, and being smaller, enclosed in an armchair, a low voice I could feel as much as hear, reading a story.

Red clicked his tongue. 'Maybe he's lookin' for you, that big old brother of yours or …'

'Or?'

'A husband, seeking his errant wife?' He took hold of my left hand, and I let him. I let him raise it and turn it over, inspecting my fingers as if he meant to read my palm. His skin was rough and dry, like the belly of a snake. He frowned. 'What d'you know? I don't see no ring.'

'Maybe I was robbed?' Red's thumb caressed the base of my finger.

'Maybe …' Red closed my fingers into a fist, held my fist in his hand. 'It ain't left no mark, no tan line or nothin'.'

Did he know, was that why he was asking, looking for the ring he knew he'd not find? Oh hell, why didn't I just come out and ask him? 'When you first saw me …' I paused, immediately not sure I wanted to ask after all. 'When I first saw you?' Red's gaze fixed on mine. 'When you saw me here, yesterday … what did you think?'

'Well now, since you ask, I thought as Christmas had come early.' He laughed.

'No, I mean, I thought … I thought that you … I thought you recognized me …'

Red shifted his feet. 'Well now, it was a bright day, an' you were in a dark house when I saw you, half in shadow and me all sun blind an' all.' He frowned. 'Though, I must confess … there's a little something about you which brings her to mind.' He frowned.

'Your mother …'

'What makes you say that?' he said, then a smile eased his frown away. 'That weren't it, no, someone else altogether. See, that's why I figure he's out there lookin' for you.'

'Who?'

'Your husband.' He tilted his head away from me.

'But I ain' got no ring.' I moved as if to pull my hand free. He didn't let me go.

'Don't mean he ain't lookin' to put one on your finger.'

'I don't remember,' I said. The skin on the underside of my arm prickled with sensation, as if it remembered something, some echo of a touch. Red let go of my hand and moved until his words buzzed in my ear, hardly more than a whisper, hardly more than a thought passing between us.

'Darlin', sure I been one to play when the cat's away, but I'd rather know what's coming back to the mouse-hole first. Don't seem right, seein' as you don't know yourself whether you's cheatin' or not.'

His lips grazed the side of my neck. 'That would stop you?' I asked, as his laugh breathed over my skin.

'Mercy, you better watch you' self. I'm not sure as you know what you doing?' I flinched as his hand slipped onto my shoulder, turned my head away and watched his index finger inscribe a circle on my shoulder where fabric met skin, staring as if he were caressing something that was not part of me, letting him as if we'd done this before, as is this was something we did.

'I don't know nothin', remember?' I said, as my pulse throbbed in my neck.

'I don't believe that.' His finger slowed. 'But you better watch out I don't turn my mind to teachin' you what you's forgotten. You think you's playin' with a mouse, girl, but you might find I'm a great big ole Tom Cat.' Red's finger slid under the strap of the undershirt I was wearing, and eased it down.

'Red …' I jerked away from him, but he gripped the strap. 'Red, this isn't…'

'Oh, I know, but part of you ain't so sure, is it? Part of you don't want me to stop.'

'Red …' His grip tightened, dragging the shirt against my neck.

'I think you done talking for now. You better just listen up.' He brushed my throat with the fingers of his free hand. 'See, I been watching you all this day, and I ain't sure how much you know and how much you care to remember, but you got to ask yourself, what if you're better off not knowin'?'

'Knowing what?' My heart hammered in my throat, my breath caught in the squeeze of my lungs.

'I thought about it, while you was lying in your deep sleep.' He reached up and brushed the side of my face with his knuckles.

'No …' My mouth was whiskey-dry; I swallowed, but even that felt treacherous, provocative. His smile creased the edge of his eyes.

'Sure thing, seein' as we's being so honest n'all. I took a long hard look at you. It would have been right easy – right easy, slippin' you out of them nasty ole' clothes while you were out cold.' I should have pulled away from him, shoved at him to get off me, but the sense that this was a game we'd played before pulsed in me. I exhaled, forcing myself to do it slowly, making myself stare straight back at him. I could almost imagine that I was watching us, me and him, together on the floor of the shack, two little creatures crawled out of the dark. It was as if I wasn't alone with him after all. I felt a smile curl onto my lips, wicked, dark, daring him to just go ahead and goddamn well try it.

'Know what? I figured you might even have liked it, my hands on you when you didn't have to pretend like you minded, when you could forgive yourself.' His words were thick and black, tar sticky. 'Who would have minded, just you and I, in the wet, subtle heat of a lost afternoon,' he murmured, his lips moments from mine. 'But …' He stood up in a great rush and sent me sprawling onto my side. 'But hell, like I said, I don't want t' waste my time on a mouse-hole, when I don't know what other rat's been sniffin' round now, do I?' And he laughed.

Anger and humiliation flared in me as I struggled up off the floor.

'What the fuck was that, what the hell do you think you're doing?' I yelled, clutching my arms round myself while he grinned at me – anger, humiliation and what else? 'You had no right to …' And disappointment?

'What you pissed for?' he asked, arms spread wide. 'You pissed 'cause of what I said or 'cause I turned you down?' Goddamn him! His smile faded. 'I did you a favour. You might not remember squat, but you sure as hell don't want to remember messin' about with me. You better learn comin' on like a two-bit whore ain't the best way of going about things.'

'Don't call me that!'

He jabbed his finger at me. 'I never said as you was, I said you were startin' to act like one. If your daddy were here, he'd tan your hide.'

'You're not my daddy,' I said, and folded my arms.

'I sure as hell ain't,' Red said, then something in him softened and he raised his hand. 'Look, we both got cabin fever here. Trust me darlin', if you knew who you were, what you was about, I'd love to entertain you, take you to dinner and what-not, but that ain't the way it is.' He padded off to the kitchen. As I watched, as the house exhaled, he ran water into the sink. I peered at him in the gloom; the stranger who thought I was a criminal, or a two-bit whore, or a little like someone else, I wasn't sure any more. I wasn't even sure who I thought I was. Maybe this was all I'd ever been, a girl in a stained shirt alone in the world, sitting in a bleak house craving human warmth from an old soldier.

We watched each other, perhaps trying to decide which of us were the bait, and which the trap, and all the while we did, I was sure there was someone else there, watching the both of us.

CHAPTER 7

RED PUT THE BOTTLE on the counter by the kitchen door, and rubbed his eyes with his hand.

'Listen. If you wanna take my room …?'

'No, this is fine,' I said, the hard edge of the key pressing against my leg.

'Really, you're the one with the busted-up side, I'm happy with the couch. The bed ain't much, but it's a bed.' But I didn't like the thought of him lying in wait down here; I wanted to get that door open.

'What about the other room upstairs?' I asked. 'Is that another bedroom?'

'That?' He glanced up. 'That's just empty. That's nothing, I keep it locked, floor needs work,' he said. 'What's the matter, you didn't think I mean to bunk in with you?'

'I'd prefer it down here,' I said, the key I'd found making me bold. As soon as he was out of sight, as soon as it was quiet, I'd have the door open and be gone. As long as he thought I was down here, the night would give me cover, even if I walked with blistered steps. I felt giddy, both with the whiskey and the sense of imminent escape.

He shrugged, perhaps too weary to push the point.

'Suit yourself, I'll wish you sweet dreams then. You can keep the lamp, 'case you wanna read or something. I got my flashlight, anyhow.'

He picked up the sleeping bag and walked to the foot of the stairs. He took a few steps up, then looked back at me.

'Look,' he breathed out, his hand flinched and relaxed. 'I'm sorry.'

'For what?'

He licked his lips and might have been going to smile. 'For the accommodation.' He walked upstairs.

I lay on the couch and listened. He went to the bathroom, the water clanked and wheezed through the ancient plumbing, then the floor creaked his passage into the bedroom and the door closed. In the kitchen, something scuttled across the floor, out of sight if not out of mind, then something else came after it.

I counted and waited for as long as I could stand it, then I made myself wait even longer, lying on the couch under the blanket, pretending Red was watching me.

'Count to ten, count to ten, then he'll go away again …'

When I could stand it no longer, I sat up. My feet touched the floor as if it was sleeping and might wake. I tiptoed to the kitchen, deciding to get the door open first and then worry about what I might take with me. I slipped the key out of my pocket, took a last look round and tried it in the padlock.

It did not fit.

I tried it again, and it still did not fit. In frustration and despair, I pressed my face against the door. I'd assumed it was the key to the padlock, because my fevered, beaten up brain was focused on nothing but the padlock. I closed my eyes and swore at the wood. Then I forced myself to inhale slowly, straightened up and fetched the lantern. I inspected the chain threaded through the door; it was solid. I could force it, perhaps lever the door off the hinges, if I could find something long and strong enough, though right now there was nothing obvious to hand.

I turned the key over in my hand. It had been placed under the couch with care, left for someone to find. Looking at it more closely, it did not look like the padlock key I'd held earlier. There was something domestic about it, something small. The locked room upstairs, the one Red said he didn't use … could it be for that? He wouldn't be deep enough asleep yet not to hear the noise of the padlocked door being forced; in the meantime, I might find something in there to do the forcing with, as there was nothing obvious down here. With the lamp throwing shapes against the wall, I crept up the stairs.

The light showed me the ceramic doorknob, painted with pink flowers, into which the key fit snugly. I paused, visions of Bluebeard's chamber flickering through my mind, the doorknob like the virgin's egg in my hand. I did not have to go in, but even as I registered the thought, I turned the key and heard the click of the lock.

The door opened towards me, and for a moment I thought it was going to be nothing more than a linen cupboard, but it wasn't. It was a small bedroom, with another, smaller iron bedstead, a grey striped mattress and sagging pillow. As the light washed the room, there was more scurrying. I caught the whisk of movement and a sharp, acrid smell. There was a tall, top heavy wardrobe, with fancy carving that the lantern-light turned into the face of an owl, two eyes and an ornately scrolled beak. There was nothing much else, just a huge floral bloom of damp on the faded, nursery print wallpaper, ducks in bonnets and baby rabbits eaten away by shadow.

Was this once a family home, out here in the backwoods? Was this a room where a child slept, little feet in summer shoes slapping up the stairs, running in to climb on the bed? I let go of the handle, stepped in and sat down on the mattress. Little feet running up the stairs with a secret, something they wanted to hide. Something joyous, or terrible, or stolen, or found? Little pearl buttons on blue velvet.

'I've got him, it's okay, it's okay – I've got him!'

I put the lantern on the floor and turned the flame up as far as it would go. The floorboards under my feet were dark and grained with age, though they looked firm enough. I straightened up and, as I moved my foot forward, felt one of the boards give and heard it creak. There was a knothole halfway along just big enough for a little finger, big enough for my little finger anyway, even with the nail. I pulled, and the board came free after a moment's hesitation. Kneeling down, I peered into the space below. Inside was a pink fabric bundle, printed with a delicate floral design and a luxury brand name. I eased it out; it looked like a jewellery roll. Buried treasure? I glanced up and slid the lantern closer before I worked the tiny gold buckles open.

Nestled against the soft pink lining was a small glass vial of clear liquid, a syringe, a length of tightly folded and bound nylon rope, and a set of handcuffs. I sat back against the bed, hand on my mouth. What the hell was this place? What did Red do here? Then something else in the alcove caught the light from the lamp. It was a snub-nosed revolver. I picked it up and checked the safety and that it was fully loaded, all before I realized that I did so instinctively, false nails clicking against the metal. This was familiar to me, this gun, or a gun like this. I knew how to load it, I knew how to shoot it, though I'd no memory of ever doing so.

'You gonna shoot me, you crazy bitch?' The image came to me again, my hand, those nails, holding a gun. This gun?

I dropped it like it was burning me, stood up and paced round the room, walking on the side of my feet, trying to calm the panic rising in my throat. A gun, Jesus, with these nails too. Gnawing one of them, I looked back down at the cache. The jewellery roll was very pink, and very feminine, despite its sinister contents. Would a man like Red keep his secret torture kit in such a pretty thing, when ex-army camouflage was so much more his style?

I rolled it all up again, my fingers shaking, the buckles stiff as I refastened them. I went to force both gun and roll back into the alcove, then decided against it. Not wanting to leave the tell-tale recess in the floor open, I moved the plank back into place, after which I was panting more heavily than the effort warranted. I leant on my hands to catch my breath then glanced under the bed, meaning to shove the things away against the wall, but the lamplight hit upon something protruding from under the mattress, caught between it and the bed frame. It was a hard, grey point, flat and thin.

Not sure if I wanted to know, but unable to resist, I touched it, then pulled it free, drawing it out like a splinter. It was a grey document bag. It looked as new as the roll, untouched by the fetid, creeping damp that had gnawed its way up the walls. I knelt on the floor with it, drawing the lamp up close, unclipped its straps and flipped it open. Inside were sheets of white paper, printed all over in dense type. I read the first few lines on the first page.

Message "mailto:alabasterbaby@hotmail.com" alabasterbaby@hotmail.com to "mail-to:nemesister@gmail.com" nemesister@gmail.com

Yes, it's me! I am so, so sorry I haven't been in touch sooner, but what with everything it's taken me this long to even get my feet back on the ground. You got my text right, so you know I'm not dead or nothing?

For a moment, I wondered if this was meant for Red too, then knew at once it wasn't. Just like the jewellery roll, this was all too feminine for him. I flipped through the pages; words jumped out at me but at first, none made any sense. My eyes fogged over and when I wiped them, I realized they were watering. When I blinked and looked up, the owlish wardrobe looked back at me, as if it had seen it all before.

I folded my legs under me and, with the tick and crack of the house and the shadows lurking on the walls, I began to read:

Sis, I know I screwed up. I know they think I've ruined my life, but I haven't. I've made a mistake and I'm going to put it right, that's all.

God, I miss you, I miss you so much. Whatever I've done I will always, always love you and always be your big sister.

I have to go now, but I'm gonna sit down and write you a proper long email when I'm set and I've got time. I know they might try and hack your account like they did with mine, and I know it was them no matter what they say, so I'm not gonna tell you where I am exactly, because I don't want them to make you tell them or something, or try and find out somehow, but I'm okay and I'm going to make it work.

Tell me how you are; tell me you're okay,
L xxx

I put my finger on the signature; such intimacy in four characters, a code between sisters rendered mundane by the uniform sweep of a digital printer. I remembered what I'd said to Red as we sat on the floor, 'I'm sure I had a sister, a brother also — older? A ... a sister ...?'

'L' had a sister, one she trusted enough to write to, one who was safe; a little sister in awe of her, perhaps? Running after, loyal, feeling blessed to be included in the game; running through the backyard, running down the street on an adventure, ripe with forbidden thrill, daring the dog that always snarled at them through the fence. Little feet in summer shoes, slapping on a sun-baked sidewalk.

''I've got him, it's okay, it's okay – I've got him, I've ...' I rubbed my forehead with my fingers, squeezing my eyes shut. The words seemed to glow on the inside of my eyelids. Lisa! 'Lisa! It's okay, Lisa, I've got him, I've got him!'

My heart pounded at the base of my throat. Lisa. My hand flinched, the papers flinched; I looked down expecting to see that I was holding something else, not papers but something lost, something found. For an instant, I thought I heard laughter, a scream of delight. I jerked round and glanced behind me, but all I saw was the open door of the bedroom, now an oblong of black. The darkness seemed complete, just the glow of the lamp spreading my shadow over the wall and the bed behind me. There's nothing in the dark that's not there in the light, I thought, but that didn't help. What was there in the light, was bad enough. I got up and went to close the door and listened, and the house seemed to listen with me.

If Red came downstairs, passing the door that he'd told me was locked, he might not try it, but he might look over the banisters to the couch below. It was lost in darkness, but when I raised the lantern and a little light fell on it, you could see at once it was empty. I went back into the bedroom and picked up the old pillow from the bed. It was clammy to touch, sagged like something neck-broken, and God knows what was nesting in it, but that didn't matter. I went down the stairs slow as I had to, so as not to make them creak. Some of the blankets Red and I had sat upon were still on the floor; so, together with the pillow, I arranged them to look, I hoped, as if I was still there, asleep.

Halfway up the stairs, I looked back down. At a glance, in the dark, if you were expecting me to be there, it wasn't too bad. You might really believe it, and as I stood there, I almost began to wonder if I was still down there. The light caught on a fold in the blanket, and the pool of shadow it cast gave it such solidity, that I could almost imagine it really was my shoulder. The longer I looked, the more it seemed as if the shape below me breathed, flinched in its sleep, sighed, safe in the comfort of dreams. My good-self asleep, my bad-self up to no good. I turned away, and when I looked back, the illusion was gone. It's just got to fool Red, I thought, enough for him to relax, to make a noise if he's out here so I hear him, that's all.

The key was still in the rose-painted lock on the outside of the door. I pulled it free, closed the door and put the lantern down to lock up. But when I tried to fit the key into the ceramic knob on the inside of the door, only half concentrating on what I was doing, it wouldn't go. I bent to look, and saw the keyhole on this side was blocked. I ran my thumbnail over it, and felt a sharp, protruding edge which, if I had to make a guess, was the remnant of another key, snapped off at the shoulder. The door had been fixed, intentionally or otherwise, so that it couldn't be unlocked from the inside.

The pull of the printed papers I'd found became too much to bear, so I turned back to them, slipping the key into my pocket.

Red thought the place was locked, had said as much, so that would have to do. I had to read, I had to know.

I sat back down in the dark of the chamber. As I struggled to read, leaning close to the lantern, a creeping sensation tickled over the back of my neck, and my shoulder blades itched. The sound of my breathing closed in on me, grew loud and interior, almost as if I pushed off into water, as if I dived.

'Gentle, ma Cherie.'

The water was purple, the water was soft. It whispered of another time and another place, the scent and sound of it creeping in under the sound of the swamp. I was too aware of it, too eager for it to come, I grabbed at it, but reality snatched it away and I gasped.

'Gentle, ma Cherie, soft now'.

I shifted position, angry that I'd thought for a moment that this dream, or curse or whatever it was even existed, or could be something I could use.

'Just read it,' I muttered, then, 'am I reading this?'

'Are you?' the voice asked me, a smile at the edge of its words. 'Haven't y'always been a swimmer?'

Yes, I had. I was a swimmer, I was swimming. I could feel the water as it flowed over me, feel myself bright in azure blue, sound and light dancing in my vision and stars in my lashes. I was a swimmer, and I broke the surface into cheering. The world was cheering for me, but when my fingers grazed the hard tiles of the pool, when I bobbed up into air, I was turning to one voice, picking it out in the crowd.

'Am I reading this?'

'Or do y' feel it? You think, maybe ya don't need read the words at all, because you seen them? Or because, ya once read them so much, they dance in ya eyes like lightning bugs?'

It was true. I knew what was written before my eyes devoured it from the page. It was not like reading, it was cold water down my throat, and me gulping desperately against thirst, as if I swallowed in what I swam. Like when I'd looked at the stranger in the mirror this morning, so gradually I saw her, both as the observer and the observed. The darkness closed down the light from the lamp, and I saw beyond the words and the white paper into something more than dream, more than memory. The world of the swamp slowed, the noise of insects faded, ticking into silence. The night breathed, deeply asleep, and I slipped beneath the water.

'Ya don't have to look, ma Cherie. Ya don't have to remember. God don't like ugly.'

CHAPTER 8

OH NO, I'M SO SORRY that they did that; it makes me so angry! It's outrageous that they're not letting you have your privacy even now! At least they don't know about this, and you can message me away from home and they'll never know ...

I saw hands that I knew were mine, typing at a keyboard. An Internet cafe a block away from home, unobserved for a dollar an hour, where a fat Turkish man lounged behind the counter and people came in to buy phone cards. Nowhere I was known, somewhere our parents would never go, a place that smelled of cheap coffee and stale bodies. I could see the yellow advertising banner over the counter and the soda bottles in rows, but I couldn't see my family, just my fingers, typing.

I saw Lisa too, in another place, where the sun seemed spiteful and the nights were never dark. I saw her when she sat down and waited for the screen to be illuminated with my words – her words – and I saw her as the tears came to her eyes and she brushed them away, because she never cried. Not since we were children.

I swam, alone. Late at night, late as I could, yellow light scribbled on the surface of the water behind me. I swam, I dived, and when I came up for air, the air I breathed was dust-dry and hollow.

There was a house with four other girls. Pink nails with rhinestones, because everybody has them, everybody there, all the girls in the house. They were all friends, and they were great; it was as though she'd known them forever, as though they were real friends, not like all those losers at school. All of those sent-away-to schools.

Do you like them? I got them done yesterday, everybody here has them. Cute or what?

There was a fleece blanket tacked over the bedroom window to shut out the light, both night and day. The floor was tumbled with hair straighteners and half-read magazines, and pantiehose, and ground-in lipstick, all in the glow of the pink blanket at the window, like waking with eyes closed and sensing the light.

Promise me you won't let them treat you like they treated me? Get money together and get away, as soon as you can, promise me?

There was a job at a casino, a good job because you could make your money in tips, like double, on a good day. But it was more than that, it was the first rung on the ladder, because it happened every day at casinos, people got discovered. She read it in the magazines, and all the girls in the house said so. Catching the bus in the morning, when the sky was high above and the heat hadn't yet drawn the spike of the cold, that was what she told herself: first rung on the ladder.

I do my face at work, in the restroom, because they give you nice soap and stuff.

And because there's no room in a house full of girls, always someone else in the bathroom or waiting. She does her face, and as she does, her reflection shows her eyes, mouth, nose, the same face she'd brought from home, the home she doesn't let herself remember. Her hair is blond, but then she dyes it, because it's that fair kind of not-quite-brown or blond colour people call mouse, and she's not a mouse, whatever else she is. The brush pulls, the brush snags before it comes free, and she tells herself this is the first rung of the ladder.

Was this my memory of who I was then, recalled by who I am now? Because I'd changed, I knew that, but the thing was, so had she.

'Ya know what they say when the sun shine but the rain fall? They say the devil's beatin' his wife.'

She fetched drinks, she cleared tables, she saw the lights of the city as they caressed her face and painted her in. The light caught in her eyes and dazzled me. She looked at the people who passed the window of her coffee shop, as if she watched fish in an aquarium, all bright colours and strange shapes. She watched the world like that, as if there was a layer of glass between her and it, and she longed to go swimming.

There was an acting class once a week, out in the suburbs where the sheep come down from the mountains. They call them sheep, but they look like goats, and sometimes she saw them from her bus, furtive brown bodies moving over a children's playground, grazing in the dusk. The grass was smooth and perfect, smooth and perfect as a green carpet as seen from under a bed. The class was good, the class was the bright spot in her lit-up week, but the last bus home was twenty minutes after the class finished, and she always had to run. One night, she didn't want to run, she wanted to stay and talk to the other people in the class, to be with people who had the same dreams as her, after a week of tables and beer and the buzz and click and hum. So she missed the bus. She missed the bus and she waited outside, not sure what for, reading the timetable over and over.

'Can I give you a ride?' It was nice of him to offer, the tutor. It was nice to sit in his car and talk about acting, to feel he saw something in her, other than waiting tables. 'Can I give you a ride?' It was nice of him to buy the coffee, while he explained that really, he and Susan, his wife, were all but over. Well, she knew how it was, after the kids, after they leave home; you look round and hey, there you both are, more like brother and sister than anything. It was nice of him to explain, so she wouldn't feel guilty.

Home, eventually, to the house with too many girls, but something's wrong. She was late, and that made her look worse, somehow. Things had gone missing, and well, it wasn't Cathy, now was it? Or Jules, with her arms jammed tight across her chest, or Candy, or Lauren, or Katie, or Tyler – is wasn't any of them, now was it, Lisa? They're all friends, they all know each other, like, for real, like forever? They wouldn't do it, not steal from each other.

Christ, I've never stolen a thing in my life, why the hell would I steal from one of them? Like I fucking care, living in that shit-hole anyway. Good luck getting another idiot in to cover my rent, I'm so out of there. I'm doing alright anyhow, I earn more than all of them, just fucking jealous. I've always been the same though, always get on better with men than women, you know?

She moved to a motel, a new place, smaller room yet more expensive. She calls the tutor to explain, because now there's no money for the class any more, or the bus or the coffee shop, half hoping he'll say it's okay. Half hoping he might leave his wife.

'Look, it's probably for the best, Lisa. Susan and I? We're going to try again, you know? I've really enjoyed our time together, you're such a special person, really you are, but, like I said, we're going to give it another go. Thought we might take a week in Cancun, at my brother-in-law's place. Look, don't worry about coming to class any more, because hey, maybe there's nothing left I can teach you ... You're a very talented actress.' That was nice of him.

Her face in the mirror of the motel room, was lit by the glow of the sunlight through the curtains. This glow was yellow, hotter than before, and just four walls, one bed, one window, and a rug with the corners kicked up. The black square of a silent TV, coin slot empty, and the drip of water in the silverfish-scuttled bathroom. She told herself that this was better, hey, there was even a pool, though they were waiting for the cleaners and it was closed.

'Ya always been a swimmer.'

I have more time to myself, which is way better. I sit and listen to the people here, because you can hear everything through the walls. I don't mind, I kind of try and imagine what they're like, so I can draw on them when I have acting jobs.

At night, there was the sound of the people next door. Lisa listened to them, for want of money for the TV. There was a woman who cried, the sound hollow and gasping. Lonely, so lonely, like she was crying for two. Lisa couldn't stand it after a while, so she put on the white worn-through slippers, thin as prison gruel, and went to the door. Hand on the latch, she made up her mind to do it, only then there was the crack-slip of footsteps coming closer, the man's tread, then the sound of the door in the next cell opening, closing. She stood by the door a moment longer, then went and sat down again. The woman stopped crying, so it must have been alright. All better now, only Lisa didn't take off her slippers just then.

There is a grey patch on the wall and it looks like a map of the state or something, like I should be able to stick a pin in it and say 'I am here.' But I can't, because some days I wonder if I'm here at all.

I saw him coming before she did, in the way the sky changes as the storm approaches, if you know what to look for. Lisa didn't know, she was head-down working, but I saw him. I called out, but I was talking in my sleep, from the wrong time and the wrong place, and she could never have heard me. I couldn't even hear me.

'The Devil's beatin' his wife.'

She woke in the hard yellow light of the afternoon, to wash among the silverfish. She walked to catch the bus, shades on, passing the door of the neighbouring room. All was quiet. She caught the bus to start her shift, and the sky above her seemed bruised – that odd colour that promises rain. She's never seen it rain there before.

Two in the morning, six hours in, and there were five guys in the corner of the casino, the spot where the cameras couldn't reach. College kids, about her age.

'Hey doll, we were wondering …'

Ignore the sniggers, she told herself, ignore the grin, ignore the implication. Set down the tray, unload the drinks, slide the bill across the table. Do not make eye contact, do not rise to the bait. Serve the drinks, that's all.

'Hey doll …' Big, raw faces, good teeth and nice hair, skin bronzed or scarred, or still white with library pallor. Money in his hand, a lot of money. More money than in the tip jar.

'Look, I'm just a waitress.'

'Come on, you're killing me here!'

'Hey, let go of me.'

They closed in on her, out of sight of the bar, out of sight of the cameras. Two o'clock, not many people in, just the man with his paper and his beer; the man who smiled and was polite, the good tipper, who said, 'Thank you, darlin'. Change is all yours.'

The college boy had money too, folded in his hand. 'Now look, doll, this is two hundred bucks. More than you make in a night, right? It's his birthday, and we promised we'd get him something special, so play nice, okay?'

'Fuck you!' She piled the empty glasses onto the tray and turned her back on the chorus of catcalls, face hot and humiliated. She went to leave. One of them put out his leg, and the others saw, and hissed with laughter. Everything crashed down, glasses, tray, dignity, all of her sprawled across the floor.

The good tipper gets up, leaves his beer. He folds his paper and takes a moment to put it on the table, before he comes over.

'Get off me, get off me—'

'Hey, easy … what's up? Sein' as you're on your knees, you might as well.'

'Go fuck yourself.'

'Hey,' and the college boy puts his finger on her forehead, as if one finger was all he needed. 'Did I say you could get up?'

The college boy didn't see the good tipper, until the man took hold of him, one hand being all he needed to make the boy squirm in his grasp. 'What the fuck—' One of the others flinched as if he meant to go help his friend, only he didn't. Good Tipper fixed him with his gaze, fixed all of them, and then somehow, none of them were going to help. Good Tipper bent the college boy's arm backward.

'You're goin' have to forgive me, son, but I ain't been servin' my country, so some little pissant like you can bad mouth a lady. You better apologize, before I go break your arm.' College boy squealed, his face blubbering and snivelling.

'Hey, dude,' one of them said, anxious, keeping out of reach. 'Hey dude, you hurtin' him.'

'That a fact?' Good Tipper let the boy go, and the whole pack scampered off, shaking themselves, trying to make it no big deal, trying to look cool, and see that they were not being followed.

'Now, may I give you a hand up, miss?' Good Tipper asked, hand out.

'No, really, it's alright.'

'Please? There you go. Now, I must apologize on their behalf. Boys will be boys I guess, but that ain't no excuse for takin' liberties. Sure, you're just tryin' do a job of work, aren't you?'

The noise of the bleating boy brought the security man over. There were explanations, there were apologies, Good Tipper shook the man's hand and made everything quite alright, one professional to another, and suddenly, Lisa's shift was over. The security man even gave her the twenty for a cab. Outside, Good Tipper was waiting.

'Excuse me miss? Hey, I don't mean to frighten you, forgive me for approaching you in this manner, but I'm just concerned, after the incident earlier?' She smiled, because she kind of knew he was going to wait.

It was nice when he took her for coffee. When he talked to her long into the morning as the dawn snapped awake around them, when he told her things she thought too precious for him to give away lightly. She told him things too, nothing real of course, just things that sounded real – about the schools and being sent away from home, and running back there only to run away again, and the running away this last time, and the being in the house with all the girls. Not the acting tutor, though. But some of it, some of the real stuff, as if it was a confessional, always half watching to see his reaction, waiting for the disgust to show on his face, only it didn't. She looked into his eyes, and I felt the warmth of the smile he gave her hot on my cheeks. It felt like forgiveness. And as she talked, the voice she used there, her valley girl voice, was quieted by the roll of his vowels, until something of her real voice, with its clipped, New England staccato, played about between them, and she thought how good the two sounded together, how nice the counterpart.

He told her first his name was Rooster, which made her laugh. When he saw her laughing, she blushed and told him it was because of the old movies she and her sister loved, and because Rooster was a character played by John Wayne. They always watched Westerns, she said; she and her sister would make a teepee with towels over the airer, and use their mom's lipstick for warpaint. They wanted to be Red Indians, wearing their hair in braids like the Indians in the films.

To prove they were brave – because they read somewhere you had to before you could call yourself a warrior – they'd dared each other to run past the nasty dog that lived three doors down. It barked and barked at them through the fence, until the mean neighbour who owned the dog shouted at them to stop. That dog though, they were both so scared of it, she and her sister. Her sister always made her walk next to the fence while it snarled at them because it frightened her so much. They had to hold hands and run together, or they'd never have made the school bus. That was in grade school, of course, before the sent-away-schools that came later. Silly, really, because it wasn't that big a dog, not when you thought about it.

He paid for a cab to take them both all the way, and made the driver wait while he walked her to the door. She was ashamed about the stinking pool with the covers on, and the vending machine at the foot of the stairs; she didn't want him to see. But he didn't seem to notice, and walked her to her door and asked if he might see her again. She wasn't sure if she was more excited about that moment, or that now she had something nice to write about.

We just talked and talked, and I told him everything, like I couldn't help myself. And he listened and he made me laugh, and then it was morning already and the sun came up. For this first time since I arrived, I saw how magical it could be here.

He asked if he could see her again, and she said of course he could, Rooster, of course. And he laughed, and then he kissed her hand, just like they do in the movies. He kissed her hand and he said, 'you don't need call me that. Them that knows me, calls me Red.'

You are Red, Rooster Levine, red in tooth and claw.

CHAPTER 9

THE FORCE OF THE WORD had me sprawling back against the bed as if he'd hit me. I broke the surface of the vision with a shock, my cry harsh, the sound of it echoing in the soft, damp space of the room. I was on my feet in seconds, wanting to run. I grabbed for the doorknob, then snatched my arm back and forced myself to stand still, hand jammed over my mouth, other arm hugging my chest.

The echo of my movement died in the instant, and around me the little room waited for the night to creep back in.

It was him, it was Red, in the emails, the messages. He knew me, he knew me all along, and I knew it, I'd felt it, but this? I tried to swallow against the tightness of my throat, tried to think. The images I'd seen, mixed with the words … what was that? I tried to pick at them, to bring them to mind; they were all new and raw and tender underneath, like fresh skin exposed under a loose scab.

No.

I wasn't the girl, the blond girl. I knew her, I knew her eyes; but like I'd known mine would be hazel when I looked in the mirror, I knew hers were blue. But he was Red, he just had to be, this man who'd saved her.

The urge to run swelled inside me. I looked at the closed door, and thought of the padlock below, and how there might still be something in there to force the door with. I went to the owlish wardrobe. Its door opened without protest and revealed another, small, grey little space, running with damp and rot. There was a metal rail across the top, which looked good and heavy, but was held in place by two brass clips. They themselves were also plenty good and heavy, good enough not to budge. The ends of the rail were decorated with ornate bulbs of metal, all very fancy and all speaking of a once far finer home, but as none of it seemed about to come loose without a great deal of noise, not much use to me. If I'd swung on it and pulled, there was a chance the wood might give way, rotten as it was, but I couldn't imagine how much noise that would make. The whole thing might splinter apart and topple over, and that would wake Red for sure. So I closed its door again.

I told myself again, that if Red wanted me dead, he could have killed me while I was unconscious, or gone for the cops. He could have locked the door and walked far enough to raise help, or flag down a passing woodsman, or whoever the fuck might hang out in a place like this – all of that he could have done and yet he had not. There was something he wanted from me, I was sure, just as sure that the girl he'd met in – well, it had to be Las Vegas, now didn't it? Yes, the girl he'd met in Las Vegas waiting tables, was not me, but my sister.

I could see the barking dog too, feel my fear of the damn thing, its nasty, snarled up face and how it always went for me through the fence, and the neighbour saying how I just had to be brave about it, that it could smell fear, that was all. I could picture myself hiding under the bed. But from whom, or what? The dog? All that green carpet and me and Lisa hiding there, with it scratching at the door, whining and snarling to get it. I turned to stare at the mouldering iron bedstead in the flicker of the lantern light.

Lisa and I, under the bed, because the dog was coming for us, the dog was bounding up the stairs to get us. No. Lisa and me though, Lisa and me hiding under the bed together. In a big house, in a quiet street, in a cold city, far from here, far from Vegas. Hot summers, but winters blown white with snow and ice, and iron skies, and vents in the streets billowing smoke, along a river that sometimes froze right over, froze right to the bottom. I longed for it, that cold, for the crunch of snow up to my knees, up to my elbows, covering everything over and making it cleaner, brighter, whiter. I stood in the dark, damp, room, stifled with residual heat and the itch of memory, and I tried to think of Lisa.

I saw her crying. I saw her crying on the bed, not underneath, and I knew that I knew why. I tried to say something to her, something like, 'It'll be okay, Lisa. He's gonna find him, Daddy's gonna find him,' but she didn't believe me. She looked up, her face pink-swollen and tear-bubbled, and her desolation was complete.

'He's back,' I'd said then, because I'd heard the sound of the car, and we both knew how odd it was, Daddy driving, because he really didn't care to; he liked Mom to drive him, but she was out, and that was a problem, because though Mom would have gone, we didn't think he would. But he had.

I went running down through the kitchen and out through the side door, sprinting to the front path, because I couldn't bear not knowing. He was getting out of the car, taking forever to unclip the safety belt, to adjust the seat back to where Mom liked it, to open the door and ease himself out. Tall man, stooped even then, brown coat with the collar up and the smell of lemon and leather he had, moving slow because of the pain.

'Daddy, did you get him? Did you find him, Daddy, Daddy?' He reached inside his coat, and smiled at me.

Then I was running back to Lisa. Daddy had given it to me and I'd hesitated, because surely Daddy wanted to give it back to Lisa himself? But Daddy held it out to me, and said, 'Oh, hey, you take it, sweetheart,' and I did, I snatched at it and I ran without thinking.

'Lisa, Lisa, I've got him, I've—'

My hand flinched – what was it? I stared at my fingers, seeming bright and white against the dark of the room, and I tried to remember what it was that had mattered so much, but all I kept seeing was the dog, that goddamn dog, its lips all snarled up, teeth clashing. It was fading, the images running one into the other: Daddy, stairs, dog scratching, whining, hiding under the bed, Lisa crying, Lisa happy. My eyes hurt in their sockets, as if I'd been gazing too long at a screen. I blinked, and night was back round me. A screech owl began to call in the trees outside, the sound acid-bright against the endless insect throb. I let my hand fall to my side. I looked down at the papers. A bug pinged against the lantern, and while it threw itself at the light over and over, I sat down to read the emails again.

CHAPTER 10

THE ROOM IN THE MOTEL was yellow, and the heat through the blind seemed warm for the first time, seemed joyous. The city became starbursts, churned into song, spinning round and round.

I remembered Lisa on a carousel when we were children; the music, the lights and the faces all whirled and tumbled together. They called her to come back, said it was time to go, it was late, but she wouldn't. She clung to the neck of the horse, and they had to get the man from the carnival to hold up the ride and help them pull her off. She wanted so much to be the girl on the horse, the girl with the lights in her hair, and that was how it was for her again, that time. I felt it, through the words she wrote to me, words churning and tumbling from the page, excited, lit up, the carousel taking her further and further away from me.

They weren't just for me though, her words. I'd thought it then, and the thought came back to me: they were as much for her. They were a story she was telling herself, as if by writing it down, it might make it real, might make her the person on the page, the girl on the horse.

I didn't want to ruin our last night, so I put on a pink dress and he took me to dinner to this amazing place.

Pink dress, pink nails, the camera flash in the mirror blanking out her face, so that she was all girls, and no girls; all of the girls who wait at tables and go to acting classes, and who believe. She was the girl that sneaked a lace tablecloth from the linen closet, and ran with it to the end of the yard.

And after the meal, he just suddenly said it.

She hardly talked about home, about us, though he asked her. She told him she was an orphan, with a sister back east, who lived with an aunt. She wrote me into her story – like when we were Indian braves, like when we were mermaids – she gave me a role. She killed both our parents at a stroke, easy, no mess. She even told him how, one day when she was set, she was going to come get me, how she'd build a big house and I'd get to live with her, and it would be like when we were children. And then he asked her to marry him. Well, you know how romantic soldiers can be, how sentimental.

I'm going to ask him to send you the airfare and you can come and be my bridesmaid. Yes, for real, like we used to pretend, with white lace and flowers and everything!

White lace and flowers, an old lace tablecloth yellowed with age and smelling of damp and mothballs. A negligee, white satin, condemned to the dressing-up box because of the stain on the front.

'Where'd you get them flowers? Mom'll kill you!'

'I don't care, I'm the bride and you gotta be my bridesmaid. Go on, you gotta pick up my train.'

I was angry with her. I wanted to scream at her – get away from him; nothing you could have done would be so bad that you couldn't come back. It was just your pride wasn't it, because you were sure that Mom hated you, or didn't love you enough? Or was it Dad, was that it, was it him you hated, or both of them, or me? Was it me, was that why you ran away and left me all alone with them and Franny …? Yes, that was it, our brother, Frances, who hated that name, and became too busy and too grown up to speak to me, the baby. What happened to us, what was so bad, that she went with Red when he asked her?

In the shivering house in the swamp, something stirred deep inside me, but did not wake. Our brother, Franny and, and … didn't we have a sister? One only I could see?

'Tell me who ya love, Cherie, an' I'll tell ya who ya' are.'

The air of his hometown was wet and pulsed with spice and gasoline. When Lisa stood in the shop and tried on her dress, she was a thousand miles from me.

'Is it unlucky?' she asked him, stood on a stool in the middle of the shop, with the boxes and drawers spilling pearls and lace at her feet. 'Is it unlucky?'

≈

He took her to his house, his father's house where they were to live. It was big and white and like something from a dream, ringed in sad trees that were draped in vines and seemed to weep and, at the rear, a large and splendid lake. He drove her there in his big black car, and wound down the window and showed her his world; told her his stories of when he was a boy, made her laugh. And his father laughed too; his father in his crisp, white suit, sitting in the big black car as they took Lisa to their house. He laughed too. His name was Jean, but everyone called him Papa Levine. He gritted his teeth and he smiled at Lisa, the little scrap of a thing his son had brought back from Las Vegas.

It took hours to drive to his house, I wish I could send you a picture of it, I will when I get a new phone – it looks like a palace, it's all white and has three levels, with pillars and huge windows and stairs.

A big old house, renowned in the parish, sitting high and dry above it all.

I could understand why Papa Levine might have his doubts, because you could fit even our house into his three times over, and I have no luggage to speak of. I remembered one of my acting classes, and pretended I was a duchess in a play.

The first night she stayed in the house, Red told her it was called Carillon, which means, he said, a peal of bells. He held her hand as they walked together through its echoing rooms, watching as she stared, seeing it as she saw it. Lisa made it into a palace for him again, and he was transfixed by her. That's what she gave him: the gift of his world again; water on the dry ground of his soul. He had been so long away from this world, so long without company.

He called my room the 'blue room.' They've got so many they all have names. I thought, here I am, standing in this beautiful room with the windows open, everything outside green and growing. My clothes looked so mean and sad in the wardrobe, but Red said as how he's going to take me shopping and buy a dress.

The night she first slept in the blue room in the white house, she woke after only an hour. She was jet-lagged, and she slipped down the stairs to fetch a drink, little bare feet silent and secretive. She saw the light under the door and heard voices, and she listened, just like Daddy told me not to.

'You gotta remember, I ain't getting any younger,' she heard Red say. 'There comes a time in a man's life when he needs to remember what he's fighting for, Daddy. A flag just ain't enough.' The light in the room flickered as he moved, as he paced up and down.

'Son, I see she's a pretty little thing, right enough. I see she appeals to your ... your senses boy, but when it comes to it ... where's she gonna stay when you go back? You ain't got that long.'

'Here, I won't have no wife of mine in army quarters, she'll live like a lady.' Lisa put her hand to her mouth, laughing and terrified. 'I got one more tour, Papa, then I'm done. A year from now, just over a year and I'll be a man of leisure. I don't wanna come home to an empty bed. Daddy, when I look in her eyes, I see the same beauty and gentleness that Mama had, and I ain't never seen that in no other grown woman. You think I'd bring some slut into your house?'

Listening at the keyhole, Lisa bit her hand to stop from making a sound.

In the house in the swamp, I bit my hand to stop from making a sound.

꒳

In the little shop where he was known, where his name was enough for them to flip the sign over to closed and bring out their best, she stood on the stool in front of the mirror, turning and turning, like the doll on a music box. The dress she chose had pearls on the sleeves, and little buttons on the back; and she wished her sister could be there to fasten them for her.

He brought her his mother's veil that night, and told her how she died. Lisa stood in the blue room and looked at her face in the mirror, her face through his mother's veil.

'You saw her, didn't you? You found her, in the water?' As he told her, he held her in his arms.

'I was the one who discovered her. And that is not what a young man needs to see, when he's at an impressionable age.'

The bridal suite was white, a big white bed with drapes around it, covers spread with pink and cream rose petals. As Lisa ran them through her fingers, her mouth was dry. Red came to the door. He looked so smart in his suit, but his eyes were distant.

'Do you love me, really?' She wanted him to hold her, came towards him, but he kept her at arm's length, hands gripping her shoulders. 'Do you love me?' His smile lingered behind his teeth. 'Really?'

I didn't want to watch, to have this in my head but the carousel kept turning. The ghost of his hands haunted my skin as he laid her down, as he raised his mother's veil over her face. I could taste the tulle, the dry, mothball smell of memory and worn-out promises; taste the legacy of his mother's skin and her perfume from forty summers before. Red kissed Lisa through it, and the white, gritty feel of it was forced into her mouth as if she drowned in lace and sand.

'Do you love me, really?' he asked and she nodded, blinded and consumed, unable to speak as she clutched the counterpane. Her body was treacherous; it preened under his touch. One hand on her throat, Red pulled the little pearl buttons from the dress. 'I think you's about wetter than a rain cloud in August, darlin.'

As she heard them scatter on the floor, she turned her head and pretended it was raining.

I wanna ask you something. Can you keep all these emails? One day, when we're both older, I'm gonna take all this and make something of it. I don't know what yet – but if you keep all this, then you can give it to me one day and then all of this can be real.
I love you.

Did she love me, really? The floor of the shack seemed to tilt and roll as if I were not in a flyblown bedroom of tired ghosts, but in a ship, turned and tossed on the sea. I tasted sand and lace as my fingers traced her words. Red took her hand and he took her round his world, and everywhere he took her she tasted it too, lace and sand.

And she was so busy after the wedding, with all the people she had to meet, all the hands she had to shake: old hands, fat hands, rich hands, gloved hands, and hers naked without their pink nails.

There are lots of people here I have to meet, from the army and all the friends they have. They are all so fine and refined, I never know what to say but they're sweet and nice to me, like they understand.

He's going away again. Neither of them speak about it, but it's there, the cloud gathering against the fire of the horizon, until all their days are rung out dry.

He's got to go back soon. It doesn't feel like a real war because it's so far away.
Papa Levine spoke to me. I was on the veranda with a juice,

and he came and put his hand on my elbow. He said that he had his doubts about me because it was all so quick and all, but that he can see I am a sweet girl and I will do right. He kept his hand on my arm for a while.

I told Red I didn't know what I would do all day when he was away. He said he was just worried about going, not because he's scared of the war or nothing, but because he doesn't want to leave me. He lay down with his head in my lap and he begged me to tell him that I loved him.

Maybe when Red has gone you could come and stay, I'll ask him. I write to you when I drive into town, I like writing to you from the cafe instead. I've remembered to attach a picture though, so you can see how beautiful the house is. They are expecting hurricanes soon, I haven't been in one before and I am quite scared about it. It rains nearly every other day, and when it does, Red comes home and his shirt sticks to his skin.

But he tastes of lace and sand.

'I did you a favour – you might not remember squat, but you sure as hell don't want to remember messin' about with me,' Red had said, but I did, I did remember.

He bought her a car, a white one. He bought her clothes and he bought her pearls, then he left. She watched him at the base when it came time for him to go; his pearls at her neck, wearing the clothes he bought her. All the soldiers looked so fine as they marched, so strong and she strained against the sun to see him, the one among the many.

The house had grown vast when she got back. She lay on the bed in the blue room and she knew that she missed him, but she was frightened that she missed him only because now she was alone. The room was neat and clean and the garden outside whispered, and she was alone. Some nights she walked through the house and listened to the rain and the wind as it rattled on the window. Sometimes she walked wearing nothing but the veil, tasting lace and sand.

There are groups I can go to for support while he is away, but I don't think I will. I haven't really got to know anyone and I don't really want to hear about their husbands anyway. Because he's an officer, the other wives who have husbands who are officers are a lot older than I am, so I don't know what to say to them.

After it was all over, I just came home and lay on our bed and wished he were back. I spent the day in bed and didn't eat anything to show how upset I was. Then I had to sneak down to the kitchen later because I was so hungry and ate cookies like a kid.

If I sent you the money, if I could buy you a ticket on my credit card, would you come, come and see me?

I never went to see her. I built her face from the words she wrote. I saw her ghost shadowed against the hot, blue sky over Red's big white house but I could not see her face. She was wearing her wedding veil for me also.

Do you think I have made all of this up as some sort of sick joke? Yes, I am married to a man you have never met. Yes, I live in the big old white house in the picture — yes — yes — yes!

'Hell, maybe this is the only thing that is real. Maybe we's the two last livin' souls on the planet, you and me Margarita?'

I am so lonely here without Red. I miss him, and right now he can't write or anything. Papa Levine is still real sweet to me, but what the hell do I say to him? He must be nearly seventy or something, and sometimes he looks at me and I don't much like the way he looks.

Do you remember how like when it was Christmas, you'd be all excited and then the day would come and it would go past so quick, then the holiday season would drag on and on …? That's how I feel now.

I made it to the cafe anyway, so I can write to you. There's a guy on the corner, he plays a guitar and he's pretty good. I think he's a student or something. He smiled at me when I came in.

A smile that tickled all the way to her toes. In the clothes that Red bought her, driving the car he bought her, of course he smiled at her. The lonely burned off her like a flame.

I stood at my window last night, and I listened to the night. It throbs with noise here, like it's all the thoughts of everyone sleeping around me. I don't know how much longer I can take it. It's like Red just took me up and left me here, like the tide, washed up and alone. When I stood at the window, I wanted to take my clothes off so that the air could touch my skin. I almost thought I could hear the girl from the motel crying again; I almost wanted to hear her.

I saw the man again the other day. He had no shoes on and he was playing his guitar. I was wearing big shades and a new dress, and I put a fifty-dollar bill in his hat. I asked the girl behind the counter, but she said she hadn't seen him for a few days. I hope he's all right, I don't know why I keep thinking of him; he's just some sort of drifter I guess.

It was a hot day on a lonely road. She was driving in her big white car and she saw him, the man with the guitar. What harm would it do to stop and offer him a ride? Or did he wait for her at the cafe until she'd finished her sad little letter to me? Did he nudge her, trip and catch her as she stumbled? He was sorry, he made her laugh, his hand on her back. It was a long, hot day.

I was just drifting about the house, not doing anything much, and I went out the back through the kitchen. It was so hot I thought I'd get some air there. Then I got into my car and I drove for a long time, until I wasn't sure where I was, and then I saw him. We were back in town in no time, I talked and talked, and I pulled over because I was laughing. We started kissing and I know it's wrong but it felt so real and so normal, and like we were just two kids. Then he said we should stop and I said I couldn't, and he said that there would be trouble, and I said I didn't care.

For the first time in weeks, months, she laughed like it was nothing she had to think about first. Whichever day it was, he had her from when he made her laugh. She kissed him in the back of her car, once she'd driven far enough away to think she was safe. When she went back to Red's white house, it looked smaller, diminished somehow. As she lay on the bed in the blue room, she fell asleep before she'd noticed, and dreamed of Paris.

I'm sorry, really I am. I won't see Paris again. I won't.

If only she'd meant it. There was a storm coming. She stood at her window and felt the warning in the air, followed by a hard rain.

CHAPTER 11

A SOUND CRACKED and shattered my memory. The shock brought me back to the room in the swamp with such force that I expected it to knock the breath from my lungs. Before I'd time even to think or listen, I scrabbled for the lantern and forced down the flame as far as I dared, shrouding it with the papers. The room slunk into blackness, the trace of the light dancing across my eyes. I held my breath.

Sweat prickled across my body, the sensation of it almost painful where it broke out under my arms and down my sides. There was the sound of paws and claws running between the walls, the see-saw rasp of insects, the whisper of trees at the window. When I was almost sure it had been my imagination, when I was about to release the breath I was holding, it came again. The sound of a footfall on the landing. It was so slight, I think I was only aware of it because the floorboards under my feet transmitted an infinitesimal movement. I felt rather than heard that Red was there. Red was outside the door.

My heartbeat seemed to pulse behind my eyes. He didn't move, as if he were listening too. He could be waiting for his eyes to adjust to the gloom, needing the bathroom again, I told myself.

He doesn't know you're in here; he's not going to try the door.

A line of light flashed through the darkness. I'd been staring into inky nothingness for long enough for it to seem startlingly bright and confused, almost a lightning strike. I couldn't help it: I shuffled back towards the bed, desperate not to make a sound and just as desperate to reach its sanctuary. The instinct to crawl under it was so strong that I didn't stop to think about what else might be lurking there, waiting for me. I slithered under, catching the edge of the frame with my hand to save cracking the back of my skull on it.

Almost at once my feet impacted against the wall and I coiled myself out of sight. Everything felt wrong, awkward, I was too big for the space – as if the world I was expecting had shrunk in my absence.

The light did not come again. It had been Red's flashlight, momentarily lighting up the landing outside. What the fuck was he doing? But I knew what he was doing… He was checking on me, just like I'd thought he would, and had risked the flashlight to see if I was still on the couch, without chancing the stairs' creak.

Another step, another half-felt, half-heard sensation of movement outside the room, his weight transferring from one foot to the other. He was still there.

Being under the bed, however awkwardly I fit, gave me a sense of security, until I remembered the gun. In my panic, I'd completely forgotten about it, and it was now somewhere out in the dark. I reached forward, aware of the lantern by the glow-worm wriggle of light that escaped the papers, feeling against the floor for the weapon. I found it, but with the back of my hand; and instead of grabbing it, knocked it away. It skittered across the floor, its metallic sound buzzsaw-loud.

The light flashed under the door. He couldn't have heard it, he couldn't – but I froze, not daring to breathe, swallow, think – just a spider at the skirting. I heard him move again, take another step, but which way? Toward the stairs or back towards the bedroom? A spider at the skirting, taking a step over a knot in a green carpet, testing its path, looking for traps. A green carpet, under a bed.

I blinked.

He moved.

The light did not flash again. He turned away from the stairs, and I heard the door of the neighbouring room creak, a sound I'd have missed if I'd been deep in the emails, if I hadn't been taut as a wire. I don't know if I heard the bed frame in his room thrum as he lay down, or if I just imagined that it did, but I let go of the breath I'd been holding with a gasp, and pressed my forehead to the floor. I lay still, then I smiled. He hadn't heard me, and the illusion of my sleeping form on the couch below had reassured him. I still had time.

I reached for the papers, turned up the light, and continued reading, not quite ready to leave the shelter of the bed just yet.

CHAPTER 12

PAPA LEVINE IS ANGRY. He went banging around the place, shouting about how the government asks men to die for them, and yet sticks knives in their back. I went in and asked him what was wrong, but he shut up like a clam and just said that Red is coming home and the army has turned its back on him.

He said, 'You just make sure as you're ready to welcome him, because he ain't gonna get no hero's parade 'cept from us, and that boy deserves one from the president himself.' He had loads of things coming up, events and so forth, and I heard him cancel them all.

What if he knows what I've done?

I knew what Red was doing. He was in dark, dry places, fishing in the air. There was a storm coming, and Papa Levine thundered, and Lisa put her hands over her ears and counted.

Red's back and he's very quiet. He's sleeping in one of the other rooms, like before we were married. He won't say why. I asked him what had happened, why he came back alone without his platoon. He wouldn't say at first.

He had to get drunk before he could tell her, and even then, he hardly told her anything. An incoherent tumble of stories, of names she forgot and relationships she couldn't follow. In their room late at night, the rest of the world asleep outside the window, he tried to make her understand while still keeping his secrets. He cried, and she didn't know what to make of his tears, other than to feel guilty because he didn't know how she'd betrayed him. She felt sick at herself, for being the thing she'd always been told she was, the thing she'd tried to run away from. When he got angry and marched around the room, shaking his fist at god, she was frightened, because she knew he should be angry at her, that it was her who deserved his fury. He told her how he was being made a scapegoat, that they'd saved him just because of who he was, and how the men beneath him, those who'd gone down with him, now thought he'd betrayed them. The word betrayal rattled about in her mind even as she held him, even as he slept.

In the house in the swamp, my hands trembled. The sheets of paper were eroding, so few of them left. I curled onto my side, clinging to them. The storm was breaking, and I could feel the rain.

'Ya know what it mean, when the rain fall but the sun still shine?'

I don't know what's happened, not really. Red either hardly says a word to me, or asks me if I love him over and over. He says he needs me, but he's still sleeping in the other room. He keeps saying how his men all hate him, and that he was only doing his job. I asked him what had happened, came right out and asked him, but he went cold and didn't speak to me for a whole day. Do you think he knows?

I try and go out, but sometimes my car keys are gone, and sometimes the gates won't open. I'm trying to be strong for him; I'm trying to be a good wife. I miss you so much.

Everything watched her: the eyes of the house, the eyes of the staff and his eyes, cold and hurtful. She went to go for a drive, but the keys for her car were gone. The garden was quiet, the gate was locked and the storm was locked in there with her.

Red didn't sleep in their bed any more, but came in at night when she was asleep. He was nice and polite in the morning, but in the night, the wolf was in his eyes. She wanted him, because if they were to make love, or have sex, or fuck, it would mean he still wanted her, or that he really didn't know about Paris. She didn't think he knew, but she feared it, and the longer it went on, the drought between them, the more she was sure he did know. It was worse when he came at night, because then she thought he did still want her and believed she was good and clean and nice, but then he wouldn't touch her and would leave without a word. Then she was sure he knew what she was, that he'd found out somehow.

It's as if he finds me disgusting, as if he's thinking about everything I said. I can see it in him, in his eyes; he thinks I'm dirty, used up, broken.

They fought. She made it happen, she wanted it to happen, because the sky was heavy with rain and the heat built up and up, until the weight of it was unbearable. She picked and nagged and worked at him, until he snapped at her, teeth bared, and she flew at him, screaming and crying, claws out.

Hooker's claws.

She flew at him, and he caught her, held her, then let her go. And she ran. She ran through the house with all its fucking rooms, all the closed doors and the stairs that never seemed to go anywhere. She ran until she found a room with a closet, and shut herself inside, and waited for him to find her, hoping he wouldn't, desperate he wouldn't.

I'm so big I can't hide anywhere any more. Please, I'm so scared, please help me! If only I could talk to Paris again, one last time. There might be a chance next week.

Then there was a break, a gap in the words. The dates were weeks apart and I felt the echo of my panic as I checked them – three weeks at least. Under the bed, in the room in the swamp, I tensed; I drew my knees up to my chest, hiding because she couldn't hide, not in the end.

There'd been no word from her, and I'd gone to the cafe every day and paid my dollar and gone online, but there'd been nothing. I built imagined horrors for her, reading the words she'd sent me over and over, all of it coming back to me in the swamp at the turn of the page. There was even a blank page in the papers, a memento of that dreadful, echoing silence. In my cold city, I'd started running, running to the cafe at first, and then just running, and then buying training shoes so I could keep on running. It had started then, in the pause between her words. Running, when I'd heard that I'd flunked my first year exams, when I had to tell Mom and Dad, and not caring at all, if only I could have heard from her. I rang the number she'd made me promise not to ring, but it was never answered. I even ran past the neighbour's place, though the dog had died years back. I wished it had been there, so I could prove I was brave. Barking dog, pearl buttons, an old lace table cloth.

I haven't been able to get out for days.

Days! It had been weeks, surely?

Red is watching me all the time but he won't come near me. I don't know what to do. I'm going to try and buy air tickets. I told him I needed cash the other day for a dress, but he just said to tell them who I was and he'd pay them later.

Her credit cards were gone, and she sat in the blue room and looked at the jewellery he'd bought her. She felt the weight of her wedding band in her hand and saw how the diamond caught the light. All of that, all of those things piled up around her and none of it any defence against him, against what she felt, and me, running, running to the coffee shop because I couldn't run after her, I couldn't save her again, just like when we were kids.

She found her car keys. She took the key that opened the gate at the end of the drive. She didn't have her jewellery but she thought she'd try, just see? Maybe she'd have come back, maybe she was just seeing how far she could get; a kite tugging at its string?

Had she told me this? I looked at the paper in my hands. The words were not there, but I could see them, feel them. I could see her.

'Tell me who ya love, an' I'll tell ya who ya are.'

He caught her – he must have, I was sure he had. He caught her in the garage and demanded to know where she was going, what she was doing. She tried to get into the car, but he caught the door and pulled it open. He was someone else, the strength in him something living and hungry, something she'd only toyed with before. You thought he was going to pull you out, hit you, but instead he ripped the keys from the ignition and slammed the door shut. Then he locked it, clicking the key twice so the mechanism thudded into place.

I imagined how she beat against the glass, white hands flat against the glass, and how he just stood there, watching her. Then in my mind she saw movement, a flash from behind him in the well of sunlight, and his father was there too. Cut out against the sunlight of the garden, the old man watched her for a moment, watched his son watching her trapped in the big, white car. Then he turned his back and walked away.

He's always there, Red's father, watching me and watching me with him, both of them all the time. He never says anything to me. There's so much silence, I can't hear myself think.

How long did they leave you there, alone, in the dark? Did you cry, were you scared, trapped in the bell jar of the jeep, hands like wings beating against the glass?

We fight all the time, and I can see Red's holding himself back and that it's a struggle. He wants to hurt me. He's going to hurt me.

Or was that at night, in the blue room as they called it? Was it there that Papa Levine saw her locked in and walked away, the click of the key loud as a gunshot? A thousand miles, a thousand years away, I wanted to scream at him for his cowardice. Or it was me who turned away, me who didn't – couldn't – stop him?

Please can you tell Mom and Dad where I am, I don't care any more, please?

Did I? I thought desperately, trying to force the memory back – did I tell them? I could have killed Red then and there for what he did to her, dug out that jewellery roll and killed him for all the things I thought he'd done.

Please can you tell Mom and Dad where I am?

Had I told them? How could I tell them this, when I hadn't told them about everything else? Had I thought that she was making it up, telling stories like she had before, getting me into trouble, Little Red Riding Hood crying wolf? That was what Dad said: just Lisa and her stories, Lisa making a fuss, buzz, buzz, buzz, with a bee in her bonnet.

The click of a key in a lock, loud as gunshot.

I'd hated it when they'd said that, hated them laughing at her when I knew she was right, knew she hadn't made any of it up. Why hadn't I told them?

He's always watching me. He's always on edge, checking the windows whenever he comes into a room, not letting me open one no matter how hot it is. He's making sure I can't get out, I know he is.

I never told them, because of college. I never told them, because of Dad, because of the smell of him, of decay and sickly sweet morphine, and the shuffle of his feet against the floor as he tried to get up. I never told them, because I left home instead.

He's outside now, in the car, watching through the window. He's watching me as if he knows what I'm writing. He's got a gun, I've seen it. He's waiting for proof, I know he is, he's waiting to catch me out and if he does—

I saw them as if it was the first time, our family. Not their faces, but their worries and words and voices and the slowly increasing distance between us, which I'd never, ever been able to bridge. Lisa had made me hers and then she was gone and I was as far away from them as she was. I knew she did it to try and protect me; and she had, she'd made me safe at her expense. I knew they were never going to come and save her, they'd already let her go. A deal had been made without me. Without knowing why, I'd just kept on running.

I saw us then, saw the view from under our bed in the beautiful big room we shared. She was a shadow against the light and we were hiding. But we were not playing a game. A savannah of green carpet, a barking dog coming up the stairs to find us – no, not the dog.

'I didn't mean to do it. I'm scared, Lisa. Will he find me, will he?' I was crying. I couldn't remember what I'd done, only that it was something unforgivable.

'Shh.' She put her finger to her lips, her little angel face cold with a fear she didn't want to show me. 'Remember the rhyme?' she asked and I nodded, too frightened to speak.

The click of a key in the lock, loud as gunshot.

'Close your eyes,' she commanded and I did, though I heard the footfall on the stairs. 'Say it.' She gripped my hand in hers, and I remembered her fingers, hot and hard and clammy all at once. 'Say it!' she hissed again as the door of the room creaked open. 'I'll say I did it, just close your eyes and say our song.'

'Count to ten, count to ten, then he'll go away again. If you get to twenty-one, then you'll live to see the sun.'

It is true, all of it. Please, you have to believe me. You do believe me don't you? Please say you believe me!

The pages were nearly gone, just two more sheets thin and insubstantial. If I did not read, then maybe she'd be okay? No. If I put the pages back and closed the door and locked it again, if I went back down and lay on the couch, if I even went into the other room and woke Red and let him fuck me or kill me or killed him – none of it would change what was printed on the last two pieces of paper.

I'm getting out. If I ask, you'll do everything you can, won't you? He's going to kill me, I know he is, if I don't get out. He hates me, or he thinks he loves me, but it's really hate. I screamed at him to let me out, let me go and he went crazy – banging doors, punching the wall – saying over and over it wasn't safe – but it's him I'm in danger from. I tried to push past him, to run, but he grabbed for me and pulled me back. I tried to get away and hit out at him, and he hit me and I fell down. He tried to say he was sorry, but then his Papa came and I got away. He didn't say anything, Papa Levine, not a damn thing! I should just go, but I can't, I've nowhere to go.

Had she run? She should have, she should have just run away from him then. But she hadn't. There was one more page.

I saw Paris the other day and he made me talk to him. I only had a moment. I told him what has happened. He saw the bruise

under my glasses. Paris says he's going to get me out somehow.
Then I'm going to get you and we'll be free for real.

The house shivered and waited. From under the bed, from a childhood far away, Lisa pressed her face to my ear and whispered.

'Say our song and it will be okay. Say it for me, please!'

Very quickly – Red is away next weekend, and I'm going to get all the jewellery I can, and meet Paris where I first picked him up on the road. Paris said to bring other things, he knows what I need to get, stuff we can sell and then we can be together.

I'm going to get all the way back to you and then we can live together, all of us, and we're all going to be happy I promise. Have faith in me. Please know that however hard it gets, however long it takes, I'll come back to you, I promise. I can trust you, can't I?

I closed my eyes under our childhood bed as Lisa had asked me to. I said our song, the one we'd made for when it happened.

'Count to ten … count to ten …'

I felt her dragged away from me, I heard her scream and kick at him, and the slap as Daddy hit her. I pressed my hands over my ears and my face against the hard green carpet and tried not to hear the rest of it. I closed my eyes, I looked away: I pretended I did not see.

'Count to ten, count to ten …'

'Was it you, or her. Lisa, you or her?' I heard Daddy hit her again. 'It was you, wasn't it, you filthy little beast!'

'I'm sorry Daddy, I didn't mean it.'

'It's always you, isn't it?'

'I'm sorry Daddy, please!'

'Are you? 'Cause your words are saying sorry, but Daddy knows what a liar you are.'

'I ain't lying, I promise.'

'You best come here and show your Daddy you're sorry. You come here now, and show your Daddy you're sorry.'

I was the one who'd listened, I was the one who'd kept her story safe, and now it had finished. The last page of the text slipped from my hand and landed with a sharp clip on the floor. I watched it fall.

She'd saved me, she'd taken it all on herself to save me.

I reached back into the void under the bed, right into the far corner. My hand closed about his body: firm, velvet, so familiar. The little pearl buttons on his jacket were cold, so too his black button eyes.

I drew myself out from under the bed, and I looked at him. I saw myself running upstairs with him, when Daddy had driven all the way to the depot, when Lisa forgot him on the school bus. Mr Pooter, her toy rabbit. Mr Pooter, left for me to find under the bed, in the locked room, in the swamp. The air became heavy with the scent of sandalwood and cinnamon, with the brush of silk on my skin and perfume on an old fur coat. As I read Lisa's words, it wasn't his face I saw any more, not Rooster, or Red, but Daddy, my Daddy, our Daddy. It was him.

I am a swimmer, I thought. I am a swimmer. I pressed Mr Pooter to my face and breathed him in. With his scent, the darkness of my memory shattered, and I knew who I was.

'A key fit only the lock it were made for, Cherie.'

CHAPTER 13

I HAD THE KEYS IN MY POCKET. I opened the front gate and felt its squeak vibrate through the metal. I didn't let it clang, but caught the lock and closed it softly. The maple in the front yard was in full leaf, dappling the sunlight and dancing with stars when I looked up, leaves like hands. I didn't let myself stand under it and enjoy its scent like I wanted to, because I didn't really want to. I only wanted to do it, so I didn't have to go in yet.

The high pitch of the gable lent the house, my home, a slightly surprised expression. Ours was grey and white. The neighbours had gone all-out pastel, lilac and peppermint green, with a fountain in the front yard, too big for the space and looking more like a giant spinning top, abandoned.

'Would you believe, it even lights up at night?' Mom had told me about it, as it had arrived just after I'd left, and at least had given her something safe to call me about. 'Like Walt Disney's castle, pink and blue. I mean, I don't mind a few lights at Christmas, but do they mean to have this on all year?'

I meant to skirt round to the kitchen, but there was a neat little truck already parked out front, with 'Smarter Party Catering' on the side. So instead, I walked up to the front porch, and got the big door key ready. Close up, I saw the blinds in the parlour were pulled half down, so the house looked both sleepy and surprised, as if I'd woken it up.

In the entrance hall, I could hear noise from both the kitchen to the right, and the parlour to the left. The people from 'Smarty Party' must have gotten busy setting things out on trays and polishing glasses, and from what I could tell, Mom's sister Elsa was talking to Francis in the parlour. I wasn't ready to speak to either side, so I closed up the door with long-practiced stealth, stepped out of my broken-back sneakers and tiptoed up the stairs.

I had my good shoes in my bag. I thought about going into my old room and distracting myself by looking through what I still had to collect, when I heard her crying. I paused at the top, still on my toes. She was crying the way Mom always did, like she was really hoping nobody would hear, but if they did and came in, then at least she wouldn't be quite all gone to pieces. Wouldn't be in too much of a state, so nobody would feel awkward about it.

She didn't hear me of course, stockinged feet and all. One side of the double doors to their bedroom was open, not all the way, but enough. Everything still smelt of the carpet they were having put down as I was moving out; but it was the other smell that made me falter, stopped me from letting her know I was there. Cigarette smoke.

The scent of it took me right back to when I was eight or so, younger perhaps. Summer, light strong so that Mom was almost in shadow, and me at the door like this, watching. She was wearing a slip, something delicate with a frill at the hem, and she was smoking, flicking the ash into a cut-glass ashtray on her dressing table. Even then, I knew this was unusual, something other mothers didn't do.

I had Mr Pooter in my hand, Mr Pooter to give me courage, but

I hadn't been able to speak. I'd stood there and there she'd been, seeming to watch the smoke as it curled in a grey tendril between mouth and nose. When she looked at me, I saw she'd been crying, tears rolling over her cheeks.

'Mamma's got a headache,' she'd said.

She hadn't seen me this time yet. She wasn't at her dressing table either. Now she was on the corner of the bed, half turned away and in a simpler, more austere black slip, and what I could see the most, was the dress she'd laid out for today. It was black crepe with a high neck and short puff sleeves, a dress that was half old lady, half little girl. She could wear better stuff, she had the figure for it, but it was what he'd have liked, how he'd have liked her to be.

I don't think I make a sound, but then she was aware of me and looked round, 'Oh, hello,' and she was fussing to reach for fresh Kleenex from the nightstand and sitting back down to dab at her eyes. 'Oh, goodness, I didn't see you there. I'm such a state!'

I went in. I couldn't see the ashtray or the cigarettes, but found I was scanning the room for them, as if I was doing a dorm check for narcotics.

'I won't be a moment,' Mom said. 'I was just, well, I was just going to get dressed. The caterers are here. Francis let them in, but I don't want him snitching all the—'

'Mom, it's okay,' I said and I sat down next to the dress. 'It's okay for you to be upset, you know?'

She looked at me as if she wasn't sure why I'd say such a silly thing, then nodded and allowed herself a smile. Her eyes were puffy, the skin that was only just beginning to soften into chiffon creases, plumped out by grief. She was good at sad, I thought, good at melancholy. It did her good, like the way the sun calms some people's acne.

'How was last week?' she asked.

'What?'

'You said you had to go out of town, take flight, for work, wasn't it? Weren't you at the airport or something when I called?'

'Oh, sure, yeah. It was fine.'

'Was the flight good?'

'It was coach, Mom. It's never good.'

'I suppose not. Such a long way though, you must have felt quite the Yankee down there.' She smiled at me. 'You look nice, dear. That dress suits you.'

'I got pumps,' I said, as if she might have thought I meant to go barefoot, but she flicked her hand – of course she hadn't thought that. I looked down at myself. 'Hey, it's not like I don't got a whole lot of black. Funerals I can do; I just suck at weddings.'

I kind of expected her to tell me off for trying to be funny, but she didn't.

'It's your colouring,' she said. 'You've got your father's skin tone, so you can carry bold colours. You should wear more of them, red and blue, because you could, you know, you could carry them off.'

'Mom, please,' I said and I got up, because I didn't want to hear that again, that I've got his colouring.

'But I was just saying,' she said, and she sounded hurt and fragile, and had the ball of Kleenex all twisted up between her hands, working it tight. 'I was only saying because you're so pretty, dear, and you always wear such dull colours, such—'

I put my hand on her shoulder. 'It's okay Mom. I get it.'

She let go of the Kleenex with one hand so she could touch mine, then leant her head against my side. We were silent for a moment. I thought about asking about her smoking and didn't, and then the silence started to feel awkward. I heard footsteps as someone crossed the hall below, and voices, which sounded like a question, and Francis and Elsa discussing the answer. They didn't know, I decided, and as I thought one of them was probably going to come up and ask Mom, I started to say, 'Hey, look, is there anything you want me to—' but she cut me off, all in a rush.

'Do you know where she is?'

CHAPTER 14

THE SHOP HAD BEEN what I'd expected, what I'd imagined by reading the name alone. It had tiny windows full of symbols from a different faith, another world, not my world, the world where I was rational and calculating and prepared. The world I'd taken a plane to see, three days before my father had died.

An artifice had been created inside the shop, a stage set to prepare the receptive; books and charts and objects in jars, in boxes. It was an Aladdin's cave of the occult, and I wasn't sure why I was there, other than I had to be somewhere while I waited to speak with the Sheriff.

'This time ya' here in more corporeal form.'

I'd been looking at some jewellery draped across a wooden hand, and I jumped because I hadn't heard her appear. Her voice was thick and heavily accented, which I took as part of her costume, along with her richly decorated turban and the regalia of beads clattered about her neck.

'I'm sorry?' I asked, but she ignored my question.

'Ya head much better, no?' Before I could reply, she brushed her forehead and closed her eyes for a moment. She smiled. 'Ya must forgive me. I realize as how ya won't understand, because y'are ...'

She paused, searched the air for the word. 'A little out of time.'

'I'm just here to look around,' I said and smiled, fearing she was going to sell me something. She came round from behind her counter, moving as if her hips towed her body in their wake. She paused a few feet away and looked me up and down in such a direct, open manner, I was unsure whether to be annoyed or impressed.

'Ya come back to me,' she said and held out her long, elegant hand. 'I see the good in ya, but ya must be careful.' I took her hand, and the slender, cool fingers closed round mine as if they held something wounded.

'I was just looking for someone,' I began.

'I know,' she said, 'an' he's seen ya.'

'No, it's not a man ...'

'He passed ya by just now, when ya was walkin' along the esplanade.' I made a gentle move to pull my hand away but she did not let go. 'He passed by in his big black car, an' he looked at ya, because there was something in ya form, in the way ya walk, which made him think of her.'

'Who?' I asked.

'Who ya binlookin' for, because him binlookin' for her also ...' she closed her eyes for a second, forestalling my question. 'Now, him binlooking after da way ya gone.' She let go of my hand.

'Look,' I said, and began to rummage in my bag among the papers and the pictures and the fragments of Lisa I had with me. 'She's a few years older than me, and her name is Lisa; she's blond, well, she was blond, I have a photo of her, perhaps ...'

'Non.' She placed her fingers on the mouth of my bag. 'I have not seen her, ma Cherie – but here ...' she reached inside her robes. 'Ya'll know him when ya see him. Ya ever heard what it mean when tha' rain fall when tha' sun shine? Mean the devil beatin' his wife.' She held out six silver dollars.

'I don't want money ...' I said, but she withdrew her hand and slid behind her counter without a backward glance.

'Go get yourself a coffee,' she said with her back to me. 'Little place on the corner, name of 'Mademoiselle's'. Tell them as I sent ya, but hurry ...' She risked one long glance back. 'Ya don't want them to run out of sugar cookies before ya get there.' The beaded curtain over the entrance to the back of her shop parted.

'What's your name?' I asked, reaching for her. For a moment, I felt the loss of her as keenly as my sister's.

'Angelique.' The beads clattered, and she was gone.

'Mademoiselle's' was on the corner as she'd said. If the wrought iron sign over the door had not caught my eye, the rich thick smell of coffee would have drawn me there. The floor above jutted out, following the corner of the block and supported by an iron pillar with a filigree of leaves at its point. I skirted the small collection of ornate tables outside and went in.

There was a long glass-topped counter, surmounted by a parapet of glass cake domes. The menu on the wall behind was almost as esoteric as the sigils in Angelique's boutique, special blends chalked up in pink and blue. There were three baristas serving behind the counter, the espresso machines sang and hissed, the low buzz of chatter and laughter was as warm as the air.

'Good morning darlin', what can I get for you today?' The barista who turned his radiant smile on me, was a little over forty and a little overweight.

'I'll just take an Americano, thank you.'

'Sure thing, can I get you somethin' to go with that? We got a new batch o' praline ready just now.'

'No, I'm good thanks,' I said and then I remembered what Angelique had said. 'Someone said that your sugar cookies were good?'

'They sure are, I'll look some out for you. They're a dollar apiece, or I can give you six for four.'

'That would be good, thank you.'

The cafe was not busy, not the hive of caffeine seekers as it might have been at home, but there was a regular flow of people in and out even in the short time I lingered. There were a few tables inside, one of which was occupied by a man reading a newspaper.

As I waited, I caught the movement of the paper as the reader folded it away and stood up, scraping his chair on the tiled floor. He walked toward the counter and stood a little to my left, waiting to pay for his coffee and the ornate cake box he took from his server. I glanced sideways and saw a man, in his late thirties perhaps, with an angular face and blond and brown hair. He'd tucked his paper under his arm, and was whistling between his teeth as he waited for his change.

The barista handed me my coffee and a brown paper bag neatly folded round the cookies.

'That'll be six dollars,' he said, and I counted them into his hand. As the man with the paper turned to go, he nudged my arm reaching for the coffee.

'Whoa, forgive me darlin'.' He smiled. 'I hope I didn't spill nothin'?'

'No, I'm fine, thank you.'

'Glad to hear it,' he said, and the light caught on the teeth behind his smile, before he turned on his heel and walked out into the sunshine. I looked after him, sure that there was something familiar about him, though not quite sure what.

⸾

The Sheriff had a neatly trimmed moustache, which gave him the air of an old prospector from the Klondike. I wondered if he cultivated it on purpose to go with his swagger and the uniform, which had a crease pressed into each sleeve. The image of old west charm was only spoiled by the bluetooth earpiece he was wearing a little self-consciously.

'Please, sit down,' he said and smiled warmly. 'You're fortunate to be visiting us outside the hurricane season; though mind you, not everyone sees fit to inform the hurricanes when they can or can't stop by.' He smiled at his joke, his office as neat as his uniform.

'Did you read them?' I asked. He looked a little deflated by my lack of ceremony.

'Sure ma'am, I read them.' He took the folder I'd sent him from a tray on his left and placed it firmly and squarely in front of him. He folded his hands together on top as if he were scared something might escape it.

'What do you think? Did you speak to him?'

'Ma'am ...' the Sheriff paused, unlaced his fingers and traced a circle on the folder. 'I can see that, to read this, would be concerning for anyone.'

'She said he hit her,' I said. 'Look ...' he didn't move fast enough, so I snapped open my bag and shuffled through the tattered copy I had. 'Look, here, she says he locked her in, stopped her from leaving? I mean, that's kidnap, right, false imprisonment? That's illegal, even down here, right?' I shouldn't have said that, it riled him, though he tried to hide it.

'Miss, please. I personally take a very dim view of any man who is violent towards a woman ...'

'So, what's this then?'

The Sheriff raised his hand. 'Miss, please, I'm tryin' to explain that I'm on your side here, I share your concern.'

'Then what have you done?' I said, standing up and pushing my chair away. 'Did you go see him?'

My outburst prompted the Sheriff to resort to a double hand raise. 'Miss, I understand your distress, but can I ask you to please lower your voice and remain calm?'

'Did you?' I repeated.

'If you sit down,' he said, 'if you sit down and give me a moment, I'll explain to you what I found.' In a lower tone he added, 'Look miss, I'd slap his sorry ass in jail tomorrow if I thought I could get away with it, just to amuse myself.' He risked a smirk under his moustache.

His confession had the desired effect on me and I sat down again. When he was sure I was calmer, he got up and closed the door ostentatiously. He did not return to his official chair but drew up a plastic one from the side and sat down near me.

'What you got here,' he said nodding toward his desk, 'what you got is nasty, nasty stuff, and I ain't takin' it lightly. Like I said, I don't have time for excuses, violence against a woman is second only to violence against little'uns. The problem is, there ain't much I can do with this.' He raised his hand a little as he saw I was about to interrupt again. 'It's hearsay, if you want the legal term, but I done what I could for you, trust me, Miss – took it as far as possible.' He glanced towards the door again.

'Did you go see him?'

'Yes, I did.' He sniffed. He smelled clean, as if his wife still used starch in the wash. 'Most folks round here know of the Levines, they're pretty much what we've got for aristocracy in this parish, so I'm askin' you to make me a promise before I go any further.'

I frowned at him. 'A promise?'

'That you'll not repeat anything that I say to you, because by rights, I shouldn't be takin' you into my confidence.'

He was just like all of them, I thought, trying to take care of me, trying to pretend like nothing had happened, trying to protect me.

'If you won't help me, what use is what you tell me anyways?'

He shifted a little in his chair. 'I guess it ain't, for now, but hell, I ain't sayin' that things might never change, and you shouldn't think it won't. If you go poking round you could ruin any chances I might have of one day sortin' this out, if more evidence comes to light.'

He means a body, I thought. He means Lisa's body.

He looked seriously at me, and we both pretended that I'd agreed to what he'd asked.

'So, what did Rooster say?' I said, pulling my fingers through my hair. 'Was he surprised to see you?'

The Sheriff cleared his throat. 'Mr Levine was ...' He smiled at the memory. 'He was a little surprised to see me, but he made time in his busy schedule. His Daddy was out, so he was able to ...fit me into his diary.' He gathered himself and drew his brow into a frown. 'Anyhow, well, I said as how the absence of his wife had been brought to my attention by some of her family, said as how I'd been asked to make enquires, as she had not been heard from in some months.'

'How did he react?' I asked, leaning forward as if I could see what he'd seen if I only got closer to him.

'I asked him how long it had been since he'd had word from her.' The Sheriff tilted his head. 'His timescale ... basically coincided with yours, he seemed ...' He inhaled. 'He seemed surprised but not overly hostile. I would almost have said he was ... prepared.'

'You asked him if he hit her?'

'Miss, trust me, a direct accusation like that right now, would have done nothing but make him clam up. I asked him to describe the nature of his relationship with his wife, and Mr Levine openly admitted that they'd been havin' ... serious marital problems after he returned from his tour of duty.'

'Yeah,' I muttered.

'Guess his homecoming weren't exactly what he'd planned,' the Sheriff said, and then registered my expression. He coughed again. 'According to Rooster, she admitted she'd had an affair, though he said he didn't know with whom. They fought, she packed her case and left, with a quantity of jewellery and cash.'

'Of course he'd say that,' I said and my voice sounded petulant in his neat, well-starched office.

'Ma'am, there ain't much else in the way of evidence, and Mr Levine was ... refreshingly honest with me.'

'How the hell would you know he was honest?'

'He admitted to me that they'd fought, and for some time,' I gripped the arms of my chair. 'He admitted the fights could get pretty physical, said as how she hit him 'n all ...'

'Well, poor old him!' I snorted.

The Sheriff ignored me. 'But without your sister's testimony ...'

'What's this?' I flicked the papers in my bag.

'This is upsetting to read, sure, but this ain't gonna get Mr Levine arrested, certainly not convicted.'

'But this is not just my word against his, or her word. Look, she talks about meeting this man Paris. He was involved. He must know that she was being hurt; she says he saw the bruises on her!'

The Sheriff sat back and drummed his fingers on the edge of his desk. There were flecks of grey at his temples, and the top quadrant of his forehead was paler than the rest, presumably where his hat was habitually perched.

'Well, I'll be honest with you, though Paris ain't all that uncommon a name round these parts, what with the French connection n'all, from them few lines I gotta pretty good idea who she was talkin' about.'

'So you could find him?'

The Sheriff pulled his moustache back in an apologetic smile. 'Now see, this young fella I think was mixed up with your sister, he's ...' he decided on a smirk. '... he's not exactly the biggest fan of my department. I've had cause aplenty to speak with him on all manner of occasions and he ain't never been what you might call forthcoming.'

'I guessed he was some sort of drifter?' I said. 'But he might still talk to me, right?'

'Miss, I couldn't advise that course of action. This man, Paris? I wouldn't call him a drifter, though that suits him pretty good when he needs to look in want of a square meal.' The Sheriff slipped his hands into his pants pockets. 'He's what I'd call a cheap con; he hustles people, mostly women with nice jewellery and men who like to gamble. I've had him in on a few counts of fraud and disturbing the peace. If I were you, I'd be as concerned for your sister's choice of boyfriend as husband.'

'But he didn't hit her!' I said.

'That's just what this says.' The Sheriff nodded to the folder again. 'Don't mean it's the truth. What I see here, is a bad marriage gone worse, then I see a woman plannin' to take off with plenty of cash and jewellery, to meet with a known con-artist, who may well play the guitar, but who ain't some happy drifter.'

'So you think she's lying too?'

'No, I do not.' Then came the pause I'd expected. 'But she may not be tellin' all the truth, or the truth she don't want to acknowledge. If she were here, I'd have Mr Levine behind bars tonight I promise, I don't believe in letting things slide no matter who I'm dealin' with. Hell, I'm from an old army family, but I ain't got no time for no one who breaks the law. Regiment or no regiment I'd see as he got what was coming to him, but while she's not here, then …' He exhaled deeply and his moustache quivered in the jet stream from his nose.

'What if she's dead?' I asked, hoping that the words would have had more impact on him than they seemed to.

'I hope she ain't, really I do, and without a body in my book, she ain't dead. Hell, you hold onto that miss, she's probably out there, just got her reasons for not getting in touch. I had her logged as officially missing, and I don't regard that as kicking this into the long grass. I don't like leavin' people on my missing persons list; I find they mess up the place. If we get hide or hair of her, then we'll be right on it, you got my word on that, and I'll let you know the second we got something.'

I slumped back in my chair, unable to meet his eyes. 'So, you don't think it's suspicious that in her last email she's scared and alone and planning to run away, and then nothing?'

The Sheriff got up slowly and tapped the edge of his desk before walking round behind me and tweaking the blind at his window open a little.

'Honestly miss, I think it's damn suspicious, but if you want my opinion, I'd say there's a lot more that them emails ain't tellin' than what they is. I got a budget, I got crimes with bodies and shootings. I even got a missing kid, and that's pretty much all we're thinking about round these parts.'

I closed my eyes and waited for him to say it like one waits for a door to close or the sound of footsteps leaving. I knew there was nothing else he could do, that he'd already done more for me and crossed more lines than others in his position might have, but hearing him say it was still dreadful.

'Miss, if you don't mind me sayin', if I were you, I'd hold onto what you got and remember we'll keep lookin', however long it takes.'

'Right,' I muttered, gathering up my papers and shoving them back into my bag.

'Miss …' he said, a warning note creeping in his voice. 'I don't wanna hear you've gone near any of the other parties in this case.' His avuncular air dissipated as he narrowed his eyes at me. 'Neither Mr. Levine nor the other are what I'd call safe for a nice young lady such as yourself to go messin' with. You might think as how you'll make things happen faster, but trust me, all you'll do is drive them further underground and get yourself slapped with a restraining order, if you're lucky.' He watched as my hand paused over the page of notes from his interview with Rooster Levine. 'It's me what'll be enforcing the restraining order, and much as I like you, the law is the law.'

I reluctantly withdrew my hand from his file.

'Don't worry sir,' I sighed. 'If you find anything, anything at all, you will tell me won't you, please?'

'Sure, got your details right here.' He tapped his shirt pocket as if he wore them next to his heart like a bible. 'You heading home now?'

'My flight leaves in an hour,' I said and stood up.

'Then you best make sure you catch it.' The Sheriff folded his hands together behind his back. 'An' if you have cause to find yourself this way again, make sure you stop by and say hello. Make yourself known to me.' He smiled. 'Save me worrying 'bout you too.'

Lisa would have liked the cookies. They were different shapes, a teapot, a coffee mug, each intricately frosted with crisp sugar shell. In the taxi to the airport I unwrapped the brown paper and bit into the first one.

I saw Lisa, in her summer dress, running to the park we played in. I saw the castle she made us from air and imagination round the monkey bars; saw the treacherous sea studded with mermaids, in which we clung together. I saw the teeter-totter, red and bright in the sun, me high in the air with her facing me.

'I don't wanna do it.' I clung to the metal handle. 'Let me down, please don't bump me.'

'I won't bump you.' She got up slowly, lowering me down until she was on her tiptoes and I was safe.

'See, you' all safe down now.'

'Do it again,' I laughed. 'Do it again!'

I brushed the sugar crumbs from my shirt, and paid the taxi driver. Then my cell flashed with the word 'Mom'.

CHAPTER 15

MOM'S LEFT HAND kneaded the tissue ball in her fist. Her right hand held mine, and when I tried to step back from her, she wouldn't let me go.

'Do you know?' she said again. My heart began to beat tight in my chest, and I knew I was blushing, could feel the heat of it itching at the roots of my hair.

'No,' I said, which wasn't a lie, which wasn't quite a lie, because I didn't, I really didn't, and the not-knowing burned in my stomach like it had been doing for weeks. Mom was looking at me and, under the beam of her gaze, her blue eyes peeled clear and clean with crying. I wanted to say something.

Don't, I thought, trying to swallow as the words crowded into my mouth, because you can't. You can't tell her what you think, what you're terrified of, not now, not today. It wouldn't be right, she couldn't take it, not after all this time, not today of all fucking days, not—

'What will I say?' she said, and because all I was thinking about, was what I couldn't tell her, I didn't get what she meant. 'When people ask today, ask where she is, what do I say?'

I pulled my hand free of hers. So that was it. Whatever will people say – all of the neighbours and all the other fusty old college professors from his work, and Dad's family; his brother from upstate and his aged mother, Grandma Johnson. Oh, and thank you, by the way, to the whole fucking Johnson family, for saddling us with that one – thanks for the moment in grade school when that name was rendered forever snigger-worthy. That's what she was worried about though, Mom, not where Lisa was, not what had happened to her, but what people might say because she wasn't there. I knew she didn't know, I knew she didn't know any of it, but what the hell did she want? Me to tell her the truth now, today? That I thought Lisa might be dead?

I wasn't going to. I wasn't going to tell her, not until I knew for sure. She could be angry as hell at me, but hey, so the fuck what? As long as the neighbours didn't find out. Besides, so what if they did? She could have two terrible daughters to weep about and be sorry about, couldn't she?

'They won't ask,' I said. My bag slipped from my shoulder, so I lifted it up again, deciding that perhaps I would wear my shitty trainers after all, and why the fuck not? Why the fuck shouldn't I be comfortable?

Mom looked at me. 'Of course they'll ask,' she said. 'Besides, she ought to be here. He was her father too, even after everything, even—' but even she hadn't got the fucking nerve to finish that one.

'Really?' I said. 'Look, Mom, the family won't say shit, and everyone else? They won't probably even remember he had another daughter, will they? They're academics, they don't notice anything not in a book or dug up from the ground. It's not like she was ever around much, was she, what with all her schools, and everything?' And that hurt her, and I saw it hurt her, saw the spots of red burn on her cheeks and her shoulders hunch, like she was flinching away from me. I should have been nice, but I couldn't be, because, I realized as I looked at her, to do what I needed to do, I kind of couldn't be around them, and I kind of needed them not to want me to be around, either. So I said, 'Besides, I'm not going to be there either.'

'What?'

'I'll go to the church, okay, to the service, and I'll stand there and bite my tongue, and shake everyone's hand outside. But I'm not coming back here after, okay?'

'Why ever not?' Mom said. 'You can't mean to—'

'I'm not going to spend all day lying about everything,' I snapped. 'I just can't.'

I left without giving her a chance to answer, the shoes in my bag slapping against my back as I thumped heavy-footed downstairs.

What the hell did she expect, me to tell her everything now? Christ, let her hate me, let Francis sneer all the fuck he liked at me, all big brother moral high ground if he wanted to, and Nana Johnson, and Uncle Gene, and all the fucking neighbours from their big fucking 'oh, look at you now' houses, all secretly glad that, hey, at least their family wasn't our particular kind of cluster-fuck. If they talked about me, then perhaps they really wouldn't ask Mom about Lisa, and I might have a chance to find her, so that when I told them about her, it wouldn't be about her being dead.

Not looking where I was going, I walked smack into a guy in a white smock, who was carrying an empty tray from the dining room back into the kitchen.

'Whoa, hey, miss!' he said as his tray hit the stone floor with an almighty crash, enough to bring Francis and Aunt Elsa to the parlour door.

Francis barked out my name, but I ignored him. Catering guy put his hand on my arm to steady me.

'Hey, no harm done, miss,' he said, the words 'Smarter Party' bright in red stitching on his white lapel. It's only when I saw him squint down at me, his saggy, grey stubbled face all crumpled-looking in concern, that I realized I was crying.

'I'm sorry for your loss,' he said, and I wondered how he knew about her, only of course he didn't. He didn't really know why I was crying.

CHAPTER 16

WHEN I FOUND PARIS, I told him my name was Margarita.

'That ain't your name,' he said and he laughed.

'Yeah it is, what's so funny 'bout that?'

'It suit you too well; salty sweet and hits you right between the eyes. Nobody gets a name that right on the mark.'

'Maybe I grew into it?'

'Hell yeah, maybe you did too?' His smile was warm and inviting and dangerous. 'Guess I know what you want then?'

'Sure you do,' I said. 'Make it a Tom Collins.'

He was what I'd expected. He was nice. He was easy to be with, easy to slip in beside and feel like he'd been waiting just for you. A dog wagging his tail.

'What you do then?'

He shrugged. 'You really wanna know?'

'Sure. What, you gonna tell me you's a tax inspector?'

'I ain't that bad, Shoog!' He laughed. 'Naw, I'm a convicted fraudster.'

'What?' I had to admire his honesty.

'Straight up, done time for it too. You still want that drink?'

'Hell yeah, I wanna hear all about it!'

Who wouldn't, sitting there in the small friendly bar, with the street hot and the day lazy outside? Nothing else to do but lounge in the warm air and listen to the lilting, rolling swell of voices and laughter, and let the cocktails work right down to your toes. Nothing to do but have this man – this handsome, dark skinned man – turn the power of his wide, white smile on you. Listen to him tell you about all the bad things he'd done, and make it sound easy, like a schoolyard skipping rhyme.

'So what, you gonna con me then?'

'Naw.' His smile warmed his cheeks. 'I ain't gonna con you.'

'Why not? Maybe you are already, how'd I know?' I twisted my ankles together, leaning back in my chair.

'Hell's teeth, girl, I can't see as you got nothin' I want that bad.' He grinned. 'Well, not money, anyhow.'

'I might be some sort of lost princess!' I said, hitting his arm. We were drinking long, pink drinks, something sweet we sucked through striped straws.

'You ain't lost, even if you is a princess. Anyhow, you can only make the con work if you knows what drives the mark, and right now with you? I ain't so sure I've worked you out yet.'

'Yeah? You work people out easy, do you?'

'Sure thing.' He leant back in his chair, stretching his long legs out under the table between us and folding his hands behind his head. The day had darkened his t-shirt against his skin, brushed his upper lip with beads of moisture.

'That's what you gotta do, read people. You can con anyone. Hell, you can con a man outta his last dollar when he's starvin', easy as shake his hand. But what's the point of that? All you got then is one dollar. Same amount of work goes into liftin' a million dollars, so if you're gonna work, might as well make it pay. It's all 'bout knowin' what the other man wants, and makin' him think as how he's gonna get it. You can con the starvin', but it's a whole heap better to con the greedy.'

'Is that what you look for, greedy men?'

Paris took a toothpick from the small wooden jar the waitress left, after we'd eaten our catch of the day, and fitted it between his teeth.

'Sometimes, depends on what they hanker after though.' He settled his hands back behind his head, pulling his body taut as he did so. 'Some men, all they want is money, for no good reason other than they do. Some want pride, some have pride and then you gotta make them think as how you got more pride, and they can take it from you. Some, they got the lust in them, I can't do nothin' with but you … you know more 'bout that than I do.'

'Yeah? You think I could con someone?' I asked, biting into the cherry from my glass. He flicked his arms from behind his head with laughter, and slapped his knee with his wide, flat hand.

'You? Why, you's been doin' it since you was born.' He dropped the toothpick on the floor, and drank his ridiculous pink drink.

'You think I'm pretty then?' I asked, a child begging for a sweet.

'Sure, you's the prettiest thing in this place; though mind, that ain't sayin' all that seein' as where we's at. But, you'd be the prettiest thing in most places, but that ain't it.' He leant his elbows on the table and rested his chin on his hands. 'You're gonna have to forgive me when I say this, but what you got it ain't 'bout pretty. You're lookin' like a cool drink on a hot day right now, but you ain't, like, magazine pretty.'

'Cute! You think you're gonna pull with that line?'

'Yeah, but that's my point,' he said, tapping the table with his finger. 'You take them women from the magazines, with all their … their clothes and hair 'n' all. You get them and you in a bar like this, anywhere in the world, wiv' sweat drippin' down the walls and beat pumpin' and hell, they're gonna go home alone, 'cause they look like you'd break 'em just shaking their hand. But you … you ain't that sort of pretty.' He shook his head. 'Naw, you're what a man want, he don't want no china doll, he want a woman makes him think how good she'd be to get with. That's what you got, you got something worth your weight in gold.'

'Hell, that's gotta be the nicest way anyone's called me a tramp!' I laughed, my skin burning with his words.

'I ain't callin' you a tramp,' he said, feigning hurt. 'I sayin' you got the power to make a man think as you is. Think as he's gonna get so lucky, you done gone twisted him round your pinkie twice before he's noticed. Hell, you're that good, he'd still think you're kissing him when you's driving off in his car.'

'You think I'm that twisted?'

Paris leant closer, and I noticed his eyes, or I remembered noticing they were dark blue, not brown. His lips were moments from mine when he said, 'You might well be, but that's my point, I don't care if you's the devil hisself, right now.'

He kissed me and the heat of the street beat at the windows and my heart thudded deep and dark inside me. It was pathetic, really; he was pathetic. Give a man an hour's attention, pretend you think he's something special, it's too easy. What was that about if you knew what a man desired, you could con him?

That first night, we walked back to the place I'd rented. I'd been there for a week already, making it look like I intended to stay. I only had days left, my contract was short on purpose. I needed to watch him, I needed to meet him and then I needed to be homeless so I needed his help.

I didn't turn on the lights. The moon was big and heavy in the sky, full to the brim with expectation, shedding light enough for us both. I touched his face, the edge of his cheek, then the hollow where his skin smoothed under his collarbone. I went to kiss him, but he took hold of my wrist and smiled.

'You really wanna?' he asked. 'We don't got to do nothin' here, maybe we've already got the best of it. I can go now, I don't mean to impose on you none.'

'Do I wanna?' My cheeks flushed.

'I'd be careful, opening your doors to strangers,' he said, but he wasn't a stranger, I'd been watching. I thought I knew him.

'I'm pretty good at lookin' after myself.'

'I dare say you is.' He let go of my wrist and slid his hand round my waist, rocking me gently as if we were dancing. 'So what now? We gonna see how good you are at takin' care o' Paris?'

I guessed he was lonely. I guessed he liked me. I guessed he was already doing the math. I guessed that he needed me almost as much as I needed him.

'Whatever,' Margarita said, 'you got him. That's all we need.'

The first place we stayed together was long and low, a scatter of whitewashed buildings under a neon sign that buzzed on, buzzed off. It shone through our window, painted us from blue to shadow over and over.

He told me – he told Margarita – he was the baby of the family, just like me. Not Margarita, she didn't have any family, not one she was going to admit to yet, anyway.

'Baby of the family, Momma always said so.' She always said he was the clever one too, and that was the thing, people never understood that. Paris was clever.

'You only got to look at him to see it, but he just don't fit the way they think he should. Not school clever,' he said, doing her voice, a smirk at the corner of his eyes. The youngest of the family, all those sisters he named and I couldn't remember, and aunts and cousins, all there to baby him. I imagined their men, solid, monosyllabic, part of the family and yet somehow outside, circling like basking sharks.

He said his mother said he was clever, but they just couldn't see it – when he was in detention, when he didn't make his grades, when he got into trouble. He was clever at school though, just not in the regular way, he said. He learned how to make money.

'Always ways to do it, even if it were only nickels and dimes. Bug racing, holdin' my hand up for things other people done wrong, takin' their punishment, passing love notes. Nickels and dimes.' Which it had been, at the start. There was never any money at home, certainly not for Paris, however clever – and he hated it. He hated the hand-me-down clothes and the homemade lunches, of whatever his mother could find, and the welfare that was never enough. She did her best, she really did, and when he told me that, the smile was gone from his eyes. She cleaned, worked two jobs, three when she could, with five of them still at home, and their father drifting as if caught in a riptide.

'Nickels and dimes, then dollars, just so as I could bring something home. Slip it into her purse when she were asleep on the couch, closing her eyes after work.'

I wasn't sure, but the way he talked, it seemed as if they'd moved from place to place when he was a kid, the father finally getting lost on the way, dropped on the kerb and nobody bothering to go back for him. He told me about one place, out in the sprawling, put-up put-down suburbs, a camelback owned by a friend of an aunt, long, low and painted pink place, that stank all ways round. There was a hole in the roof, and the stairs ran with water when the rain came, and the smell of gasoline and drains, of a tide gone through and gone out. No matter how his momma scrubbed the place, and all of her children, they could never get the stink out.

'Back then, she were cleanin' house for this rich old,' and he paused, only a half second, but enough for me to know he bit back the word white '… old lady, livin' in one of them houses in the nice part of town. One all painted and iced-up somehow, like a wedding cake: white windows, blue walls. Sometimes, me an' Sally May,' who was, I think, the sister next in age to him, 'we'd get the bus over an' walk round to the place, 'cause the lady there didn't mind us if we kept to the kitchen. Momma didn't like us bein' in that pink stink-house alone; said the wires weren't safe.'

They'd drink milk from glasses that weren't plastic, through candy-striped straws. The old lady even let their mother give them cookies, on real china plates that matched, so long as they didn't make crumbs.

'We crept through the house once,' he said. 'When the ole lady got Momma to drive her some place. Momma told us to stay in the garden, which we didn't. Took our shoes off and went all through, lookin' in that, poking in this. Didn't take nuttin', because we was too scared Momma might lose her job if we got caught, but we looked all right.' I thought of their little fingers, and their eyes: Sally Mae's brown and Paris's blue, wide and white rimmed, silently looking into that fancy kind of furniture you get in old people's houses, with fusty names and the smell of mothballs. The squeak of long closed drawers, summer dresses still in dry-cleaner's plastic wrap. Black bare feet on a polished wooden floor.

'Didn't last though. Momma found the old lady dead, and that were that. Her family had the place sold from under her, 'bout the time I started Junior High.' Where he learned how not to be there when he didn't have to, and not get caught, and how to spend the endless summers keeping out of the sun.

'I has this friend o' mine, smaller than the rest of us. Only white kid in our class.' He was called Jude, or Jute maybe, this kid. They were drawn to each other, both on the edge of things, both cleverer than the world seemed to give them credit for. One time, they'd been picking pennies from the sidewalk, heads bowed for the glint of metal in the gutter. They'd done well and got themselves an ice cream to share. Only, in turning away from the stand, a woman in the queue behind had caught Jude's arm with her bag, and Jude had dropped their cone. Splat – white exploding against the asphalt.

'She was all upset about it, o' course,' Paris said, 'oh my, look at that, you poor thing,' and Jude, smaller than Paris, young looking, burst into tears. 'So she bought us both another, sprinklings an' all.'

'Your first con,' I said, rolled in sheets that crackled with static, that made the hairs on the back of my neck dance.

''Suppose,' he said. 'That summer, it was all snow cones, an' king cake, an' cotton candy, high as hogs we were. Worked with him, him bein' all l'ill, an' white, seein' as nobody was gonna give the time o'day t'some raggedy ass black kid, now were they?' Like his momma always said: clever, just not school-clever.

He got up and went to the bathroom, his long, lean arms loose at his sides. He ran water into the basin and washed his face with his hands. It wasn't a big room, so he wasn't that far from me, and I could watch the droplets of water trace his dark skin darker, drawing down his spine, all of him touched with the blue of the neon light. On, off, on, off.

'Better than picking pockets,' he said. 'Dippin' gets ya caught in the end, same wiv' shop liftin', no need for it. People come with money to spend, might as well spend it on a bit of local colour.'

He was taller than Jude, looked older. They hadn't been friends for long, hardly knew each other by the next summer. He thought Jude's mom had gotten suspicious of something, said she didn't like them hanging out together. That's just how it goes, he said. By the next summer, he'd made a whole lot of new friends and was selling weed – nothing big, just dollar wraps here and there, more to get talking to the herds of college kids and out-of-towners there for a good time, more for a way in, than the money. Then he was taking tips to find them the best tables for an authentic slice of the city, and the best bars for blues and jazz, and the hookers in the walk-ups, one step above the street girls. He was hanging round the edge of places, learning to play cards, craps, dice, running messages, keeping a look out. A lot of money to be made, when you were too clever for school.

'Helped Momma get her salon, when I could. She started doing weaves an' shit at home, when the mall she worked at closed, an' she lost one of her jobs. Got to invest, I told her, make something grow; gotta put the time in.'

'But not you,' I said.

'Naw, not me,' he said, 'I ain't got the time for it, waitin' round for something to happen.'

It meant there was always somewhere to go, once Momma had the new place over the salon. The salon was something permanent, anchored and weighed down with all those sisters and cousins, and the neighbourhood women coming and going, because his mother, Beatrice, let them pay what they could when they could, knowing as she did that sometimes a wash and set was all that got a woman through the week. All those women, all sure he'd been there when he said he had, should someone come asking after him. Why, hadn't they seen him come in, taking his time to say hello to them all, each and every one? Such a nice boy, so kind, polite, good to his momma. Sure, he'd been there, well, they were almost sure he had been. As sure as made no difference.

In the motel room, he ran a bath in the narrow, tide-marked tub and got in, his knees up above the soap bubbles like dark cliffs in an arctic sea. I went to the mirror, leaning over the basin to pluck my eyebrows, naked but for the static from the sheets. He watched me, and behind my reflection, I saw him settle his hands behind his head, elbows high.

'Pop, pop, pop, firecracker,' he said, his smile flicked over by the neon blue buzz from outside. 'You's all fourth of July.' I smirked at him, just to let him know I was grateful I was.

'You ever work with someone else, someone now?' I asked him, turning round to lean against the cold rim of the basin. 'I mean, I could be like that kid, the one with the ice cream?'

'Hell, I dunno …' he lowered his arms, sat forwards in the water.

'Oh come on, you can't always work alone, right?'

'Hell, I ain't alone. Haven't I been sayin', I got my Momma, my—'

'You know what I mean,' I said. 'Think of all the shit we could pull together, what we could do.' He was laughing, shaking his head. 'Oh come on, don't say you haven't thought about it.'

'You wanna get rich quick too?' he asked.

'You think you're rich?' I said, and I stepped right in there with him, water boiling and spilling onto the floor, him struggling to make room for me, laughing, sure the tub was gonna split open on us. 'I got a thought 'bout that – us getting real rich, real quick.'

He was so fucking easy, I almost felt sorry for him.

CHAPTER 17

IN THE MONTHS BEFORE I arrived, I'd been busy. I'd immunized myself to fear. The first time I walked alone into a bar, bought a beer and sat on a dirty plastic stool, my heart pounded at the back of my throat as if it were running the other way. I forced myself to stay put, till a man looked at me and smiled, then I scuttled back to my car.

I made myself talk to them, as I thought Lisa had. I picked out a man in the crowd and saw if I could get him to come to me, to sit next to me, to buy me a drink. Some of them were repugnant, some of them were good company. It didn't matter. What mattered was how soon I could make them come to me, then it mattered how quickly I could get away.

Paris was different. He was nicer, more charming, more handsome – nice enough to make it a pleasure. A pleasure for Margarita anyway. He was right up her alley, quite her cup of tea. I might have thought him attractive, after a fashion, in passing, though perhaps only Margarita would have slept with him. It didn't matter; I could only have met him as I did, lounging in a basket chair in the heat of the afternoon.

'You got the most amazing eyes,' I told him, my lips brushing his cheek. And he really did, dark blue ones, which I'd never seen before.

'Momma always said eyes are like birthdays. Women take more notice of 'em.'

I could see that moment suddenly, sharply, so bright it hurt. The shiver of his mouth on mine, the memory of the heat of his lips so real I touched my mouth. I gasped, pressed the back of my hand to my face, a sob caught in my throat.

He was with me again, but frozen, trapped between the gaps in my memory. Like fireflies, recollections were scattered through the house in the backwoods, eluding my grasp.

Paris – where was Paris?

I remembered the motel, the 'Pelican Inn', stretched out along the side of the road, far enough from everywhere for no one to mind much about it. Two floors of orange walls with copper green roofs, a scaffolding of plaster columns and vending machines. There was even a pool, and it was open.

I'd had my hair cut in preparation. Paris hadn't wanted me to, but he'd agreed to it in the end, after a perfunctory argument. I knew he would, I was good at reading him before I met him, and two months in, I thought I was a past master at it. We'd been testing each other, seeing how far we'd go. We'd both gone further than we'd intended, or so I thought. He didn't know my real name, but he knew me. Well, he knew Margarita.

It was a nice pool, better than the place that surrounded it. I was a swimmer, and Paris wasn't, so when I swam each morning, I knew I'd be alone.

'Did you get it?' I asked when Paris came into the room. I looked up when I heard his passkey in the door, and my hand lingered over the gun in my vanity bag until I saw his smile.

'Next time, you can get this sorta shit.' He grinned. 'You shoulda seen the look the clerk give me.'

'Who cares what she thought?' I said.

'She? You weren't there, he thought I was going to look real pretty!' Paris hooked his hand on his hip and struck a pose. 'Real purdy!'

'Stop messin', I said, laughing at him. He threw the bag at me and closed the door.

'This why you got your hair cut, why you so set on bein' blond?' He came into the room and threw his jacket on the chair. He stretched his long, limber arms up above his head. 'Sure is hot out there today, you's gonna be sweatin' in that thing.'

The wig was wrapped in a plastic bag, with a smiling woman looking back at me from it. I took it out and jammed it on my head, my vision fogged with platinum strands until I wiped them clear. My sister's face looked back at me from the mirror over the vanity table.

'Shoot,' Paris said, and I knew he saw it too. He sat heavily on the bed, looking at me.

'What you think?' I said, unable to resist the urge to make him slip up.

'I'll take me the brunette,' he said. 'I think I like her more.'

'Really?' I stood up and came over to him, reached out with my finger and touched his shoulder. 'You don't want to cheat on me with me?' I put my finger in my mouth and bit down.

'Aw c'mon, please …' I climbed onto the bed, onto his lap, and he couldn't resist, couldn't help getting hold of my thighs as I encircled his neck with my arms.

'Come on, don't you want a piece of this …?'

'Sure, but that wig …' He smiled at me, shaking his head, his thumb idly slipping under the edge of my shorts.

'It ain't for your benefit.' I smiled, eyes wide and watching him.

'It's for old Red Rooster and his Daddy, so he thinks as I'm a sweet li'l thing what needs his help.' I reached up and gathered the wig into bunches with my hands. 'You think this is too much, or is it just the right side of white trash?' I laughed, but Paris didn't. He let go of me and leant back, elbows on the bed behind him and looked away from me.

'Take it off,' he said. 'It's too hot for it now, you gotta wear it tomorrow. Anyway, like I said, I prefer you dark.'

'What's eatin' you?' I said. 'Look, this all an act, you know that?'

'Sure I do.' I made a move to get off his lap, but he grabbed hold of my waist. 'I said take off the wig, not get off o' me.' He grinned, but he didn't look in my eyes until I'd dropped the wig on the bedroom floor, then he turned the full power of his gaze on me.

'Why you gettin' all freaky?' I asked, running my fingertips along the edge of his neck. I traced the hard line of his collarbone, his skin made velveteen by the bloom of sweat.

He took hold of my leg. 'Freaky? Hell, girl, I'll show you freaky.' His thumb ran up the inside of my thigh, letting it lead his fingers underneath the leg of my shorts. 'If you's in the mood for a li'l freaky.'

'You know what I mean.'

Paris laughed, his smile deep and wide as he pulled me closer.

'Oh, I know what you mean.' He twisted off my shirt, and we made love in the dirty heat of the motel room, with the sound of the road outside and the whirl and buzz of the air conditioning, until the money ran out and it juddered to a stop.

We lay wrapped in the embrace of the afternoon, trying not to feel the day slipping inexorably toward tomorrow. I let myself imagine I was pretending we were there just to be together, like we were real people in a regular world. I laced my fingers through Paris' and lay with my head on his chest, watching where our bodies met. I heard a laugh rumble within him.

'What?'

'Hell, I know what you're doin'.'

'What d'you mean?' I asked, and the warmth and the light of the moment evaporated as guilt prickled my skin.

'I see you,' he smiled. 'You's just like all the other white chicks.'

'Excuse me?' I sat up and gave full rein to my indignation, glad of the distraction of a row. 'What the hell d'you mean by that?'

He was still laughing at me, shaking his head. 'I see it, you's lying here just looking as your lily white skin next to my rough ole black skin, and you's thinkin' as how I make you look all li'l an' white, an purdy ...'

'Stop it,' I said, and went to hit him, only he caught hold of my wrists, grinning.

'Oh, yeah. I is such a big strong black nigger; I make you feel like all the covers of them cheap paperback books you get in the airport down here.' I got free from him as he laughed at me.

'What the fuck you mean?' I demanded, grabbed up the pillow and hit him with it. Laughing, he fended me off.

'Oh pleeze missus, don't hit me, I's a-beggin' you!'

'Don't you fuckin' pull that shit on me; that just ain't funny.'

'Baby, chill!' he said, still laughing but alert to the tone in my voice. 'Hell, I was just messin' with you!'

'Is that what you think of me?' I pushed past him and clambered off the bed.

'Oh, shit, Shoog ...' he said as I wrapped myself in the hotel's bathrobe. 'What's you' problem?'

'My problem?' I yelled. 'Shit, you know how that sounds? What, you think bein' with you is just some ... some fuckin' game I'm playing?' I said, knowing full well it was. 'You think, what, I'm with you 'cause you make me look good?'

'No, I don't think that, you crazy bitch. I just sayin' as how some white girls think like that.'

'No you ain't, you were sayin' that's how I think!' I turned to the dressing table, and with a sudden, burning rush of anger, swept everything onto the floor.

Paris jerked up from the bed as an explosion of hairbrushes, make-up and lingerie hit the floor.

'So what?' I turned on him. 'What if I said as how you's only with me, 'cause you think how white woman's easy, how they don't give a brother no shit and take everything you give 'em, cause they's too fuckin' hog-tied with guilt to stand up for themselves?'

'Now hold on a minute, I ain't ever said as how I think that ...'

'Is this why the wig freaked you out? Made you think I'm getting' too white for you?'

'That ain't it!' Paris retorted.

'Oh, you tell me what it was then, where all this is comin' from?'

'Don't do this,' he warned.

'What is it?' I screamed.

He gripped the back of his head with both hands. 'It fuckin' makes you look like his wife!' he bellowed at me.

'Whose wife?' I demanded, though I knew, I knew at once who he meant, and the thrill of it jabbed through me. 'Whose wife?'

'Red's wife.'

'What? How'd you know?' Lisa, I screamed at him inside my head, say her name. Say her fucking name!

'Cause I fucked her!' He flung his arms down as if he'd thrown the words on the floor between us. After he'd said it I laughed, the relief of finally hearing him admit it was so immense I was almost dizzy with it. I could have said it then, I could have told him and maybe he'd have understood, but I turned my laugh into a snort of incredulity as he sat on the edge of the bed, elbows on his knees.

'You what?' He didn't look at me as I glared at him. 'So that's why you've been gettin' fuckin' cold feet. If there's a problem with what we're doin', you better say something, 'cause this thing's on now, and …'

'Damn it, girl.' Paris looked at me at last. 'It was nearly a year ago, it were nothing.' He held out his hand, fingers spread.

'What?' It sickened me to think of him with her, how vulnerable she must have been, how he must have charmed her, but that at least made my outrage convincing. 'Why the hell didn't you say nothin' before now?'

'Well, it ain't something I'm proud of …'

'Jesus, you bastard, there's plenty you ain't got to be proud of. Oh, fuck, does he know who you are?'

'It ain't like that … he never knew me,' Paris said, frowning. 'I ain't a goddamn amateur …'

'How d'you know that?' I demanded, hands on hips.

'Trust me. He 'n' his good ole' boys' would have found me already if he knew.' He put his hand on his chest. 'Seriously, they'd a' hung this nigger's ass from the nearest poplar tree soon as look at me!'

'You better be sure. What if he's plannin' on a klan reunion on your behalf?'

'He don't know me from the next guy.'

'What happened?' I said. He held out his hand to me, but I remained standing.

He stood, picked his pants up off the floor and began pulling them on. 'You knew what I was when we first met. You been runnin' these cons for the last month, so don't you start getting' all uppity.'

'Don't you run out on me,' I said taking a step toward him. 'I just wanna know what's goin' on here. You say we're okay to get one over on old Red Rooster, but then you sayin' you've already been with his wife?'

'Okay.' Paris zipped up his fly and turned back to me. 'Look, she was just some girl half his age, I never knew who she were or nothin'. An' yes, I went wiv' her cause she put a fifty in my guitar case, and she had designer shades on. It weren't right but it were for the money, that's it.'

I sat down on the dressing table stool. 'Where's she now, then?' For one glorious, desperate moment I wanted him to just come out and tell me, to say that he'd driven her to the airport, or the train station. Or left her in a motel like this one, with tiny soap and irregular cleaning rosters. Or taken her down a thin, dry road, somewhere the land melted into swamp, and shot her and thrown her in. Something, anything that might have meant this was over, that I would know where she was.

'I don't know,' he said, and pulled his smile into a frown before he went on. 'We was supposed to meet, but she never showed. I waited, but she never came.' He exhaled, and hooked his thumbs into the loops on his jeans.

'You were going to go off with her? She was going to leave Rooster for you?'

'Guess?' I pulled a face at him. 'Okay, course we were gonna go off together; we were in love.' As he shrugged his shoulders, shifting his weight casually from one foot to the other, my rage erupted.

'You stupid fuckin' …' I tore myself up from the stool and sent it flying '… two timin' …' I snatched up some of the debris from the floor and hurled it at him … 'bastard!'

'What' wrong with you?' He deflected a hairbrush on his forearm. 'Crazy bitch, what the hell's gotten into you?'

'Shut up!' I screamed. 'Liar!'

'What da' fuck you—?'

'Because you said you loved me!' I screamed, because it was what I should have said, had all of this been true, had I really been Margarita. I ran to the bathroom and locked the door. I sat on the floor with my back pressed against the door, hugging my knees. I needed this, I need him to really think I'd fallen for him, and a good old-fashioned fight was perfect.

'Fuck me girl … why y'all bein' like this?' he said on the other side. He sounded crestfallen, like a guy who really didn't quite get it, but thought he really ought to apologize. Part of me was starting to feel sorry for him. He was really starting to enjoy the two of us together, getting used to having me at his back. And we were good together, we really were. I could see it from his point of view. I could see our potential.

'Don't you go getting sentimental,' Margarita said. 'This is business, alright? Fact that he's pretty wiv' it … that's just a bonus.'

I stared at the space under the pale pink washstand. There were cobwebs on it, and one of the motel's complimentary slippers curled up like a discarded cocoon. On the other side of the pedestal was my make-up case, the soft pink suede decorated with the familiar, expensive pattern of brown flowers interlaced with elegant script, part of a set. One that came with a jewellery roll.

'Open the door please, darlin'. We can't sort this out with you in there.'

'You tell me what happened first,' I said, pressing the back of my head to the door, eyes closed. It wasn't going to change anything but I wanted to hear him say it. Lie to me, I thought, lie to me, because I'll know it. I know you too well.

'You really wanna hear all that?' I didn't answer, because both yes and no would have been the wrong answer. I heard the sound of him sitting down on the other side of the door, heard his sigh of resignation.

'I never knew who she were. I was just doin' my tourist game – you know, playin' my guitar wiv' my bare feet n' all.' He laughed. 'Hell, sometimes I think they was just pleased to see a good lookin' man on the street; we's pretty thin on the ground round these parts!'

'And?' I said, glad he couldn't see I was smiling.

'She just went by me one day, dropped a fifty in my case. What's I suppose to do with that, give it back?'

'You followed her then, you marked her out?'

'No, it weren't like that. She give me a lift one day, saw me walkin' back. Hell, couldn't really drive my car 'bout now could I? Didn't go wiv' the act.'

'Then you slept with her?' I dug at the carpet with my finger, working my nail into the pile, picking and picking at it.

'What's the matter, you feeling jealous?' Margarita asked.

'Sure, I slept with her, in the end. I ain't no saint. I could see she were unhappy, I could see she were rich. I ain't proud!'

Neither was I. 'But you told her …' dig, dig. 'You told her you loved her?' dig, dig, dig.

He paused, and I could hear him wondering what to do. Lie to me, lie to me, please, I begged silently.

'I didn't mean it,' he said eventually, sounding like a little lost boy caught out. I slammed my fist into the door, because I should have been angry, real angry, if I'd really fallen for him. And because I was angry at him, real angry.

'What the hell?' he shouted.

'If you lied to her, how'd I know you ain't lying to me?'

''Bout what?'

'That you love me!' I closed my eyes and clutched the carpet under each hand.

I was back there, for a moment, in our special place under the bed. I couldn't remember which of the thousand times we'd hidden there it was, but there was a chill in the air, and we both had on winter stockings and hand-knitted crew neck sweaters. Lisa had Mr Pooter in her hand, when his little blue velvet jacket with the pearl buttons was new.

'You'll be okay, you know?' she said to me. I didn't look at her, I just shrugged. She was going away, not for the last time but the first, and right then I'd thought it would be forever. 'I'll write, I promise.' Even that didn't elicit a response from me. Lisa was going and I was being left behind, and I could see how guilty she felt.

'I don't wanna go,' she said and she reached out and put her hand on my shoulder. 'But he won't hurt you, I promise. He only hates me.' And she smiled a light, wan smile and I did also, because we both knew she was right. I was not scared for myself; I was scared for her, though at the time I did not know why. She held out Mr Pooter to me, and after a moment, I took him.

'You can have him now,' she said, her eyes wet but determined. 'I mean, just to look after till I get back.'

'You sure?' I said, squeezing him gently, feeling the delicious, firm resistance of his body.

'Sure,' she said, and we smiled a sister's smile.

'You are comin' back, aren't you?' I asked her.

'Course, I want him back; you're only looking after him while I'm away.'

'Shoog?' Paris said, as I had been silent for a while. I reached across and picked up my make-up bag. 'You remember when we met?' I heard the creak of the door as he moved again, changing position, his back to mine with the wood separating us. 'You looked so pretty, wearin' that li'l dress, with your hair all down and them big eyes of yours. You know, I ain't gonna pretend, I just thought as you was a honey, y'know? Then we kinda started doin'

them cons n'all, and thought hey, you got, you know, potential?'
He chuckled, then said quickly, 'But you's more than that now.
Hell's teeth baby, you's the nearest anyone's ever come to makin'
me wanna give this shit up. You just say, say it now, and we's gone,
we's gone a thousand miles away from all of this.' I looked at the
bag and unzipped it. Mr Pooter looked up at me with his one eye.
I closed the zip again and put the bag back on the floor.

'You tell me you lied to that man's wife 'bout lovin' her, but I'm
supposed to believe it when you say you love me?'

'I know how it sound, what d'you want me to say? You think I'd
have told you 'bout her, if I didn't mean it this time?' He sounded
more disgruntled when he added, 'Why the hell d'you care so
much 'bout what I said to her? It didn't mean nothing!'

'So what the hell does it mean, when you sayin' it to me?'

'It means I love you, you crazy goddamn bitch!'

'Well I love you too, you asshole!'

I sounded pretty convincing. Perhaps for a moment I'd meant
it, in a way. Perhaps I did love him, because I needed him. What
is love, anyway, but needing someone else? Whatever, I had to act
like I believed it when he said he loved me, because I needed him
to love me back.

'I think we got him,' Margarita said.

CHAPTER 18

WHEN I RETURNED from my interview with the Sheriff, it began.

I lived my life the way I had been: set on automatic. In between, I began to prepare. I put away the money that my paternal grandfather and maternal grandmother had left me, in an online savings account innocently titled 'road trip'. Frances – he'd stopped being Franny at last – was furious to discover that he was to get nothing, and tried to get me to lend him five thousand dollars to help him open a vintage record store, just weeks after the funeral. The arguments made it easier to reduce my contact with all of them to the barest minimum, without the need for further explanation. I went to work, I went to the gym, I went to the store and I came home. In between, I was Margarita.

I got her a new laptop and I built her life on it. I invented people on Facebook, and they made friends with real people, real people who then added Margarita to their lists, when an algorithm suggested it might be a good idea. I found her a mother and a father and two brothers; I couldn't quite bring myself to give her a sister to usurp Lisa's memory, but she had a school record, even a group photo from the year she'd graduated. I found one from a high school across state that had a Facebook page; there was a girl at the back no one had tagged who could have been her, so I uploaded the picture to Facebook and tagged it as Margarita. Some of the other people from the photo wrote and said hi, said they liked the new name and that I was looking good. One, who called herself Mary Contrary, even told me a story about her from high school. It sounded just like something Margarita would do. That's what I wrote on her wall, anyway.

Margarita had two boyfriends: one whose picture I lifted from a London tattooist's website, and the other a bass player in a local band. She broke up with both of them, and they both left heartbroken messages on her wall, while her relationship status switched to 'it's complicated'. The musician even wrote her a song, but she just laughed about it. Some of her friends joined in – they were quite cruel – and despite often going on record as wishing men would show their feelings more, they tore his to shreds. I nearly felt sorry for him, but he hooked up with a groupie pretty soon afterwards and moved to Boston, so he was okay.

I started to buy her things, as if preparing for a new baby. I filled the cabinet in the bathroom with her brand of skincare products and make-up. I consulted consumer reports stratifying our society and predicting what products any particular socio-economic group would buy – it helped out at work also, and netted me an Easter bonus. After a while, I knew exactly what she would buy from any store I went into. My apartment had two bedrooms, and I dressed the smaller one as she'd have liked, until I could walk from one to the other and almost believe I had a flatmate. She left her underwear pegged to the Venetian blind over the open bathroom window; it was always me who had to put it away for her, and it was always more scanty and cheap looking than any I'd ever wear. It itched. She was a lot less tidy than me, and sometimes she'd leave the cap off the toothpaste, which started to annoy me, along with her habit of leaving mascara smudges on the mirror.

Margarita liked working out and swimming too, but her activities had more purpose than mine. She joined a shooting club, then kickboxing and circuit training, as well as our thrice-weekly swim. She was louder than me; she played her music at full volume and she drank, but she was confident in a way I envied.

I was top of the self-defence class; my personal instructor Ralph was impressed. He offered me some one-to-one tuition, which was really beneficial, but then Margarita slept with him and it got kind of weird after that. He was nice, I liked having him round, but Margarita just wanted him to show her different moves, to spar with her, to have him hold her down and see if she could get free. It got awkward in the mornings when I met him in the bathroom, knowing what he and Margarita had been up to the night before. I wished that he was seeing me, wanted to say that I wasn't really like her, but it was Margarita he was more attracted to. Then she really freaked him out, when she began begging him to hit her and he said that he wasn't into that sort of thing and, though they'd had fun and all, he felt that they were kind of over. They had a blazing row, which got quite physical; and so after that we had to find a different class. She broke one of my favourite plates too, throwing it out of the window after him.

'Why did you do that?' I asked her.

'Who cares?' She sniffed. 'It only stuff, an' stuff don't mean shit, end of day.'

Sometimes, when I couldn't sleep, I would question her about what we'd planned to do, marching round her room asking her over and over again.

'Are you really going to do this? Are you sure you can? You can't go there and do all this and then not go through with it, not if you're gonna get away.'

She'd argue with me, her hip jutting to one side, hands out like she was in a street gang, adopting a stance.

'You know what Red did to her ...'

'Sure, but—'

'He beat her, locked her up, maybe even raped her, all of it in front of his Daddy.'

'Yes, but ... but why hasn't she called, why hasn't she—'

'You read the emails, right? You saw what she said, you sayin' you don't believe her now, huh?' She would suck on her teeth, slapping the air at me or kicking at the bed. 'You callin' your sister a liar?'

'No, of course I believe her!'

'Yeah? Well sometimes you act like you think she ain't worth it, like she's just makin' trouble, like what Mom and Dad used to say.' Arms crossed, chin jutted forward, glaring at me, daring me to argue.

'You weren't there. You don't know how it was!' I'd say, a hot, righteous anger blazing in me, the words 'circle of trust' crashing about my brain.

'Well, tell me how it was then, 'cause I don't get it sometimes. How come Daddy did what he did to her, but he never touched you, huh? What, you special or something?' Was I special? Hell no, not me. Not special at all.

'I'm not special ... it's just the way it was.'

I'd sit down on the bed, hands in my lap, all the fight gone out of me. There wasn't a reason, not a reason I could see, it was just how it was, how it was all the time, until Lisa went away. 'I read up about it, you know, it can go like that; families give each other roles, and one of them can be given the role of victim. It's a recognized phenomenon.' And what had there been after she'd gone? A wall put up and best left in place, in case removing it tumbled everything down for the whole family, all of us. Never the right time, what with Dad getting sick, and Lisa in tough-love camp, and crazy-kid camp, and bad-girl camp. Never the right time, because then I messed up too, in my own slightly less spectacular way, throwing all my exams, then my retakes, then year one of the third-rate college that finally took me. There wasn't time or space to risk the havoc it would have wreaked, not with the holiday home and all.

'Yeah, well, all I see is that you ain't stickin' up for her no more,' Margarita growled, 'like you always said you would. Ain't that a recognized pho-nom-ina, ain't that call' lying'?'

'I am sticking up for her, and I am gonna find out what happened, I swear it!'

'Oh, you know what happened, girl,' she said, her voice dark and quiet inside me. 'You know old Rooster Levine killed her, and there ain't nothing no one's gonna do about it, but you.'

We had a file on him, on old Rooster Levine. It's amazing what you can find out when you're motivated, and when you've got a nice, distinctive name like that to play with. His Daddy also, because there was a lot more about him, and his political campaigning, and his charity work, and his financing of this and that. He was the sort who cropped up in local newspapers and websites, who opened things, who pronounced on local affairs, who could be relied on for a sound bite. There was a paper trail for his son Rooster too, but it was an altogether thinner, more insubstantial thing than Pappa Levine's. He was not exactly a ghost, but he was not a man much versed in social media, nor was he a prominent feature in his father's world. Reports mentioned his service record, the unit he was most recently affiliated with, but the details were vague. He'd been decorated sometime around the millennium, which flashed the image of fireworks and fairy lights through my mind, as if Red were a kind of Christmas tree. He'd seen action 'overseas and in the

Middle East,' but that was all. He was back, I worked that much out, but there was none of the fanfare one might have expected for the return of a conquering hero. I had a handful of pictures of him, mostly indistinct, mostly looking away from the camera as if avoiding my gaze. But there was one, one where he had to face me.

It was in the local paper, the 'T.P', in their social column. There he was, under the only headline to bill him as a 'war hero', smiling out at me, with Lisa beside him in that dress with the high lace collar, and all those little pearl buttons that would sound like rain when they scattered over the floor. It was pinned to Margarita's bedroom wall, with all the other scraps and snippets about him, and about men like him, and about the war in Iraq, and men and women from his unit, everything I'd found. Together we looked at him, and he looked back at us, Rooster Levine, while he held my big sister's hand.

'But, do I have to kill him?' I asked Margarita, after we were both quiet for a long time. 'For Christ's sake, look at him; he's a solider, a goddam Iraq veteran. Do you seriously think I can take him down, alone?'

'No.' And she'd smiled. 'But you're not alone.'

I went to bars and hung around at the jukebox, feeding quarters into them relentlessly, watching the room from the corner of my eye, under the cover of the chink of coin. I walked through the battlefields of the gender war, through empty parking lots, back alleyways, shortcuts through ill-lit parks. I went armed, I went prepared. I went to lose my fear. But I never went alone.

It happened first when I found a truck stop on the freeway, forty miles out of town. A lonely bubble of light and coffee in a long, cold night, under a neon sign with a herd of big rigs clustering for warmth. I filled up, then parked in the muddy ground out back and went into the store.

There was a small group of tables huddled round some vending machines, and a narrow shop counter, where I bought cigarettes and chewing gum. Three isolated men watched me as I entered. I felt their gaze on me, hungry and lost. I moved casually, looking round as I waited for the clerk to find the smokes I'd asked for, and sized them up. Which one would it be, which would be unable to resist?

The clerk glanced at me when he'd found the cigarettes.

'You got a restroom?' I asked.

'Out the back.' He nodded left.

'Thanks. Put my smokes on the side.'

When I found it, I watched my face in the mirror as I ran water, and deciphered the graffiti scrawled over the sink to calm my mind. The tap dripped brackish liquid into the chipped basin, plink – plink – plink. I counted as I waited, slowing my breathing until it was in time with the noise. Plink – plink – plink. I lingered long enough for the idea to take hold in one of them, and when I came out, one of them had gone. He'd made his choice, as I'd made mine.

I nodded at the clerk and paid. As I walked back to my car, I slipped my hand into my pocket and fit my fingers into the brass knuckles lurking there.

You don't have to do this, I said to myself, but I wasn't talking to me or Margarita. I was talking to him.

Which one are you? The one with the red plaid shirt and the blue cap, turning his spoon over and over against the tabletop, or the thinner, older one, with the bald head and the tuft of white hair behind each ear? Neither. It was the third one: blue shirt and grey pants, the toes of his camel brown boots buckled and stained with oil. He was a family man, he'd been at the counter when I paid for the cigarettes, folding his change into his wallet. For an instant I'd seen a picture, a child and a woman inside. He'd stood close to me, closer than he might have. Maybe he thought he recognized me; maybe he was just showing paternal concern for a young woman alone in the night.

For a moment, as the cold air touched my face, I let a thrill wash over me. So it's you, I thought as I heard his step behind me. You're the coward, you're the one who just can't help himself. How will you explain the scratch on your face, which is all you think I'll do to you? How will you answer when your wife asks you why you smell of my perfume? She'll be angry, suspicious – she'll accuse you of cheating on her, she'll think that's the worst you're capable of. You'll dust the mud from your jeans when it dries out, leaving only a stain on each knee that your wife will wash clean for you. Even if she suspects you, she'll never know you. Not like I do.

'You all set, doll?' Margarita purred inside me.

I was six feet from the car, and he must have thought that I'd reached for my keys, because he quickened his pace. I let him come, my heart rate slowed and a cold expectance tensed my muscles.

'Come on, girl,' he said from behind me. 'You best not be out here on your own.' He grabbed my shoulders and pushed me forward against my car, unaware that I went limp as he did, dissipating the force of the impact, because I was ready for him.

'Yeah, what we got?' He pressed onto me, urgent and filthy. He wanted me to scream, he expected me to scream, so he clamped his meaty hand over my mouth. But I didn't need to scream. I was not afraid. His other hand clutched the crotch of my jeans. 'Yeah, what we got here? We gonna have us a fine time, you 'n' me, girlie.' I let him touch me. 'That's it,' he said, his breath shuddering over me. 'You hush up, and I don't gotta hurt you none.'

The moment came, and I was ready for it. Overconfident at my apparent submission, he leaned round and tried to force his left hand down the front of my pants. As his fingers clawed at my flesh, I snapped into action and stamped my heel into his ankle.

'Bitch!' He crumpled sideways. I twisted and slammed my elbow into his ribs, then smacked my brass-clad fist into the side of his neck. Women always think they'll knee them in the balls, but that's a mistake; a second's hesitation and you've given your attacker your thigh to hold, you're off balance and then you're on the floor. You go for the eyes, the nose or the neck, all of which are routinely exposed, and all of which react with involuntary spasm to pain. The man sprawled across my car. I jerked back, then punched him as hard as I could in the small of his back, the brass thudding into his flesh – once, twice, three times.

'Jesus, fuckin'—!' I twisted round and kicked the back of his knees, sucking air into my lungs as he crashed to the ground, hugging the driver's side wheel.

'You run then,' the voice of my instructor Ralph came back to me. 'You don't stick around to see if he's okay or to teach him a lesson, ladies. You run and get the hell out of there.' That's good advice. That's what you should do if you're a victim of sexual assault, or any kind of assault. But I wasn't.

I dropped and forced my knee into his side where I'd already hit him.

I punched him twice in the face, and felt the bones in his nose twist and splinter. He screamed. I forced my hand over his mouth as his face gushed blood. 'You hush up,' I hissed, 'and I don't gotta hurt you none.' He sobbed, his fleshy lips squirming against my palm. I ground the brass into the side of his head. 'You done?'

He whimpered, struggling against the pain, then he nodded. I pulled my hand away from his mouth.

'You done this before?' When he didn't answer, I grabbed a handful of shirt and wrenched his head up.

'No … no ma'am.' I hit him again. 'Oh, Jesus my face, my fuckin'— yeah, I done it before … bitch!'

I pulled his head up as far as I could. 'Good.' I slammed him back down and stepped away.

You know why they say get away when you can – to run, don't look back, don't try and teach them a lesson? Because the moment you do that, the moment you turn back and stamp on the head of, or kick the side of, or spit on the face of some dirty fuck who's done this to you, you stop being a victim any more. And that will lose you the sympathy of a jury. He might not get off, if they catch him, if he doesn't take a plea; but then again, it might just stop the DA seeing you as a safe bet. If you want to get a conviction, you need to be a victim. You need to be a good girl.

Not caring if my victim was conscious or not, I walked round to the passenger side door and climbed across to the driver's seat. I had to force the brass knuckles off my fingers, which were already swelling with the pounding I'd given them. My hands were bloody, more of it smeared on my jacket. I pulled it off, wiping my hands on the sleeve, then balled it up and stuffed it in the footwell. I drove away.

The freeway arced away from my headlamps, a seemingly endless grey ribbon snaking through darkness. As I drove, the reality of what I'd done seeped into my limbs, until my hands shook and the breath struggled to escape my chest. I managed to get to my exit, pulled over when I could, and threw the door open. I ran to the trunk, leant against it and was sick. Afterwards, I pressed my forehead against the cold metal and closed my eyes.

'You' all right,' Margarita said. 'You're all right. I got you.'

There was a bottle of water in the glovebox, so when I'd thrown up everything I could, I got it and washed my mouth out. I sat in the driver's seat for a while with the lights on, engine running and my hands gripping the wheel. I felt sick, but I felt something else. I felt Margarita.

The car was suddenly illuminated by the blaze of headlights. I saw blue and reds in the rear view, then the cop whooped his siren the once. I ruffled my hair over my face, grabbed a tissue from the glovebox and pressed it to my nose when I saw the officer get out. As he drew closer, I let out the tears I'd been struggling to hold back.

'Miss ... Miss could you turn off your engine please?' The beam of his flashlight blinded me as I did as he asked, shading my eyes. He dipped the light. 'Can you wind down your window?'

'Hey there,' I managed my brightest, sweetest smile. 'Oh, goodness, I'm such a mess!'

'Miss, is there a reason you're sitting here with the engine running?' He peered at me. 'Are you okay?'

'Oh, I'm sorry ...' I wiped my eyes. 'I kinda broke up with my fiancé. I'm sorry, I just got real upset. I didn't think I should drive, you know, 'cause I was crying so much.' I smiled up at him. 'Pathetic, huh?' I wiped at my eyes, looked down at the black smudge on my fingers. 'Jesus, I'm such a mess.'

'Oh, no, we've all been there.' He smiled, and I could imagine him biting back the urge to say that I didn't look like a mess at all; that sure, with a touch of lipstick, I'd look real pretty again. 'I was just worried in case you broke down or something.' He straightened up, his radio squawked and he turned his back on me to answer it. 'It's been a busy night, miss,' he said, when he bent down to look at me again. 'Lot of bad people out there. Wouldn't feel right if I didn't make sure you were okay, now would I?'

'I'll be fine.' I smiled. He even tipped his hat and winked at me, boy scout that he was. Lot of bad people out there, I told myself as I pulled away.

CHAPTER 19

I STARTED GOING to support groups, ones for abuse victims. I wasn't sure why at first, because I never thought I was a victim, but maybe I thought being among other women who'd suffered like Lisa, might make me feel closer to her. Margarita's Facebook friend Mary Contrary joined one too – she put a post up about it, which kind of gave me the idea. I started talking to her, or Margarita did. She said she knew me from school; she said we weren't close but we got on. She said it was nice to get to know me, because she'd always been a bit in awe of me. It was nice to have a friend. Margarita called her 'doll' and they started to talk all the time.

The first group I found was at a local church, not one of the pretty ones with a spire and stained glass, but a plain, serviceable one, anonymous even, as if God were equivalent to a laundromat or a drive-through. It smelled of coffee, the instant kind, and floor polish and new carpet. We all sat round in a circle as if we had something to confess. It was like an AA meeting, where we all had to own up to how long it had been since the abuse, as if we were responsible for it. That's how it made me feel, anyway.

The woman who ran it was large. Had one looked up the word 'maternal' in a dictionary, her picture would have been there, all hair and velour leisure suits, wayward bosoms under softness, like overgrown kittens. Meow. People brought cookies – girls with bitten fingernails and scars on their arms, and ones who looked as if they'd eaten three batches already, stuffing and stuffing as if they could ever feel full. Even ones who looked like, oh, they might have eaten a cookie, you know, once, but would never do it again, they promised. Peanut butter crunch, chocolate chip, pecan and maple. They all seemed to want to bake; even the boy made red velvet cake. Well, he had been a boy, when he was a child, when it had happened. She was called Amanda now.

I wanted to be strong for them. I was strong. Well, I was silent. I listened and, when it was my turn to share, I shared as little as I could, as if my cookies were worth ten of theirs. I let them think that I was waiting until I felt comfortable, let them assume from my reticence that what had happened to me was way worse than anything they'd suffered. I thought about making some shit up, but I couldn't go there, even I felt too guilty about doing something like that. The group was unsatisfying after a while; there was too much weeping, too much picking over what had been. Margarita got sick of it too.

'Why don't they do something?' she'd say. 'Why don't they get themselves a stick or a gun and go beat the shit outta them pervs? The law don't do squat, does it?'

We were asked to leave in the end. It came out that it was my sister, not me who'd been abused, and the group leader said my influence was 'unhelpful'. She said it as if she thought it was the worst thing she'd ever said to anyone before, taking me to one side after the meeting, and hardly giving the word breath.

'Unhelpful.' She pressed her fingers to her mouth, face scarlet, then handed me leaflets about other groups, advising me to be honest from the start. 'I just want to make it clear, honesty is the key here, and I just feel that, well, some of the others feel that you've … you've not fully committed to the circle of trust, you know?'

Mary Contrary was sympathetic when we told her. She said she was joining a group online, and sent me a link or something. I can't remember which now, but it was like Facebook for the damned, people posting their true life experiences so you could comment and chat, offer support. Their on-screen names were verbs, rather than nouns – still-laughing, standing-tall, never-going-to-cry-again-forty-seven.

After a while though, you entered into an arms race of abuse, top trumps of real life horror. When I first joined, I'd read all of them with a sick sense in my stomach, but after a while, I found I was judging them. Abuse story blackjack; I was looking for a hand of twenty-one, the story that would trump all others. When I started, I was reading headlines like 'my brother touched me' and feeling angry, appalled that anyone would feel able even to write those words, let alone share them in a public forum, but after a while that sort of thing had me snorting with derision. Okay sister, so what? Get over yourself, look at this one, this one here: 'my father sold me to his friends for sex when I was eight'. Now that's abuse, that's shocking, that's worth my sympathy.

Christ, when did that happen, when did I become so immune to everything that I was scoring each out of ten, looking only for ones terrible enough to feed my rage? And when I found them, I didn't just hate the men, not just the men – I hated the women too. The ones that knew, the ones that shut the door and closed their eyes and wouldn't believe. The ones that helped hold their children down, that advertised them for sale, that helped get them drunk first. I hated them too, perhaps even more so.

I'd go running in the dark, headphones on, running and running, with their words and their stories rattling and screaming round my head, until they were my stories, until they were Lisa's story. Was I one of them? Had I shut the door on her? Had I looked away when I could have done something?

A key in the lock, loud as gunshot, my feet echoing behind me in the dark.

I told Mary Contrary about it, how I felt; she understood. It was good to talk to someone about it, someone other than Margarita. I got to hoping there was a message from her every time I logged on. Mary was an abuse survivor too, like Lisa. She'd gotten angry with her groups too, she said she was on her own now, like me, that she really liked talking to me, because I'd been there. I had to admit that it was my sister who was abused, but Mary understood that too, she said she felt my pain.

'I'm so full of rage,' she said. 'Because there was nothing I could do to him. That was it, he got away with it.'

'They threw me out of the group,' I told her. 'They said I was destructive, said I wasn't really an abuse survivor, and that I was unsettling the other members. I broke the circle of trust.'

'That blows,' she said. 'Anyway, they were wrong. Your father forced you to witness what was going on, and then he called you a liar when you tried to get help. He made you a partner in his abuse, and that's pretty twisted.'

I thought about this for a while, and though she was right, it didn't make me feel any better. It made me angrier, because I hadn't done anything, hadn't been able to do anything. Angry because I'd been a child.

'I let her down,' I said. 'I didn't do anything. Jesus, if I were back there now, if I were me now and not some scared little kid, I'd have broken his goddamn nose for him.'

'Yeah, I think you could, too,' Mary said. 'You didn't think you could do all the other stuff at first, did you, but you did.'

'Yeah,' I said and I have to confess, Margarita was grinning at me with pride when I wrote that. I'd told Mary about the man at the truck stop, about the others, even a little about Ralph the instructor and the day I'd laid him out flat.

'That's so cool,' she said when I'd told her about him, poor Ralph, and how surprised he'd looked. 'I knew you could do it, that's like … awesome – you're like a super hero!' Ralph hadn't thought so. Don't hang around to see if they're okay, ladies.

'I'm not a super hero,' I said. 'I'm scared all of the time, I throw up and everything. And I can't bring her back, can I? What good was I to my sister?'

'You were there for her,' she said.

'But I didn't stop him, and then she ran away to marry that man and now she's dead.'

'Are you sure she's dead?' The word 'dead' seemed to pulsate on the screen, white on black. Made me think of bones.

'I don't know, I think so. Why hasn't she contacted me if she's alive?'

'But you know him, who he was, this guy she married?'

'I do now. I've found out everything I can, everything. There was even a boyfriend, you know, someone who tried to save her. That should have been me; I should have saved her.'

'You should find him, this boyfriend, find out what he knows. And, you're sure he did it – her husband – you sure he killed her?'

I asked myself that question over and over as I ran through the dark, as I trained, as I swam, as I worked out at the punchbag. She was my sister and I'd let her down, but she would have contacted me if she was alive, I knew it. I believed it. Are you sure he killed her? Bone white words, dead black screen.

'Yes,' I wrote. 'I'm sure.'

'Well,' Mary Contrary said. 'So what else you doing all this other stuff for? You're going to get him, right?'

'He's not like the others,' I said. 'He's a soldier, he's bound to be real hard.'

'You're stronger,' she said. 'And he won't expect you to be. I mean, he won't be scared of a woman. They're all the same – my daddy, all of them – all think they're the boss and they can do what they want.'

'I don't know if I can do it,' I said.

She went offline then. I checked back the next day and the next but nothing, just a silence which lasted for days. When her message finally came it was a relief; it was like I wasn't just alone with Margarita, that there was someone else out there who understood.

'Go get him,' Mary Contrary said. 'You said yourself, you're sick of the way we do nothing but talk about it, the way they never get made to pay, so you go get him and you make him pay. He killed her. He deserves to die.'

That night I ran for an hour, then another hour, my feet impacting on the ground as if they were my heartbeat. When I stopped running, I was standing on a walkway above the railway tracks. I felt giddy, as if the ground were rushing away from my feet, as if someone had picked me up and placed me on a high shelf and I'd no idea how to get down. I held onto the handrail and closed my eyes. It began to hum, began to vibrate. The train came roaring out of its tunnel, and the whole bridge shivered and rang with its noise, so much noise I could almost feel it hit me.

'You ain't gonna jump, is you?' Margarita whispered in the silence after the train had gone. 'You don't want to kill yourself, do you?'

'No,' I said. 'I want to kill Red.'

'So do I,' she said, and we laughed.

CHAPTER 20

A DAY OR SO BEFORE we did it, I woke in the Pelican Inn and I saw the bed was empty. When I looked round, I saw Paris leaning against the window, a shadow against the glass. He was watching the road, and without me speaking, he knew I was awake.

'I don't want to do this no more,' he said. I waited, my heart thudding panic through my chest. 'After we done here, that's it for me.'

'What 'bout us?' I asked after a while, making my voice small and lost, because Margarita wouldn't want him to go without her.

I felt the bed subside a little as he sat down. 'You still want me, when it ain't about this?'

''Bout what?' I asked, still unsure if he meant the thing with Red or not.

'When it ain't 'bout us runnin' round workin' cons, living in motels, y'know? When it just me and you and regular life?' I went to answer but he carried on. 'I can't do this shit much more. If I get caught again, I'm goin' away for a long time – I don't want that, n' I don't want this to be the only thing that mean' you with me.'

'It ain't,' I said, sitting up on my knees, putting my hand on his shoulder.

'Y'know, when we hooked up, I first thought as how I was enjoying workin' these things with you, cause you were good at it. Then I got to thinking, I liked workin' these things cause it meant bein' with you. Now I'm thinkin', I want you to be wantin' me even if we ain't workin' cons.'

'Sure thing,' I started to say, but he cut across me.

'Don't you go sayin' just what you think I wanna hear. I ain't never been this close to someone, so you be honest. If you like this life more than you like me, then …' he bit his bottom lip '… then you take the money what we make, and do your thing. Without me.'

'Course I wanna be with you,' I said. 'Once this is done, we're gone, outta here, together. I ain't never gonna leave without you.' I was glad it was dark, because I hated myself for saying it.

'Why?' Margarita asked. Paris was asleep again, I wasn't. I was watching the pulse of light passing cars drew across the ceiling, picking out the map-work of cracks in the plaster. 'You tellin' me he ain't done the same? Told some poor dumb bitch in a motel room like this exactly what she wanted to hear, so as she'd do what he wanted?' I didn't answer. She was right, but so what? Did me doing it to him somehow make it a better thing to do?

He was still asleep in the morning when I got up and went down to the pool. Hell, all couples need time apart, even Paris said so. I swam a perfunctory length for the sake of appearance and stretched myself out on a towel. It was early, way too early for the people of the Pelican. I had the water to myself, just me and a Carolina mantis, perched in one of the shrubs in tubs.

'Hey,' I said. 'Hope you don't mind, but …' I reached into its shrub and eased out the local paper I'd hidden there a few days back, with its densely packed type and rows and rows of small ads. I hadn't circled the one I wanted, just in case. Before I turned to the right page, I looked back at the motel and the window of our room, but all was quiet, all was orange stucco walls and roof tiles.

The place I called was an early riser like me, up with the dawn to catch the night fishermen. Perhaps it never closed, one of those establishments you still got round there, where there's no need to lock the door and if no one's about, you can just leave the change on the counter, and fill up with a scoop of mealworms, or maggots, or whatever shit you wanted, knowing nobody would mind. I imagined it had one of those bells outside, the sort that rings when someone phones, so that you'd hear it if you were fixing boats out back. That morning, it rang a long time before it was answered, and the sound of it must have been loud as hell in the bright, wet morning.

The voice that answered was higher pitched than I'd been expecting. As he told me his name was Dave, Dave Delahoussaye, I wondered if he was one of those guys who looks like a grizzly but sounds like a chihuahua.

'I'm callin' 'bout the place you got advertised, page twenty-seven.' Because there's nothing like superfluous detail to make someone warm to you. 'The fishing place out in the reserve?' I listened while he told me everything that was wrong with it, and how it was for people who weren't much for creature comforts, but if you took the time to get all the necessary paperwork, well, it couldn't be beat for a spot of fishing, if that was my bag?

'Not so much,' I told him. 'I'm a wildlife photographer, got an assignment for a travel website, doing a feature on the Southern states, and...' that impressed him enough for him to talk himself down to a very reasonable price, all things considered.

'Sounds great,' I told him.

'You best come by an' check it out, let me show you round,' he was saying, and I was agreeing to do just that, when I heard the creak of the gate in the fence that circled the pool.

I was still saying goodbye to my new buddy, when I rolled round and smiled up at Paris. He was wearing the hotel bathrobe over his shorts, shades on, expression impossible to read.

'Hey,' I said, 'you up already?'

He didn't answer, but came and sat on the lounger a foot away from me. There was no way I could have hidden the paper without him seeing and so I didn't. I picked it up and flicked it over, 'So, hey, look,' I got to the section advertising beauty salons, 'I've found this place, yeah?' I couldn't tell if he was watching me or the paper, so I pretended he was looking at what I was trying to show him. 'Says it does wigs and hairpieces, a discrete service for the discerning—'

'Who ya been callin'?' he asked, petulant.

There was no point denying I'd been speaking to someone either, so it had to be someone who might be awake, and not a threat to him. In the rush to appear natural, I said, 'My sister, s'all,' just like I might have when caught out at high school.

'Ya what?' he said, frown lines creasing his forehead.

'What, you think I don't got family?' Sister. Why sister for fuck's sake? Because she was on my mind, of course, all the time I was talking to Dave; Dave who'd no idea I'd already driven by his place out in the reserve weeks before, when I'd quartered the parish, trying to find what I needed.

'You never said,' Paris said, like he was real hurt about it, because he'd gone and told me all about his family, all those sisters and cousins and aunts, and hell, I hadn't shared nothing with him in return, now had I? Which was odd, what with us being so close and all.

'So?' I folded my arms. 'What you care? She's back home anyhow, hence me havin' to call early. You rather I woke you up?' He shrugged at me, the silent treatment. So I slapped the newspaper at him. 'Whatever. You got things to get, like a wig an' all the other shit you been' banging on about. Me, I gotta go get me a white trash makeover, remember?'

He let the paper fall into his lap, then finally took off his shades. 'You wanna do this, then?' he said. 'You weren't out here, lettin' y'sister talk you out of nothin'?'

'Hell no,' I said, wishing to God I had been. 'This is the big one, ain't it? After all we've been building up to, all we done? Or what, you think I'm not ready yet, you think I can't handle it?'

'No,' Paris said, and relented and took my hand. 'I seen what you can do.'

Oh yes, he'd already seen what I could do, what we could do together. We would find a boutique, a small one, and the more exclusive the better. I'd stand outside on my cell and have an argument with my voicemail. The key was to be loud; the key was to be salacious and annoying in equal measure. I'd go in and look at a few things, start talking to the manager when she didn't want to talk to me, but had too because that was her job. I'd reveal how I'd just caught my boyfriend cheating on me, I'd get their sympathy, the knowing looks and eye rolls. I'd be irritating though, and after a while they'd be sick of me. I'd try stuff on, waste their time, text on my phone, weep, that sort of thing. I'd choose a dress in the end, and then I'd come to pay and guess what – not enough cash.

'We take cards.'

'I don't got no cards, that bastard took them all. Oh shit, I really want it, look, can you hold it for me and I'll go find the cash back at my motel?'

They wouldn't want to, they'd think that I'd skip, and I've been wasting their time and offending the other customers.

'We really can't do that without a deposit, miss. I mean, if another customer comes in, we'll have to let it go I'm afraid.'

'Look, I'll take my wallet. You hold my watch; it was the last decent thing that bastard ever gave me.'

The clerk would want me gone, but she'd want to make a sale also; they never get much commission and she only made minimum wage for all her air brushed make-up and killer heels.

'Sure,' she'd say.

'Just put it on the counter, plain sight. I'll be right back, you get me?' and then I'm gone.

Paris would come in after, in a nice suit. He'd start looking for a gift for his girlfriend and get one of the assistants to help. His girlfriend was picky, demanding, nothing seemed quite right. He'd show them a picture of her in his wallet, and then he'd see my watch on the counter.

'Hey, can I get a look at that? Now, she's always goin' on 'bout this stuff.' He'd offer them money for it; offer them hundreds because he knew they were going for a thousand dollars in New York. The clerk would say no at first, after all, it's not hers, though she'd give anything right now for it to be hers. Paris would say that he didn't want anything but that watch, not now he'd seen it.

'Hey, look – take my card,' he'd say finally. 'If the owner comes back and she's interested in selling, would you get her to call me?' And then he'd be gone, his big fat wallet going with him.

Now the shop assistant had lost another sale, and then I'd come back, her customer from hell.

I'd start saying how I didn't get quite enough cash; can she give me a discount? She's had enough now, but then she remembers the watch. At first she asks for it to cover the dress, but I'm not that stupid, I know it's worth something.

'Hell, I reckon I could get a hundred for it round at the pawn shop,' I'd say, getting real above myself. Now she thinks she's going to lose this chance too, and she's sure the watch is worth ten times the dress and commission together. In the end, she'd give me a couple of hundred for the watch and throw in the dress as well. As I leave, she'd watch me, fingering the card Paris gave her, itching to ring the number and collect her reward.

By the side of the pool at the Pelican Motel, Paris took hold of my hand.

'You don't think I'm ready for this?' I asked him.

'You? Oh, you's ready, Shoog. You's all the way ready.' He kissed my fingers. 'An' I'm ready too.'

CHAPTER 21

THE HOUSE IN THE BACKWOODS was hushed. The night air had cooled and soothed its pain, and for once it was resting. Raw and vulnerable, I remembered fragments, an outline of my journey, but the closer I got to how I came to the house, the more the pictures began to break and dissolve into grey. I held the papers in my hands, almost resenting what they'd given me, because they'd not given me everything I needed, and what they had given me, hurt. Mr Pooter looked at me, as if he understood.

Where was Paris, what had happened to him? I couldn't even remember what it was Paris and I had planned for Red, or Rooster, and though I knew what I'd intended here, I wasn't sure if I'd told Paris or not. I looked at the floorboard where I'd found the jewellery roll and knew I'd put it there along with the stack of Lisa's emails. I even knew what Margarita meant to do to Red alone, though not if I could really do it without her, or quite which one of us she was. But despite all of that, I still could not remember what had happened the day before.

'You gotta find him ma Cherie, afore he gone away down dat road.'

There was a noise on the landing outside.

'Count to ten, count to ten, then he'll go away again.'

A light flared, instinctively my hand found the handle of the revolver.

Creak.

I wanted so much to crawl under the bed again, close my eyes and have Lisa tell me that if I just said our song, it would all go away. Instead, I gathered myself into a crouching position and picked up the gun.

Creak.

The door inched open a little more, and the beam of a flashlight lit me up, writing white across my eyes.

'So what, darlin', you can't sleep?' Red said from behind his crocodilian smile. 'Or is you just dream walkin'?'

I pointed the gun at his chest, my heart thudding as cold concentration flooded through me.

Red flinched, but he regarded me levelly. 'You sure you wanna do that, darlin', seein' what happened last time you pointed a gun at me?'

'Put the light down,' I said.

'Now, just you slow down. Ain't we friends n'more?'

'Put it down, now.'

'If that's what she want,' Red said and slowly, deliberately lowered the flashlight and placed it on the floor between us. 'That's what she get.' He straightened up. 'So, seems as if you got a better idea of who you are?'

I didn't answer. I was desperately scrabbling through the fragments of my memory to try. Red flinched, and I responded by flicking off the safety.

'Whoa – okay darlin', you might wanna be careful with that thing.'

'Keep your hands where I can see 'em.'

'Sure thing – well, this gonna make for an awkward night.' I got to my feet. 'Here you are, standin' in my house, in my clothes, after I took you in and looked after you, an' all, which was pretty big of me, seein' as you done robbed me blind a day ago.'

A chill washed over me, I faltered and he saw it. He kicked the flashlight up at me, and all my preparation did not stop me instinctively ducking away from it. He darted forward, and had hold of my wrist before I'd registered his movement. He forced my arm up, and the gun went off.

'You wanna play with the boys, darlin', he snarled as he got hold of my other wrist, 'you best grow some balls!' I dug my feet against the floorboards and struggled, screaming as he tried to force my gun hand down. We twisted round and I fired again. The shot exploded the top corner of the narrow, owl-faced wardrobe behind me.

He saw his chance, let go of my hand and hit me across the face. I crashed to the floor, then he was on top of me, his weight forcing the air from my lungs as he scrambled to get a grip. I bucked and writhed under him and grabbed a handful of his hair, but he laughed at me.

'Get off me!' I screamed in his face as he pinned my arms against the floor.

'Now why the hell would I do a fool thing like that, pretty?' He grinned. 'Just when it's gettin' interestin'!' I heard the floor creak under me as the house jerked awake in the aftermath of the shots. Red took hold of my throat, his long, strong fingers gripping firmly enough to promise more. 'I suggest you stop makin' a racket, you cheap li'l bitch. I can't barely hear myself ...'

There was a long, drawn out noise from behind me, something ripping, twisting, splintering – and then impact, as the wardrobe in the corner of the room, fatally shaken to its rotten roots by the shot, crashed down on us both. Red took the full force of the blow for me, like the gentleman he professed to be. The shock jolted through me, and I gasped. There I was, smothered in dust, debris and redneck aristocracy.

The impact of the wardrobe knocked Red to one side. When I could gather my senses, I crawled out from under him and the mess of splintered wood. Coughing, I pulled myself onto all fours and saw that the old-fashioned metal coat rail, concealed inside the rotting wooden husk, had smacked into Red's temple.

I started to laugh despite the dust. 'All right,' I spluttered, looking up at the blank bedroom window. 'I owe you one.'

Red was prostrate, lying on his face, upper body covered in rotten wood. I grabbed hold of his legs and pulled, inching him free of the debris curse by curse, no idea how long I had before he came to. He was already muttering and stirring by the time I got him out of the way and half through the threshold.

I kicked the debris away from the bedstead and snatched up the jewellery roll. Not standing on ceremony, I ripped off the buckles and shook the handcuffs free of the pink suede. I straddled Red and snapped the cuffs on one wrist, then the other. I got off him, and he began coughing, flinching back to consciousness.

'Shit,' he muttered, and then realized his movement was restricted. The keys for the cuffs fell out when I ripped them free, and when I picked them up, I saw the gun and the pile of emails. The case was still lurking in the space under the iron bedstead, so I grabbed it and shoved the papers inside, along with the nylon rope. Collecting the gun, I momentarily toyed with the idea of tying him to the bedstead, but the room was still groaning and shuddering with the impact of the wardrobe and I did not trust the floor.

Making sure the safety was on, I jammed the gun into my belt, and picked up the lantern. Red had rolled onto his side and drawn up his knees to get purchase on the floor, already crawling out on the landing.

'What in the hell y'all playin' at?' he snarled.

'Stop your whining and get up.' I prodded him with my toe.

'What hit me?' He asked as he worked himself up onto his knees.

'The house,' I said, allowing myself a smirk.

'Where'd these come from?' he said as he tried to get a hand on the floor, then realized why he couldn't.

'Enough with the questions – get up.'

'Fuck you!' he snapped, so I pulled out the gun and jabbed him in the side with it.

'All right, all right. Jesus, give a woman a gun and she thinks as she's cock 'o' the walk.' Using the banisters as support, he levered himself onto his feet.

'Downstairs,' I said. 'Seein' as I don't much trust the floor up here no more.'

'Guess that's the heart of the matter: trust,' he said.

'Get going,' I said, flicking the gun to indicate the stairs.

'Shame you've messed up the place. I was quite gettin' to like it,' he said as we descended, him leaning on the banister and me keeping a few feet behind him, the gun trained on his back and the lantern swinging alongside. The light billowed crazy shadows across the damp grey walls as we went, making a shadow cage of the room below.

'This ain't your place, what d'you care?' I asked, as another groan echoed behind us.

'No, it ain't.' He paused to look around. 'Though, I'm thinking of making an offer, should the owner desire a quick sale.' He tried to wipe his face on the edge of his shoulder. 'Which he might, seein' as how murder tends to devalue a place.'

'You ain't dead yet,' I said.

'Neither's you, darlin'.' He shrugged his shoulders and went on down. I paused when he reached the ground floor.

'I should have realized this place weren't yours when I saw them things in the bathroom. You ain't got a heart condition, have you, Red?'

'Only in that I don't have much of a heart,' he muttered, and then turned to look up at me. 'Poking round was you? That how you found them bracelets?'

I pulled round one of the kitchen chairs we'd sat on to eat breakfast, and shoved it toward him. 'Take the weight off.'

'How kind,' he said and bobbed his head.

'Wait,' I said as he went to sit and plunged my hand into the back pocket of his pants for the padlock key.

'Hell darlin', I got some small change round the front if you wanna reach it.'

'Funny. Now sit.'

He smiled and took his time getting comfortable. I was aching and throbbing again after the struggle upstairs but I remained standing. When he'd sat, I threw the document bag onto the couch.

I wasn't quite sure how to tie him up and keep the gun trained on him. I managed to wrap the rope round each of his ankles, binding them to the chair legs. Aware that he might kick me in the head as I did this, I kept the gun pointed at his crotch, which seemed to dissuade him of the idea.

'You never was a boy scout, now were you?' he observed accurately. I threaded the rope through the handcuffs, and tied it off behind him. It looked like a mess, but it would have to do. Once he was tied, I went to the kitchen and opened the back door to the air and the sound of the night. Though it was barely fresher than the air inside, I had an exit. I breathed deeply and closed my eyes for a moment.

CHAPTER 22

'I THOUGHT YOU was gonna be sensible an' slip away,' he said, watching my return.

'You just think on that, Rooster.'

He grinned. 'Well, seems as you have the advantage of me again, darlin'.' He laughed, and the laugh coughed and rattled in his chest. 'I'm guessing you've had something of a revelation.'

'I've always had the advantage of you: I know you.'

'Really? You found enlightenment up them stairs did you?'

'Something like that.' I grinned.

'What's your name then?' he asked, squinting through gloom at me. 'Just for my information you understand, nothin' personal.'

'Margarita,' I said.

He shook his head. 'Oh, so you're still set on playin' these games?' He sniffed. 'Seems rather rich you feel the need to attack me, when all things considered, I got a whole heap more reason to be on that side of the gun than you.'

I tilted my head. 'What the hell you moaning 'bout?'

'Moanin'?' He shook his head. 'Hell's teeth darlin', you still playin' dumb? I ain't surprised, not as surprised as I was,' he leant back a little in the chair, 'when I see, as it were, the vixen finding the dog-pound, just when I thought the trail had gone cold.'

'You were following me?' I said, then realized my mistake. Though I'd remembered so much of my life and why I was here, when I tried to recall the last few days the images were still dislocated, muddled. He knew things I didn't.

'I was following the both of you,' he frowned. 'No, I was following my Daddy's money…' The con, he was talking about the con. He still thought that was all this was about. 'On that note, pretty, where is it?'

'Now what would it be?' I asked, though my attempt at subterfuge sounded clumsy as hell out loud.

'Well, it, would be the bag with my Daddy's fifty thousand dollars in it.'

'Damned if I know,' I said.

He chuckled. 'Now you got me wondering what you intend. In fact, I'm mostly wondering why you's still here? I thought if you remembered me, you'd be hot-footin' it away?' He narrowed his eyes.

'Maybe I like the company?' I said, sure I could feel Margarita grinning at that.

He laughed out loud. 'Hell, I wish that were the case, but I don't think so.' My fingers tightened against the handle of the gun. 'I'm wonderin',' he said in a low voice, 'if there's a whole lot more you don't remember yet, which is why you ain't done a midnight flit or took my head off already? I don't think you do know where the money is, and what's more – you don't know what happened to Paris, do you?'

I had no option but to let him have his little victory. He was right, I didn't care about the money and I didn't know about Paris, and Red knew where he was. Or wanted me to think he did.

'If he's dead,' I said, 'I'm gonna kill you right now.'

Red laughed, spittle forming on his chin. 'Now that … that's right unfair of you – I ain't had no hand in his death or otherwise, no more than your own sweet self.'

'You saw him, didn't you, when you went down the road?' I raised the gun at his chest. He stopped laughing.

'Now that would be tellin'.' His eyes flicked down to the floor before he looked up at me again. 'Your head's more full of holes than a Swiss cheese, so what we gonna do here? Sit on our thumbs till the sun come up and you start joining the dots, or we gonna make a deal?'

'No deal.' I felt the hot, dark heat of anger pump behind my eyes. I flipped off the safety again. Red saw and he straightened up in his seat. 'You're gonna tell me what happened to Paris,' I said. 'Or I'm gonna take off your left foot, and then you're gonna tell me. Your choice.'

'That's a mighty bold boast darlin', seeing as you ain't exactly a professional …' I turned the gun away and shot the right leg off the grinning side table. It exploded into a shower of splinters. We both watched as it crumpled over and came to a rest on its side.

'You wanna make a bet I can't shoot another stationary target, even closer 'n' that?' I asked.

Red ran his tongue over his teeth. 'My mouth's awful dry. You find it in your heart to get me some water? Might loosen my lips a little …'

I considered him from a moment, then I went and filled one of the coffee mugs and held it out to him. 'You may have to help me a touch,' he said, rattling his handcuffs against the chair.

Gritting my teeth, I put the mug to his lips. He took a gulp of water and I watched it slide down his throat, the muscles working under his gleaming, filthy skin. Then I snatched the mug away and threw the rest of it in his face.

He spluttered into laughter. 'Keep tryin' darlin', maybe one of us will believe you mean it – hell, I'd never have given you a drink.'

'What happened to Paris – where is he?' I tossed the mug aside and sat on the couch, leaning my elbows on my knees, the gun in my hand.

'That fine upstanding fellow? Jesus, his mama really call him Paris France?' Red shook his head, clearing his eyes of water. 'Great con – was this his idea, or yours?'

'Tell me …'

'Darlin', I figure as you're set on shootin' me, I might as well take my time, 'cause you won't do it till I'm done.' I didn't answer, so he said more softly, 'Or am I wrong 'bout that?' Of course he wasn't. I shrugged and waved him to go on.

'Like I said …' Red leant back against the chair. 'Nice con. I guess you an' he was working your way through the state, just griftin' along.'

'Something like that.'

'Cute, well, for whatever reason, you and your fine young buck Paris France, fixed on Daddy and me, when we were havin' ourselves some father-son time.'

'Daddy?'

'Senator Daddy to you,' Red said. 'A good man with a son who's been a sorry disappointment to him.'

'You surprise me.'

Red smiled. 'Man's gotta make peace with himself. We met young Paris at a game we attend from time to time. I thought him a brash young fella, fuller of himself than an egg's full o' meat.'

Something came back to me then, something Paris said.

'Best way to get to a man? Let him think as he already got you beat, let him think he's superior to you in every way – hell, best of all, annoy the shit outta him, then he gets to thinking as he's doing the world a favour if he takes you down a peg.'

'He irked me,' Red said, nodding at the memory. 'And I beat him on the turn of a card.'

'Then, you let him think he's already got you beat, let him see your desperation. If he's a good man, he'll cut a deal, let you go – but if he were a good man, he'd never be there in the first place. If you've got your mark right, he'll never be able to walk away, not when he thinks he got you down.'

'He told us all 'bout you.' Red smiled. 'Said as how all he needed was a chance to double his money, said as how you'd be there next time. Make it worth our while. You should have heard what he said 'bout you … can't say as he was wrong, though.'

Paris, the word scribbled in neon above the door. Was that why we chose it, because he couldn't resist the joke? Faux black marble, black plastic tables and chairs, the tongue of a stage lolling across the room. Everything just a little bit sticky, a little bit gritty, quite a lot shitty. Testosterone, oestrogen, silicone, little back room – private, no windows.

I saw myself then, I saw Margarita in that blond wig tied in bunches. Little denim hot pants and a white shirt knotted under my breasts. I think I was even wearing cowboy boots. I could recall looking at myself in the mirror over the vanity unit in the room in the Pelican Inn; I remembered how I stared past it out of the window to the wide, white expanse of road and the night burning along the horizon.

'You okay Shoog?' Paris said from behind me, sliding into view.

'I checked up on you,' Red said. 'Happen to know the manager. Hell, I know just about everyone local. He said as how there were a coloured gentleman and a white girl staying there, said as how they'd had something of a fight. He'd gotten complaints.'

'You let him look you up,' Paris had said. 'You let him prove to himself some part of your story, then he starts believin' the rest of it. You only need the one lie, the rest is all truth; that way the lie got a better chance of stayin' hid.'

'And there you were, Margarita.' Red tasted the word as he said it, as he whispered it. 'My Daddy's a man of old-fashioned tastes. He needs to let off a little steam from time to time, but he's got ...' he smiled '... traditional ideas, when it comes to a sweet little thing like you, with a big old nigger like Paris.' He relished the filthy word.

'Don't you call him that, you redneck son-of-a-bitch!'

'Have I offended your liberal sensibilities?' Red taunted. 'Oh hell, I know what I mean by it. You got coloured folks what go to church, black men who go to war and you got niggers what go to jail, and Paris walked in that night like a nigger with attitude on his arm.'

In the room in the Pelican Inn, Paris had brushed the side of my face with his finger. 'I gotta say somethin'. You know what we're doin' tonight, I'm gonna have to say shit I don't wanna, both to you and about you, and I ain't happy 'bout that. But if I tell you what I'm gonna say or do, you won't react right – so I ain't gonna tell you, but I am gonna say I'm sorry – understand? Only way you're gonna pull this off, only way you can do it, is forget who you is and what you are. If you don't live your lie, no one else gonna be fooled, an' you gonna get hurt.'

'Staking you in a poker game,' Red said. 'I guess that really appealed to the old man, what with you twining yourself about so ... invitingly. Your face, when old Paris said I could have you as part of the deal, just so I'd play one more hand, now that was a picture.'

'You like that candy-ass bitch? She yours.'

'What the fuck?'

'Shut yo' mouth. I'm sick of you an' yo' mouth. You shut the fuck up an' do as I ask. You goin' suck cock if I want and you goin' fuckin' like it, or you ain't gettin' no more hits outta me.' Paris slapped me across the face. I knew he held back, but it stung me just like he said it would, just like its memory stung me again. 'Sure an' she's yours, for the weekend or whatever – you do what the fuck you like with her, I ain't bothered. I pretty much broke her, anyways.'

The room in the abandoned house was still, its cool air tainted with swamp water rising from the floor. It was the dead time, the hours before dawn and after midnight, when all good things were asleep. But not us, Red and I, we were awake. We were not good things.

'Course he won.' The light from the lamp glinted off Red's teeth and the wetness of his eyes. 'He started laughing and laughing and pullin' that money into his bag. You know what, my Daddy even started to ask if you were gonna be all right.' Red smiled. 'He was concerned for you, till you shot Paris.'

'Crazy bitch … what you doin' now? You gonna shoot me?'

'I shot him,' I said, and the memory made me smile: my hand, holding a gun, with the snub end lengthened by a silencer. That's what I'd remembered in the shower, my hand holding the gun and Paris playing his part.

'Then I gave you the bag,' I said, excited now, thrilled, as the memory took shape, unaided by his words. I saw him, Red Rooster and his Daddy, saw the look of horror on their faces as Paris crashed into the corner of the room, fake blood spraying up the wall, fake blood pooling out of his body. My hand holding the gun that I'd fired, even as I cried like a child. Then I'd thrown the bag at them and started screaming, yelling.

'Get out, just get out and leave me alone! Take your money and get out!' And they'd run, because no would-be senator cares to be found in the back room of a bar with a crazy hooker and her dead pimp.

'You ran,' I said, laughing afresh at the victory of the moment.

'You bet your sweet ass we ran. Hell, Daddy likes to dip his toe in some dark water, but that … that shit ain't never gonna wash clean.'

'When did you guess?' I asked, leaning back against the couch, still glowing with the renewed knowledge that we'd pulled it off.

'Didn't take long.' Red was smiling too, almost as if he shared in my victory. 'Daddy started flappin' his jaw 'bout helping you, 'bout goin' back – I said as how he was crazy, and he said as how they were gonna find our DNA all over the place. Hell, he was even gonna call his lawyer.'

That night came back to me with Red's words, like the blood on the wall. I saw Paris in the Pelican's pink, dusty bathroom by the basin, a plastic mixing bowl inside, into which he poured a gilded ripple of syrup. I'd dipped in my finger and it came out red.

In the shack Red exhaled, still smiling at me. 'Daddy was on the point of dialling the number. I said to him to leave it, that we'd got the money. I ripped open the bag and guess what? Whole lotta whorehouse calling cards.' He grinned. 'Nice touch.'

Paris had smiled as I'd licked my sugar bloodied finger.

'This way, this way we get the time we need. You got one chance to make the switch when they're lookin' at all this red syrup on the walls. Then they'll run. They just need to think I'm dead long enough for us to get out. A minute's all we need, two's even better. If they come back in, we's already gone. Here, I'll show you how to fill the blood pack right, so as it goes off with a bang.'

As soon as the door closed, Paris was up. He turned the table over against the door, just in case, while I dragged two chairs under the air vent in the ceiling. Inside the crawl space he retrieved the cases he'd hidden there earlier, and we changed. Barely thirty seconds gone.

Seventy-five seconds, and we were in the vent, crawling to the outside. Paris kicked the outside grille to loosen it, then pulled it up inside beside us. The car we'd bought was underneath, it was cheap and it was nasty but we were going to dump it as soon as we were down the road. Paris jumped onto the roof, and reached out for me.

'Shit!' I'd exclaimed, patting my pockets as I landed next to him.

'What's the matter?'

'My passport, it ain't here!'

'What da' fuck?'

'Oh shit baby, I'm so sorry, I left it in the room at the motel.'

'Jesus Christ, what the hell we do now?'

'We gotta go back, they don't know we ain't coming back tonight; we ain't checked out yet.'

'Quickly,' he said, hitting the sidewalk and wrenching the car door open. 'We ain't got much time, first place he's gonna look.'

I knew we didn't have much time. I was banking on it.

'Paris always said how some men you could con because underneath they wanted you to,' I said to Red. 'Seems like you're one of them.'

Red shrugged. 'Maybe you' right, darlin'. Sitting on my thumbs this past year, with nothin' much to entertain myself since I left the army, I gotta say, it was fun trackin' you down. Daddy charged me with finding you, discreet like, not to make a fuss. He weren't about to go to the police, but he weren't gonna let you get away with that, pretty. He don't like getting' made a fool of, and neither do I.' He rolled his shoulders, moving his hands behind his back.

'I guess not,' I said, still smiling at the audacity of it. 'Not gonna want to be connected to a dead pimp and his ho', not gonna want to admit how we got his campaign funds either.'

'I kind of enjoyed the challenge, my special ops training been going beggin' awhile. You never knew I was there.' I smiled, because he was wrong. I'd known he was there, I knew what he'd do. 'I suppose you and he had something in the nature of a falling out?' Red shifted in his seat again. 'They say there's no honour among thieves, suppose that's to be expected. Decided you'd had enough of him did you?' He cocked his head to the left. 'Took some of his words to heart?'

'No,' I said, though Red was right, of course. But not about the words.

I'd made sure the motel clerk noticed me and my blond locks when I got my passport. I stopped and asked him where a good place for second-hand cars was, said we'd had a win on the slots, and we were gonna party and get ourselves a new ride. I'd pointed to the lemon out front – 'We ain't gonna be driving that old heap no more!' – and I'd winked at him.

Paris had pulled off the freeway, to where we'd left the new car, all without knowing I'd been advertising it. We had enough to buy it before the big con, and I'd let him choose, which felt like folding some money into his pocket and telling him to 'go get yourself something nice.' I figured we needed some sleep, and I figured the best way of both shutting him up, and making sure he did, was a little sex, applied liberally in the back seat. He hadn't seemed to mind, had pulled me onto his lap and kissed me.

'You takin' that thing off?' he asked of the wig, still in its blond bunches.

'Not till we're three states away, just to be sure.'

'Leastways he's pretty,' Margarita said, 'not like that makes it any less of a sin, though.'

The sex had worked, I'd thought, both to give him the impression that we were still in this thing together and help us catch a few hours' sleep. Trouble was it had worked a little too well. I woke up when I felt the car moving, jerking myself up as it slipped into gear. Blinking, cotton-mouthed and disconcerted, I saw Paris was driving, and was at once flooded with panic. I'd planned our escape route through the reserve and sold it to Paris on the grounds that nobody ever went that way, unless they'd plenty of time to kill, so it was the last direction Red would have considered. Of course, I'd also meant to leave enough clues to ensure that was exactly the way he would go; only all along, I'd meant to wake first, and I'd meant to be driving. I looked at my phone. There were eleven minutes to go before the alarm I'd set was scheduled to wake me.

'Hey, sleepyhead,' Paris said, glancing back over his shoulder. 'Why don't you close your eyes for a bit? I'm cool.'

'Okay,' I said, 'guess I might as well,' not sure what to do next. Paris smiled at me, like he was my older brother, like he was taking care of us. It was over, I thought, and he was all ready for us to run away together. He was looking after me, with no idea what I'd planned to do next.

Red flexed his shoulders, cocked his head to one side. He was enjoying this, telling me how dumb I'd been, how easy to follow. 'The clerk at your motel mentioned how you'd asked him all about the way through the reserve. Said it surprised him, as the two of you didn't look much like the country type, not seein' as you said you were set on buying a new sports car. Careless of you to leave that old wreck you were driving in full view when you swapped them.'

Careless, I thought, and I smiled. Little old Red, following the trail I'd left for him. Proving to himself the lie I'd told him.

'The old fellow at the gas station, said as how a mixed couple in a nice, bright red car had been there few hours before. He remembered you, darlin', but then I guess who wouldn't? Nice white girl, black man making her get the gas. Said he made some observation 'bout him not being a gentleman; said you agreed with him.'

A dry road in a wet place, I thought, lined with malformed hangman's trees. We'd needed gas, like I knew we would, and that there was only the one gas station. But I'd meant to be driving by then, so I could have left Paris behind, caused a scene, made sure Red knew where I was headed. We passed the first sign, then the second – last chance for gas this side of the wilderness. I'd half been pretending to be asleep, figuring that if I was, Paris would have to get out to pump and pay, and I could slip into the driver's seat and get away. The needle was hovering just above empty when I risked a glance. Seconds later, Paris began talking.

He was on his cell, had it cradled under his chin as he began to slow for the turning. I hadn't heard it ring, but I hear him answer, heard him say, 'Hey there, how's you?' My guess was his mother, so I pretended he'd woken me and sat up. When he saw me looking, he pulled the kind of face you do when it's your mother, and she's not going to take the hint about ringing off.

'Naw, look, I think I'm gonna be headed out of state, soon,' and then he paused, listening, as if the other person on the line was doing a lot of talking. 'I'm not sure,' he managed, then, 'hard to say, y'know?'

He pulled up by the pump and turned off the engine. Nodding, hand over the cell, he mouthed at me, 'Get the gas, Shoog?' and when I scowled, added, 'Coffee, two sugars?' with a grin. 'Sure, Momma,' he said to the phone, 'I hear you.'

Tied to the chair in the shack, Red rolled his arms, rubbing his cheek on his shoulder.

'Like I said, my truck was not happy. Should have stayed at the gas station, but I pressed on and she died on me.'

I closed my eyes for a moment. 'You stopped here.'

'Found the key out back, pushed the truck round the side.'

'And I just walked through the door.' The appalling symmetry almost made me laugh. I'd meant Red to find this place, but instead, the place had found him. 'Shit, I knew I knew you – why didn't you say something?'

Red shrugged. 'First, I thought you was just messin' with me, and you were the one with the gun. Then I saw as how you'd been shot, an' I figured you weren't going nowhere fast.' He shifted position and coughed a little. 'It amused me, seein' what you were about. I was having a whale of a time. Hell, didn't you enjoy the little performance I put on just for you?'

'The bathroom window … that was you?'

Red grinned. 'Sure was. My truck's pretty much fixed. I just been cleaning things to look busy.'

'So what you been doing?' I asked, my grifter curiosity wetted despite everything.

'Playin' with my shotgun,' he said and when he saw my expression added, 'You really are from back east. You think I weren't armed?'

'But you were inside,' I said. 'I saw you?'

'Smoke and mirrors, darlin'.' He was enjoying this far too much. 'Opened up the shell cases and laid a little gunpowder trail. Told you, I learned all kind of amusement in the army. Powder fuse to a heap of gunpowder and rocks, light the end and run. I shot out the window and the truck after it were lit, then ran inside. Gave myself a moment to shut the door and bang, bang, fourth of July!'

'Why the hell did you bother?'

Red looked hurt. 'Come on, you think you'd have stayed in here with me so long if you hadn't thought there was something worse outside? Oh, I had a whole other story ready just to see what you'd do, 'bout how there were some boys on my trail after Iraq and everything, but you didn't seem to need it. Maybe you were having as good a time I was, after all?

'Fuck you,' I muttered.

'Be my guest,' he said. He was having a good a time, despite the handcuffs. I'd had enough of him thinking he was clever. I raised the gun and aimed it at his left foot again. His face fell.

'The other day, yesterday,' I said, focusing on him. 'You found him, didn't you?'

'Who?'

I raised the gun higher. 'You found Paris …'

He looked down the barrel and did not flinch. 'Why you care, seeing as how he shot you?' The memory of pain, hot and white, lanced through my side. 'You're right though,' he said with a sigh, as if he were suddenly weary of pretending. 'I found your car. Nasty business, the driver side was caved right in. Seems he hit a boulder on the roadside. I'd say he was trapped, seein' as he never followed you, or my money.'

'All this time, you been playin' me?'

What had I done? Given in and told him? Tried to make him stop, knowing that we were getting closer and closer to the shack, and that if he drove past it, all of this would be for nothing?

'No, it weren't like that!'

Paris hit the steering wheel. 'Goddamn it, you said you loved me, you forced me to say it …' I think I'd begged him to understand, just to leave me and go, but he hadn't.

'Look, we got to pull over, just up ahead, there – can you see it?' Why hadn't he?

'No way. You think I'm gonna let you kill him, you think I

wanna get mixed up in murder?' He was looking out for me, I thought, because he still wanted the dream I'd sold him – me, him, fast car, trunk load of money – he believed me, and he was angry.

'There, that's it, pull over; pull over for fuck's sake!'

'No way, you crazy bitch, you ain't doing this.' He'd floored it, pushed the car and the road faster than he should have.

'Turn this car round, now!' I demanded, pleaded.

'No, you liar, I don't gotta do nothing you say no more!' Then he'd slowed, and I'd thought he might have been going to relent, but I'd been wrong. He carried on, not looking at me, taking me further and further away from everything I'd prepared.

'Keep the car, keep the fuckin' money, alright? You gotta let me do this, I come all this way, I come so far – turn round, please – I gotta get to that house!'

'Get off of my wheel, you ...'

I heard the tick-tick of the engine in the calm after the crash. I'd torn open the door, grabbed the bag and ran, moving as if the world were molasses.

'Come back – I'll shoot – I'll fuckin' shoot you!'

He had the gun in his hand, jabbing it through the window at me as I ran. I imagined him scrabbling in the glovebox for it, and me thinking he'd never do it, all while thinking how much he must hate me, how much he didn't understand.

Then white pain, the world turning over and over as I'd gone down. My head had impacted on something hard, hard enough to crack the sky in two, bringing dark, my own, personal night.

'Was he dead?'

'Dead?' Red rolled the word round his teeth. 'Car was a hell of a mess, inside and out. Maybe he were bleeding profusely, quite pro ... fuse ... ley. Hot day, long way from nowhere – he was lucky they found him.'

'Who?' I asked. Red started laughing. 'Who?'

'Darlin', I might be special ops, but even you would have worked it out. That thing was all over police tape and shit. Lookin' at it, they had to cut the roof off to get him out.'

'What you sayin'?'

'This road's lonely, but it's the only way through the reserve, though what they're saving other than mosquitoes, fuck knows. I guess someone did the decent thing, called the authorities, and now it's the authorities what's got Paris.'

'They've taken him?' I was almost laughing. 'Someone came?'

'I guess so. Don't know what state he was in, but seein' as they left the car, I'm guessing he was still breathin'. They don't bother rushin' off when they got a corpse in back. It's not that far up the road. Leastways, far enough for a phone signal.'

I slumped back against the couch cushion. Paris was either dead or safe. Either way, there was nothing I could do for him right now.

'So, we done here?'

'Done?' I echoed. I could see behind him, see through the windows by the front door. The sky was inky black, but silver was etching out the horizon.

'Yeah, you won, you got me. Guess you don't recall where the money is, but hell, we can just call it payment received for a fun night out.'

'You think we're done here?'

Red frowned. 'I hope so.'

CHAPTER 23

I STOOD UP and drew my fingers through my hair.

'It never was about the money,' I said, standing with my feet apart, weight even. I rolled my neck, heard a click as I flexed my shoulders.

Red raised an eyebrow. 'So what's this happy horse shit? You got something of an itch I can help you with?'

'When you first saw me …' I looked down at him. 'What did you think?'

'What'd you mean?'

'When I first saw you, when I'd lost my memory – when I didn't know your name but I still knew you?' Red frowned and narrowed his eyes. 'And before, you sure you didn't know me, when you first saw me in the back room at the poker game? What did you think of me?' I took a step forward, the gun pointed squarely at his chest. He looked at it, moistened his lips, then a smile dragged them back from his teeth.

'Not sure as I should say …' He tilted his head so he could meet my gaze. 'Not with your itchy trigger finger 'n' all.'

'Go on,' I said, heat beating in my throat, sweat clawing down my spine. I swallowed and a smile I'd been dreaming of for months curled onto my lips. 'Tell me.'

I saw the pulse throb in Red's neck as he exhaled, closed his eyes and then opened them again.

'If I gotta be honest with you darlin', I liked you well enough when you was all blond and dusted up with sugar. Hell, you looked like a popsicle on a hot day. But I liked you more when I seen you all dark and dirty and sweat stained, with blood on your face, fainting at my door.' I saw a rush of colour burn in his cheeks. 'I could barely keep my hands to myself as you lay in a muck sweat on that there couch, but you know what?' He pursed his lips. 'Right now, with your face all sly 'n' angry and you standing over me with that gun – fuck me, darlin', but you gotta be the hottest thing this side of hell. I swear, I never met a woman what could bust my lip up before, but you know what? I think I kinda like it.'

'You like it?' I felt something twist and burn inside me, a dark vanity intoxicating and rich. I moved closer to him, within reach, if he wasn't handcuffed and hog-tied. I pushed the weapon against his cheek, pressing his face so that he had to turn his head away from me. He swallowed, hard.

'If we're bein' honest, if you were to fuck me on this chair right now, you could go ahead and spread my brains over the wall after, an' I wouldn't give a damn. I'm pretty much sick of this life as it is, think you might be doin' me a favour.'

I climbed onto his lap and pressed the gun into the side of his head. His animal eyes watched me, a smile pulling his lips into a leer. My heart was shaking the bars of my ribcage; I had a hot taste of metal in my mouth, and a delicious agony throbbed through me. His body was hard and firm, his skin burning to my touch.

'What you think you're gonna do to me that I don't want you to?' he breathed, the words lit with his dry, mocking laugh.

'I'm gonna make you suffer,' I said, feeling the rise and fall of his body under me, the heaving of his lungs betraying his fear. I could smell it on him, I could taste it like salt in sea air. I meshed my fingers into his hair and dragged his face up to mine. 'I'm gonna make you feel like you made her feel.' My lips brushed the skin on his cheek, touched the barrel of the gun. 'Then, I'm gonna kill you.'

He was barely listening to me, so it took him a moment to ask. 'Like who?'

I laughed. 'Tell me who you thought of, when you first saw me. Did I remind you of anyone?'

'I thought …' but his voice trailed away. He jerked his face back from mine and I saw his pupils widen as realization shivered over him. 'Lisa?' he said, the word catching in his throat. 'But you ain't her, you can't be?'

The thrill and relief flooding through me made me laugh. I jumped off his lap and turned myself round in front of him, delighting in the look of astonishment on his face.

'You ain't her!' he insisted.

'No I ain't. I'm her sister!'

'Her sister?' He squinted at me, searching for something he'd barely registered the first time he'd seen me. 'Her sister … my God!' He peered at me again. 'Lisa – she … she said she had a sister, I remember now, but her name weren't Margarita, it were …'

'Don't remember?' I folded my arms across my breasts, the gun in the crook of my elbow. 'Frustrating, ain't it?'

'But what the … why you done all this, what's all this for?' he asked, straining against the chair.

'Don't you dare,' I said, my smile twisting into a snarl. 'Don't you dare deny what you did to her.'

I marched over to the document bag and ripped it open. Grabbing a handful of papers, I thrust them at him. 'Here … it's all here, what you did to her …'

He jerked back as far as he could, as if I was holding something burning to his face.

'Emails, from Lisa to me – tellin' me what she did after she left home, after she met you – you never knew she wrote me, did you?' He didn't answer, so I shook them at him again. 'Did you?'

'Darlin', calm down,' he said, his voice straining to sound controlled, all hint of his bravado gone. 'I don't know what she said but …'

'She said you hit her.' I threw the papers and they erupted in a flurry of white leaves, foolscap thistledown drifting to the floor about him. 'It says you locked her up – you took her away to your big old fancy house and you never let her go!'

'Now look,' he started to say. 'You best listen to me—'

'No, I don't,' I cut across him. 'I don't gotta do nothing you say. She was my sister, my sister. When we were growing up, all we had was each other.'

'She said that,' he said softly, as if now he could remember her saying it, as if she'd said it to him only moments ago and it was fresh in his mind.

'They were always down on her, always hurting her, mocking her – just her, never me.' The words tumbled out of me, glorious, painful, echoing round that damp, grey space. 'Always Lisa, pushing her and pushing her, but I was too small, too little – I could never help her, never – I was never big enough to save her.'

'She told me 'bout your Daddy,' he spat, suddenly violent, defensive. 'She told me what he did. I ain't sure as your family's got much on mine.'

'I couldn't help her,' I screamed, and there was a sob beneath it. 'I couldn't help her, and then they sent her away to all those schools in case anyone found out, in case someone else listened to her.'

'She told me,' he said, eager, as if he were pleading his case. 'She told me how she played up. She wrote you then, she did, didn't she?' He looked up, a smile on his face, a smile as if we were sharing.

'Yeah, she wrote to me, until I found out they read the letters – they tried to break us up all the time, always – like they hadn't done enough.'

'But they couldn't come between sisters?' he said.

'An' neither could you!' I kicked at the paper with my bare feet not caring how much it hurt.

'But I never …'

'Yes you did.' I snatched up one of the pages and I forced it into his face.

'I can't read that,' he snapped, twisting away from me.

'But you know what you did, don't you?'

'She cheated on me!' he retorted as I slapped the papers onto his lap. 'I was away serving my country, and she went sneaking round like a she-cat on heat!' I hit him. I punched him in the mouth. It felt so good. Like the first thing I'd done right in a long time.

'Hit me again,' he blazed. 'Go on, if it makes you feel better – it won't change what she did, your precious sister.' He spat at me and when he smiled, his teeth were bloody.

I laughed, wiping the spit from the jeans I was wearing. 'I bet she was desperate for some real, honest lovin' after being with a twisted old pervert like you – oh, we're sisters, we shared everything …' And we had, in a way. I'd read her words over and over until I could see them, lived them, until it had almost felt like I was the one he'd met, I was the one he'd married. Which was why he seemed just so goddamn familiar.

'We all got our little peccadilloes. You should know.'

'You ever find out who she was with?' I asked, enjoying the look of anger that flashed across his face, that tightened his jaw.

'If I had, I'd have killed him.'

'Yeah, Paris thought as much. He was sure you never knew.'

'Paris – your Paris?' He burst out laughing. 'Well, don't that beat all?'

'You think that's funny?' I said.

He shook his head, still laughing. 'You don't? You tracked him down to see what your sister was gettin'?'

'No, to get to you, when the police wouldn't.'

'That's why that sheriff came sniffin' round – I never could see what he was drivin' at. What you go see him for?'

I stared at him. 'Because you killed her!'

He looked at me. 'What?'

'Lisa, you killed Lisa.'

Something cold and urgent descended over his expression; for a moment he almost looked sorry, sad, as if he'd just told me there was no Santa and realized his mistake.

'Oh, darlin', no …'

'Don't deny it!'

Red coughed. 'I don't know what you think I am, but …'

'You liar,' I snorted. 'Of course you'd say that, you're a murderer and a liar.'

'I'll tell you what I told that old fool policeman: I never killed her.'

'You expect me to believe that?'

'I ain't lying. You really gonna shoot me now?'

'When I'm through hurtin' you.'

'And then what?' He rolled his shoulders, stretching his neck. 'You gonna be a murderer too? You ready to have my blood on your hands? You think just 'cause you're south of the Mason–Dixon Line, we don't got laws? Your pet sheriff's gonna be after you quicker than a hound dog, seein' as he knows you're Lisa's sister.'

'Let him,' I said, and I couldn't hide the satisfaction in my voice. 'Lisa's sister flew to Mexico months ago, and when this is all over, she's gonna fly right back in. Work was real sorry to see her go, but volunteering looks so good on the resume. It's amazing what a thousand dollars buys you in Mexico.' I clicked my neck again. 'You forget, my name's Margarita. That's who you've been following, that's who tricked you out of your Daddy's money.'

'What?' he demanded, straining to understand. 'You been planning this all the time? You ... you set me up months back, to do this?'

'I've been living this every day since I lost contact with her. Hell's teeth,' I mimicked, 'I even walked my shoes off my feet when I'd no memory, just to get to you. I meant you to follow me here, I knew you would but, thing is Red, old buddy, I'd already been here before. Got myself a head start.'

'You planted this shit, before everything, before the poker game?' He waved his foot toward the papers on the floor.

'I believed you might find them interesting readin',' I snarled. 'I even left us breakfast; glad you turned out to be a chef as well as a murderer.'

Red slumped in his chair and let his head drop toward the floor. He inhaled deeply and when he looked at me again, his face was cold and calm. 'They tell you I killed her, did they? Them letters of hers?'

'They told me—'

'They told you she walked out on me?'

'She was going to, she said—'

'Well who for?' he snapped. 'She must have told you she was seein' that man, that liar, that convicted fraudster Paris goddam France, and you come knocking on my door?'

I went to speak, then I pressed my tongue against the back of my teeth. Red spoke again, sounding neither angry nor desperate, but cool, calm, as if he were simply stating the obvious. 'Your sister gets herself mixed up with a criminal. She steals for him, she goes to meet him, an' then she ain't heard of no more. An' you think I killed her?'

'It's not—'

'What is it, then?' his voice grew louder. 'You got the evidence, you got the truth of the matter all over them papers ... So you tell me what happened! You might have spent the last few months sleepin' with her lover, but you ever think you been doin' something else? You ever stop to think you might have been fuckin' her killer all this time?'

'You think I'm that stupid?' I yelled. 'The last few months I got to know the both of you, you think I can't see what you're trying to do? Sure, Paris France is a cheap con, a thief and a liar, but he's no murderer. So go on, keep reaching – who else you gonna blame? I think your Daddy's got plenty more to answer for. You gonna say it was him next? Or your housekeeper? I believe you have one, right?'

Red shook his head. 'I don't much care what you believe. I don't care much 'bout anything no more. You can take your sweet time over hurtin' me as much as you want – you think you're gonna do more to me than what I've lived through? Hell, when they trained my unit, they beat the shit out of us more times than I care to remember, just so as we was used to it. We're trained for anythin' darlin', y'all better know you done nothin' but tickle me up a little.'

'I'm gonna make you pay for what you did. Look! Look at her words!' I kicked them with my toes again. 'You locked her in your goddamn car, while your Daddy watched, while he let you! What else did you do to her, what else while your Daddy was watchin'?'

'What?' He was laughing again. 'You got some imagination on you. Sure, why not? What my Daddy does for entertainment is his concern.' I hit him hard across the face. He spat and leered. 'Shit, that felt good, sure wakes up a man. There's some as pay double for that treatment, though not sure it's worth fifty big ones.'

'Did you hit her?' I snarled.

'That's what you wanna believe? She took my money and my car – you wanna hear me say it, I'll say it, darlin' – truth is, I did not kill her!'

'Then where is she?' I demanded, my head spinning and churning with his words.

'Ask Paris. She drove off in my car with my mama's diamonds on her fingers and the clothes I bought on her back, but I did … not … kill … her.'

In the space after his words the cool dawn air licked through the kitchen windows and breathed over my skin.

'You'd say anything wouldn't you?' I said. 'Anything to save your miserable hide.'

'Seems as I'm damned either way,' he said softly. 'Seems as you've already made up your mind. No matter how much you hurt me, the truth ain't gonna change.'

The silence of the morning crept in until he spoke again.

'You know, every day I get up and I jog round our land. If I go real hard, it takes me 'bout an hour to go all the way round, an' every time I do, that hour seems longer and longer, and you know why? Cause I got nothin' else I gotta do, and there ain't no one chasing me no more, no matter how hard I run. If I'd have known you was after me I might just have had reason again, 'cause strange as it seems, girl, these last few hours? You've brought me back from the dead.'

'You … you tell me what you did to her.' I pointed the gun at him again, held it inches from his face in both hands, ready for the recoil when I took my shot.

'What d'you think?' he asked. 'Go on, seems you got all the answers – you tell me how I killed her? That is, if you still so sure it was me?'

I screamed in fury and tore away from him. I saw the whiskey bottle on the side, snatched it up and smashed it against the wall. It splintered, leaving me a brutal edge.

'She betrayed me, your big sister,' he mocked. 'She took everything I gave her an' ran off with Paris, that li'l whore!'

I turned and stabbed the glass shard into his thigh with a howl of rage.

'You fuckin' bitch!' he screamed, 'Oh, Jesus, you fucking … shit!' He twisted against the chair and forced his scream into a laugh, going on and on until the sound was hot and red and hammering in my head. 'Oh baby!' He leered at me. 'I love the way you kiss! Tell me, it get you wet does it, you hurtin' me?

'Shut up!'

'Go on, I'm hotter than a match head; I never had so much fun when I was with old Lisa!' He laughed, his body shaking with the effort. 'I'm hard as a rock baby.'

'She was my sister,' I screamed, blinking tears from my eyes. 'She was my big sister and I let her down, I … I let you have her and you …' I ripped out the shard and threw it against the wall as he bellowed in pain.

'Put the gun to my head,' he demanded. 'Put the gun to my head and pull the trigger.' I pressed the gun to the side of his head. I wanted him to flinch, to beg or plead but he stared back at me, his face pale but defiant. 'Pull the trigger,' he said, 'or I swear, I'm gonna kill you.'

'I'll do it,' I said, jamming the gun to his temple to mask the tremor in my hand.

'You do it and you're just like me, Margarita.'

'No,' I said, 'I ain't like you!'

'No you ain't,' he said, our faces inches apart. 'There's only one of us what's gonna kill an innocent man.'

'You ain't innocent, you did it, you killed her …'

'Shit,' he said, the words pumping from his chest, his face a bloodied, twisted mask. 'I married me the wrong sister!'

There was a ripping, splintering sound. Red twisted from under me, pulling the chair back apart and ramming into me with his shoulder. He sent me staggering backwards against the couch, crashing to the floor. Fuck, he must have been working the bars of the chair loose all the time he'd shifted in his seat. I saw him hit the floor, writhing as he worked himself free of the ropes, trying to flip his legs through the loop his bound hands made. The gun skittered away across the floor; I tried to reach it but the urge to run was stronger as I saw Red's legs come free. I dragged myself up and ran toward the kitchen door.

'I'm coming for you!' he yelled. He was up on his feet, cuffed hands in front of him. I spilled out into the yard, the grass shockingly cold and wet under my feet.

'Oh, you better run, girl!'

CHAPTER 24

I RAN TO THE FRONT of the house as panic beat in my throat. Red exploded out of the door behind me; he ran toward his truck, as I limped, unseen, to the far side of the house. I pressed myself against the wall.

I tried to control my desperate breathing, straining to hear him coming after me. Darting a glance round the end of the house, I saw the side of the veranda below the steps was open, revealing an alcove under the stairs. I scrambled into it.

There was just enough space to crawl on all fours. The ground under my hands and feet was sodden and stank of mildew and rot. I tried not to imagine snakes lurking there as I peered upwards. The dawn was coming but the sky was still dark, though it was bright compared to the space under the stairs. There were gaps between the boards, striations of grey and silver above me, and then I heard him.

'Margarita!' he bellowed. He was following me, coming up on the left side of the house. 'I know you ain't far darlin', what with them feet of yours – come on now, I think we're done playin' these games.'

I saw a movement, he'd come round to the front and was standing at the foot of the stairs.

'You know I'm gonna find you – an' when I do … I reckon you owe me a whole lot o' fun.'

I prayed for him to start off down the road, I willed him to think that I'd gone that way, though I knew I'd have been obvious, a silhouette limping against the dawn.

'I'm gonna forgive you for knocking me down, takin' my money, callin' me a murderer, but I'm still gonna mess you up, 'cause I want to. You come out now … maybe I still won't be a murderer when I'm through with you?'

The planks above me groaned at Red's footfall. He was coming up the stairs to the house. He took another step, and I could see him above me, leaning against the rail that ran round the veranda's edge. His hands were still cuffed together and he was staggering.

'Margarita!' he bellowed. 'I know you're here …' I forced my hand against my mouth. If there were no snakes at my feet, there was one above my head and I'd stepped on its tail. Red swore and bent against the rail again. He coughed and I moved, but in the cramped space I could see nothing and collided into a beam supporting the floor above. The noise was imperceptible, but I heard the scrape of his boot on the wood as he straightened up. He was listening.

I eased my fingers around the beam then spread myself low against the ground. I peered at his silhouette above me as I slithered under him, and saw the unmistakable shape of my gun in his shackled hand. He moved with exaggerated care but the hollow veranda was like a drum and magnified each step he took. I'd crawled in at one end and now Red was above me; I had to get to the other side without him hearing. Misdirection, I thought as sweat coursed over my back; you gotta send him the wrong way.

I swept my hands through the soil until my fingers closed around a stone. I grasped it and inched as close to my exit as I could. I had one shot. Then I heard him singing softly above me.

'In a cavern, in a canyon ...' he took a deliberately heavy step, coming toward me '...excavating for a mine...' He stopped, listening. My eyes were slowly adjusting to the gloom – what had been black had faded to charcoal, the sky I glimpsed through the boards arcing to cobalt. 'Lived a miner, forty-niner, and his daughter ... Clementine.' He stamped. Shock ricocheted though me. I jerked and the stone, greased with damp, escaped my hand. Swearing silently, I flailed in the dirt, scrabbling through grit and gravel.

'Oh my darlin' ... oh my darlin' ...' Stamp. 'Oh my darling, Clementine, are you lost and gone forever?' I heard the hiss of his laugh above me. 'Dreadful sorry ... Clementine!' he barked. My hand found the stone.

I hurled it the way I'd come, and it clattered against the inside of the veranda. Red turned and lumbered toward the sound. I dragged myself through the dirt and slithered out the other way. I broke cover and scrambled to my feet. I could hear him yelling from the far side of the house.

'Clementine? Comin' to get you!'

I reached his truck, hanging onto it as I sucked air into my lungs. Jesus, I thought, the tyre's not even shot out! I jerked my head from side to side, trying to find a way out. I thought of running back inside the house and searching for a knife or hiding under the bed upstairs – both futile against a man with a gun.

The road behind me was hard and dry and my feet were throbbing; either side of me was rough ground and waist-high grass littered with twisted trees – to go that way would be to tie myself in knots for him.

Then I heard her again, Angelic or whatever, whoever she was; the final voice in my head.

'Water, ma Cherie; he fear her drowned face.'

I stumbled across the rough wet ground and without a second's thought, dived into the water. Its black depths engulfed me, brackish and thick. The fear of weeds and hidden rocks gripped me but I forced them from my mind and pushed forward. It felt like I was under for an hour, a day, a lifetime – but when I erupted through the surface, I saw I was barely a few feet from the bank.

I thought, or imagined I saw him as I pushed myself under the cold, viscous depths, almost welcoming compared to the thought of Red on the bank, armed.

As I struck out, my knuckles grazed wood. I had reached the boathouse. I could not bear to open my eyes, so groped blindly until I'd caught hold of it, pulling myself forward. For a moment, before my lungs began to burn, before the desperate need to breathe forced me up, there was a voice in the darkness. I felt a desire, deeper than any I'd felt before. Something wanted me to stay, something yearned to be free of all of this madness and obsession. Something in me cried out for rest, freedom, an end to all of it. I hung in the darkness, caught between two worlds as if I were nothing but a whisper.

'If she ain't dead, ma Cherie, you still ain't found her. Ain't no one else gonna bring her home.'

I broke the surface. Coughing up dirty water, I clung to the side of the boathouse against the drag of the river.

The roar of Red's truck starting up was like a monster in the dark. I flinched when I heard it, hot panic flashing over me despite the chill of the water. The headlamps blazed across, throwing the shadow of the boathouse across the river's oily surface. Crouching as low as I could, I saw the truck looming up on the bank, larger than the house, larger than the whole world behind it. As its eyes burned, the driver's side door swung open. Red got out, scanning the water. He slammed the door and I dived again.

I felt my way around the edge of the boathouse, the sound of the river hissing and sighing in my ears. When I surfaced, I was inside, hidden in the shadow that the truck's headlamps carved out for me. I could see the remains of the wooden walkway, offering another oasis of shade, which I reached seconds before I heard him above me again.

'Margarita?' he called out. 'I know you're in here, I seen you.'

I dragged myself from post to post, my feet unable to find anything but water. He fired into the wall of the boathouse, and the sound sliced through the space. Water sprayed up to meet the fall of splintered timber. In the echo and roar of the noise, I moved through the to the side of the walkway that had no barrier.

'I don't aim to shoot you, but if you get shot darlin', that's down to you!'

I took hold of the underside of the walkway as he cocked the weapon to fire it again. Summoning every last ounce of strength, I forced myself up through the water and grabbed his injured leg. With a howl of protest, he crashed into the river.

The water seemed to part as he hit it; his body severed the blackness, then it swallowed him whole. He struggled up again, his face twisted in fear, mouth open and terrified. I hung in the blackness as he went under.

I heard music, violins calling as if driven by bellows working a fire, as if the music were cranked out by the turning of a handle. Red's hands, linked with steel, surfaced; his fingers touching the beam of light from his truck.

'Drove she ducklings, to da water, every morning just at nine. Hit her foot 'gainst a splinter, fell into da foaming brine.'

Caught in the water, I saw him, a lifetime before I was born. I saw white silk, billowing up over his mother's face as his hand reached out to touch her, still with the hope in his fingers he was not too late.

'Ruby lips above the water, blowing bubbles soft an' fine. Alas for me! I were no swimmer, so I lost my Clementine.'

I heard his howl from beneath the years, his child's voice as he saw her face under the silk, her skin made luminescent, lips bruised violet, eyes closed as if she only slept.

'Ya must live with yourself, whichever path ya choose, ma Cherie.'

I pushed off from the post and struck out toward him. I caught him as he tumbled toward the riverbed, and brought his head up. He spat water, gasping, heaving against me, his body limp and shivering. I got my arm round his neck, he thrashed for a moment, nearly dragged us both under, then he surrendered.

I made the underside of the walkway, and wrapped my arm round a post. He breathed, fought to fill his lungs again, the sound sobbing and gasping through the boathouse.

'What you doin'?' he asked when he could.

'Savin' your sorry ass,' I said. He laughed.

'Why?'

'To save mine.'

CHAPTER 25

THE EARLY MORNING was cool, and for a moment, the sky was beautiful. Even the swamp seemed calm; the sing and sigh of wind and water a lullaby.

Red's blood had seeped through his pants, the stain visible in the fabric even though they were now soaked in river water and mud.

'You better drop 'em,' I said as I approached, carrying the second bottle I'd found in the cupboard over the stove. He looked up at me and a smile played over his lips. I dumped his case on the floor beside him. 'Don't push it,' I said. 'I saved you, but we ain't friends or nothing.'

'Sure thing, darlin.' He stood up, leant against his truck and unbuckled his pants, his hands still manacled together. He sat down, and I held the bottle out to him.

'You can do the rest yourself.'

'Might need a hand with the bandage,' he said.

'Call me when you're ready.'

I walked to the other side of the truck, and listened as he tried to hold in his grunt of pain as he poured vodka over his wound. I'd helped myself to his suit, the expensively made black one, and to one of his evening shirts, though I'd still drawn the line at his underwear. The pants were loose, but I'd synched them tight at my waist using his necktie as a belt.

'That looks good on you,' he said as I came back round. He'd ripped the sleeve off one of his shirts and was clumsily binding his leg with it. I knelt down and took it from him.

'Thanks.' He sat back, gripping the seat with his hands as I wrapped, tying the shirt tight on itself. 'You know, that was Armani,' he said, wincing as I tightened.

'Yeah,' I said, 'I know.'

I helped him into the passenger seat of his truck, his arm about my shoulders.

'You gonna be okay drivin', darlin', what with your feet 'n' all?'

'Sure. But you can wait for your brother, if you like?'

'I don't really have one,' he said.

'No shit?' I raised my eyebrow at him.

He smiled. 'You ever found the keys for these things?'

'Nope. Guess they washed away in the river.' I shut the door for him.

I looked back at the house as I stood with one foot on the well of the truck, my hand on its door. It regarded me with the air of one watching an unwanted visitor, leaving at last.

'You gonna be okay?' Red said as I got in.

'Sure, if I use the side of my feet, then it don't hurt so much. I took a pair of your socks.'

'No,' he said. 'I meant are you gonna be … okay?' He shrugged.

'Sure.' I managed a smile. 'Unlike Paris.'

'Oh, he'll be okay, that one,' Red muttered out of the window. 'Always said as you were too fine for him.'

'Maybe,' I said and turned the key in the ignition. 'But that's okay, 'cause I'm too smart for the both of you's.' The truck spluttered into life at once, like it had something to prove.

'Don't think I'd have done what you did,' Red said. 'Not if I were you.'

'I don't think so either,' I said, though I wasn't sure if he meant my saving him, or trapping him with the intent to kill in the first place. 'But that's 'cause you ain't me, Red. You ain't a bit like me.'

'That I ain't,' he said and slumped back against his seat. 'But… I really didn't kill her.'

'I believe you,' I said, adjusting the rear-view mirror. He rolled his head sideways against the headrest to look at me, closed his eyes, then turned his head away.

'I came upon Lisa in the garden, carryin' a valise. She screamed at me, said she never wanted to see me again. Something had emboldened her spirit. If he gave her nothin' else, I guess Paris gave her that. I've no idea if he took her life in return, though.'

'When you saw her, did she say where she was going?' I asked, watching the boathouse in the mirror, a shimmering mirage.

'Nope. I guess I realized what a fool she'd made of me … what a fool I'd made of myself. I let her go.' He looked at me again, shading his eyes from the sun. 'I am truly sorry for my behaviour toward her, but what you sai … what she told you, I never …' He didn't finish.

I pressed the gas, and the truck juddered down the dirt track. I pulled onto the grey road, that one that runs like a scratch on the surface of a marble table.

'You don't happen to recall where you hid my Daddy's money, do you?'

'Nope.'

I dropped Red off a few yards outside the gas station.

'Guess you're keepin' the truck?' he asked as he opened his door and slid out.

'You know everyone round here, you'll be all right for a ride.'

'Guess you're right.' He raised both hands so he could run one through his hair. 'Well darlin', I can't exactly say as it's been fun, but it's been real.'

'Goodbye Red,' I said and I was about to pull away when he put his hand on the hood.

'Like I said ...' He paused, his face fractured through the spider web bloom of the glass. He looked smaller in the daylight, older. 'I'm gonna forgive you for hurtin' me an' takin' my money, but darlin', if I ever catch sight of you again, I might just remember as how you called me a murderer an' stuck me with a broken bottle. Reckon you still owe me an apology for that one.'

'Yeah? That's funny, 'cause I thought you'd be madder that I had these all along.' I held up the handcuffs' keys before I pressed the gas pedal and jerked away from him, throwing him off balance. He stood in the road and laughed, wiping his mouth with the back of his hand as I swung the truck round and faced back into the reserve. I registered the confusion on his face as I passed him, saw in the rear-view that he straightened up and shaded his eyes, watching me until he was swallowed by the curve of the road.

It was an hour's drive until I reached the wreck of the sports car. Just as Red said, it was circled with a meagre string of incident tape, its front end and driver's side door crumpled round a large boulder, looking as if someone had taken a can opener to its roof. I pulled up behind and got out.

I uncapped the water bottle I'd brought with me and drank, surveying the landscape. Large birds clustered in a group of trees a little way off from the car, their white umbrella wings open and serpentine necks bent back as they watched me with boot-button eyes. Under their scrutiny, I tried the trunk of the sports car and it opened. My case was still inside on top of Paris's, though it was lodged fast and would not come free. I dragged the zip open and gutted it, piling out clothes, documents, tools of the trade, my wash-bag and a pair of shoes I could just about stand to put on. I dumped it all in the truck and walked round to the passenger side. Paris's coffee cup was crumpled on the floor, broken glass and debris scattered on the seat. I leant in, picked over the mess of the driver's side and something caught my eye. His phone was poking out from under the seat, sticky with blood. I slipped it into my pants' pocket.

I looked at the expanse of grassland rising away from the car, then I started walking, dressed for dinner and with Red's shotgun slung carelessly over my shoulder. My eyes blurred, and I went toward a horizon fractured by tears, following the ghost of the path I'd carved for myself a day or so before. The grasses hissed and sighed at my waist, and I spread out my fingers to touch them as I went. I looked back at the car and the echo of a gunshot rolled and cracked though my mind. I could see him, Paris, one long arm extended through the window as he fought to get free of the car and failed; as he yelled and demanded I come back for him, as he reached for the gun by his side and waved it, as it fired.

The rocks were invisible beneath the grass, a small, grey outcrop under the green. I bent down and touched them, saw the indentation to one side where I must have lain, for however long the crack to my head had put me out. I'd been shot, I'd gone down, and hit my head on them, and had no memory of waking up again. The bag I was looking for was tucked out of sight behind the rocks, I'd even placed a few stones on top of it, just to be sure. The ratty blond wig in its pigtails was a few feet away, where it must have fallen from my head. It looked like beauty parlour roadkill.

I stood up and shaded my eyes. The lush green land curved away from me, trees marking the line of the brackish river that eventually wound its way down to the shack. I was on the crest of a small ridge; it would only have taken a few steps to be over its peak and I'd have been invisible from the road, swallowed by the marsh as it had tipped and rolled me onward, down toward the water. I took a breath and hurled the shotgun, sending it spinning through space, turning away before it hit the ground. I thought of it lying in the grass, waiting to be discovered like some hillbilly Easter egg. Well, good luck to whoever found it.

I changed my clothes at the roadside and used a scarf I had in my bag to cover my bruised forehead. I looked more like a chemotherapy victim than anything and I figured the implication might keep questions at bay for a while. I thrashed about in the grass verge around the boulder, and my foot struck the pistol Paris must have dropped after he'd shot me, accidentally or otherwise. The pistol was a lot more my style than a shotgun, so I picked it up. Well, it was better than leaving it lying around, messing up the place.

When I passed the gas station again, no one was about: no police cars, no renegade redneck mobs. I thought of the handcuffed Red, and what story he might have come up with for the attendant, and honestly wished I could have been a fly on the wall for that one.

I drove back into town as if I were watching the world on a TV screen. I'd found my dark glasses and was glad, not because they saved my eyes from the sun, but for the barrier they formed between the world and me. There was a small family-run bed and breakfast I'd noted a few days back, and eventually I found my way there, stopping off beforehand to buy some things, a new case to put them in, and a car to put that in.

There's nothing like a cash sale to cut through the questions. The car was for sale outside a private house, a handwritten sign posted in the rear window. It was silver, inconspicuous; middle of the range, middle of the road, forgettable.

I wasn't. Neither was my story of escaping from an ex-husband, to explain the bump on my head. The cops had already seen to him, but I was getting out of town, and I didn't want no one but them to know about it. His mother was just as bad, and as he'd slept with my best friend, there wasn't anything here for me no more. The man selling the car nodded sagely, embarrassed by the flood of information, but sympathetic. I'd left Red's truck parked outside a run-down house three blocks away, with the keys in the ignition, sure that fate and the occupants would take care of it for me. The man selling the car wished me luck and hoped my ex got all that was coming to him. So did I.

The landlady of the boarding house was like her establishment: warm, friendly and over decorated. She took in my natty headscarf and shades, drew her conclusions and kept them to herself. I asked if she could bring me something to eat, said I was jet-lagged and asked not to be disturbed.

I did not allow myself to think until after she'd knocked on the door and left me a plate of sandwiches and a glass of milk, with a home-baked cookie on the side. I ate, stripped off my clothes and stood under the shower with the water hammering on my face. Then, I thought.

I thought about everything I'd done, everything I'd believed, everything I'd not done but had come so close to doing. I thought of Lisa; Lisa I'd loved, Lisa I'd lost and Lisa who Red had not killed. The world I'd created for myself, the world I'd lived and breathed and worn for months, cracked and broke and fell away from me, and I was left small and naked and curled on the floor of the shower as the water washed my tears away. Then I slept, and dreamed of nothing but the crack and sigh of the swamp.

CHAPTER 26

AN INNER CALLING prodded me awake hours later, stiff and hungry. I was ashamed to see just how dirty I'd still managed to make the nice, crisp sheets on my bed, as if even after all my scrubbing, something of the previous night had sweated out of me. I showered again, inspected my wounds – the one on my forehead now a delicious shade of purple – and did what I could with the clothes I had, to look like a nicer girl than I was.

I went down the stairs, thinking about breakfast though it was nearer to supper. I walked into the guest lounge, and was greeted by a chorus of glass-eyed stares. The place was peppered with dolls the way a freeway is peppered with roadkill: dolls in bonnets, dolls with curls, dolls dressed as Native American squaws and, perhaps most incongruously of all, a traditional cherubic Victorian child wearing a bunny-girl leotard and ears. They looked at me and I looked at them, and I got the distinct impression I'd interrupted something I shouldn't have.

Tucked away to one side of the room was a white desk, its cabriole legs painted with pink roses, and on it the familiar bulk of a computer. A lace tea cloth had been draped over the monitor, as if to remind it of its place; and above it, on the wall, was an embroidery of an austere Virgin Mary, reminding me of mine. There were a lot of moths preserved under glass, dusty and silent, as if each were trapped against their own personal windows, too tired even to flutter. I looked at the computer, and my fingers itched to get back online.

'Alright,' I told the assemble, 'I won't tell on you, if you don't tell on me,' and went to find the landlady.

She found me, coming out from backstage as I re-entered the reception area, and greeted me with a wider smile than I'd seen in a long time.

'Anything I can do for you, darlin'?'

Resisting the urge to ask for a hug, I asked if I might use the computer to check my emails.

'You sure can,' she said. 'But y'all sure it can't wait till morning? You look real done in.'

'That's okay, I slept most of the day. I feel better than I look,' though that wasn't saying much. I'd tried brushing my hair over my bruise, but I noticed her eyes flick up to it just the same. She frowned.

'You sure you shouldn't pass by the ER, darlin'? That looks more than what witch hazel can see to?'

'Already been,' I said, feeling it was the most heinous lie I'd ever told, 'and I've never been one for hospitals.'

'Alright, I done my best.' Her face settled into the resigned smile of a woman with teenage children. 'Can I at least get you something from the kitchen?'

'Coffee would be great, and some more sandwiches, thank you.'

'I'll put some angel food cake on the side,' she said. 'You look fit to faint, if you don't mind me sayin'.' I watched her pad off, and decided I didn't mind at all.

The dolls made no comment on my return, which I took as an

encouraging sign. As the computer groaned into life, I flipped back its lace shroud, and waited for the screen to go blue.

I logged on to Facebook as myself first, and updated my status with pictures of Mexico I'd stored in preparation. It seemed pointless, as everything I'd planned had, quite literally, gone south; but as I'd no idea what else to do until I found Paris in the morning, I thought I might as well stick to the plan. I spent an hour uploading fake diary entries and sending messages to my few remaining real friends to bolster my alibi, telling them all that 'it sure is hot in Wahacca this time of year.'

'You been on vacation?' the landlady asked when she brought my food, complete with angel food cake as promised. 'It just takes my breath away how people can keep in touch these days, it scarce feels as if they've gone sometimes.'

Frances had left messages about borrowing money again, along with a heavy handed reminder about Mom's birthday, both of which I ignored. When I was done, I signed out, drank my coffee and decided to log on as Margarita. Her profile jumped with notifications: a tumble of messages in her inbox and three friend requests from strange men. After I ignored most, I saw a message from Mary Contrary, the girl I'd met through the survivor websites. I smiled to myself, took a last swig of coffee, and opened it. Come to think of it, it was quite nice to feel someone cared enough to see how Margarita was doing, seeing as she'd been offline for a while.

And yes, Mary was asking how I, Margarita, was, and why she hadn't heard from me, and apologizing for not being in touch herself for weeks. She told me she was feeling much better; she was going to come into some money soon and start a whole new life. She said she wanted to say goodbye. I turned away to bite my sandwich, then read the last line of her message.

'I was wondering, after what we talked about, did you ever catch up with that bastard Red, like you said you wanted to?'

I paused, mouth full of turkey on rye. I put down the rest of the sandwich and began to scroll through her messages, my finger jabbing at the mouse. I flicked back and back, scanning the screen until I reached the first time I'd mentioned to her that I had a sister.

Red.

I hadn't used that name once, not ever, not in any message on Facebook or email. I loaded up the survivors' website and read though all the messages to the girl who'd revealed herself to be Mary Contrary from Facebook: nothing. I'd called him every name under the sun, but I'd never called him Red, not to anyone else. Hell, I'd never even called him Rooster.

Them that knows me, calls me Red.

I got up from the computer and went to the window. Night had fallen and the little garden outside was singing with insects, the air rich and verdant. Was it possible? I looked back at the dolls, all of them staring at me, their faces arch, impassive, as if they already knew. No, it wasn't possible, it couldn't be.

I sat down and read her messages again. I found a notepad and pencil and, relishing the triumph of analogue technology, I charted the times she'd asked what I was going to 'do' about my sister's husband, when she'd told me how 'they' never got caught, how 'they' deserved everything that was coming to them, how I had to 'do' something. Not once had I called him Red or Rooster. Neither had I called him Red when she'd asked about the guy my sister had slept with, and suggested that if I found him, he might be able to help. Or when she'd congratulated me on being so strong, on taking out the truck driver, on all the training I was doing. Not even when she'd told me I was amazing, that I could do what all of them couldn't, get revenge on one of the bastards.

'It's you, isn't it?' I said to the screen. She'd been alive all along, just like Red said. Lisa had been alive and she'd been talking to me, goading me, pushing me. I was wrong, she had contacted me after all. I looked at the message, it was sent seven hours ago, when I'd already left Red at the gas station. She'd slipped up, she'd been expecting to hear something by now but she hadn't, and she wanted to know, she was desperate to know. Because it was personal.

I put down my pencil, the words of her message throbbing behind my eyes. For a while I was too numb to feel anything, to take on board what she'd done to me, my big sister, my Lisa. I was aware of the hum from the monitor, the warm thrum of the garden and the cold, merciless twist of loathing inside me. The dolls said nothing, but I was sure they were all thinking it.

Of course she'd had to message me, to ask me, because for the first time in months, she didn't have someone telling her what I was doing. Because Paris wasn't with me any more. I'd been so busy convincing him we were in love that I'd ended up believing my own lie. No, worse than that: I'd believed his.

The only thing he hadn't known was what I'd intended to do with Red after the con, and the shack and all of that. So what else could he do, but go along for the ride until it became obvious. And then? Make sure there wasn't anyone else left to stop me, including himself. Sure, he'd gone a bit overboard on that – he'd probably meant to pull over and throw me out, oh, and keep the money as back-up – but he'd managed spectacularly to do what he'd intended: give me no way to back out. Fuck me, but you almost had to admire them. The both of them.

'Bitch!' Margarita exploded, 'Fucking bitch! An' that two-faced son of – that – that fuckin' bitch!'

I turned out the lights in the lounge and sat in the dark for a while.

'So,' Margarita said to me, when she was calmer. 'What ya gonna do now?' Her voice faded to a chuckle within me.

CHAPTER 27

AFTER TRAVELLING SOUTH-WEST along the freeway for some time, alone but for Margarita and Mr Pooter, my sister's stuffed toy rabbit, I became almost hypnotized by the repetitive spill of the world scrolling past. The landscape was uniformly flat to the point of modesty, as if the expanse of sky above had quite robbed it of the will to achieve anything more than hot and green. I liked it. It stopped me thinking; it stopped me asking myself questions; it stopped me from wanting to run. I felt as if the wheels of my new silver car were locked into train tracks, taking me where I had to go without my having a say in the matter.

The freeway eventually rose up on stilts at junction 311. My course took me through a dizzying spiral and onto a slip road, to be delivered into the parking lot of 'Stop Three Eleven', taking inspiration for its name from the junction. It was a truck stop built around a casino, or casino built around a truck stop; either way with all the architectural style and panache of a convenience store. A white cube with a red tiled hat, wet dark windows and the peak of a veranda shading its door. It offered an all-day buffet of mac n' cheese, fried chicken and three bean salad, where you could drink and drink for hours and yet never truly get drunk. The champagne didn't taste like cherry cola, it tasted like Gatorade and desperation. It was everything I could have wished for. I checked the exits, quartered the ground and got back into my car. I gave 'Three Eleven' a final glance in my rear-view and headed for the junction and the way back to the city.

Once there, I sat in my car outside a beauty salon in town, with treatments listed in French on a board outside. It was the kind of place more used to a style and set than nail extensions; windows shrouded in lace curtains as if hiding something from polite company.

A quick internet search had provided me with the direct numbers for the wards in the county hospital and common sense narrowed it down to three. The first drew a blank, so I rang the second. As I listened to the rings before my phone was answered, I pulled the cardigan I'd bought tight across my chest, and folded my arm under my breasts, as if I were supporting a bust ten times the volume of my own. I was sucking on two marshmallows and had the car radio tuned to the local station, turned up just a little too loud.

The woman who answered when I was put through to the ward, sounded as if she were finishing a long shift and her voice was already half out the door. I went into my rant as if she'd known me from grade school, as if there was nothing but a garden fence between us.

'I'm phoning about my boy, he been with y'all for a day or so now, he not bothered to ring home, mind. He's the name of French, Peter French?'

'Yes ma'am, we got him here, but it's really a might early ...?'

'Oh, he is, is he? Early or not darlin', I should like to tan his hide for him, so help me God!' Well, you know what boys are like, I said. If I'd told him once, I'd told him a thousand times, driving those damn fool cars like he was the only thing on the road. I'd pass by and see him, only I had diabetes and my foot was nearly took off last year, so I was on sticks, but my neighbour, the one with the ride-on and the dog that barks, well, he said he'd take me, only he wasn't gonna be free until later and I wanted to know if it were worth my while coming. 'I mean, if he's gonna be let out today anyhow's, I can just save myself the bother, now can't I?' Well, she understood. She had two boys herself and was worried as hell about the eldest, getting mixed up in gangs and what-not; you hear such terrible things. She wasn't really sure if Paris was being discharged yet, but sure, she'd check her notes.

While I waited for her to return, I refreshed my marshmallows, slurping a drop of pink goo as it escaped my mouth a second before she picked up again.

'Well, you didn't hear it from me, but he's gonna be signed out some time after four.' Well, I was mad as hell with him, stupid boy, but he was okay, wasn't he? He was. It was nasty but superficial, she told. Yeah, I thought, that figures.

Peter French, the name Paris always said he used when he had to sign anything official, had been in for twenty-four hours, sleeping for the most part. He'd gotten a wound in his side where the steering column of the car had pinned him to the seat, but it hadn't hit anything vital, flesh wound, that sort of thing – well, thanks for that, she was an angel, really she was.

I'd prepared to ask if I could speak with him after all, but she was way ahead of me.

'I shouldn't really, seein' as how it's before visiting times n'all ...' I heard the noise as she leant forward. 'Yes ma'am, seems as if he's awake.' She dropped her voice, I could almost picture her wink. 'You want me to pass him the phone?' She chuckled.

'Oh bless you,' I said. 'But don't you go sayin' who it is, then he ain't got time to hide under the blankets like when he were five.'

I unbuttoned the cardigan, flipped down the sunshield and watched myself in the mirror as I swallowed the marshmallows.

'Paris?' I said out loud, hand over the phone, then coughed. 'Paris?' No, still not quite there. I had a bottle of water in the glovebox; I snatched it up, swigged a mouthful and spat through the open window. 'Paris … it's me.'

I listened to the woman's progress as she clipped her way through the institutional soundscape, trying to compose myself until I heard her muffled voice telling him he had a call.

'Hey?' Paris said, after I'd counted to six, imagining him watching until the nurse was out of earshot.

'Paris, it's me … Lisa.'

'What?' Was he expecting me, was he expecting her? 'Lisa … Y'heard something, she reply?'

'I think so. I'm worried.' I put my hand to my mouth, cowering my shoulders, thinking myself back to under the bed.

'Baby?' he said. 'Baby, you there? What happen, you gotten a reply?' I closed my eyes. What would he expect Lisa to say? He'd want something to have happened, he'd want her to have something to tell him, because why else would she risk calling him?

'I got a message, but it just said be lucky. Do you think she's okay? Does that mean …?'

'That all it said, you sure, what …'

'Paris, I'm scared,' I said to distract him, as I'd no idea what message he'd been hoping for, and what he might make of 'be lucky'.

'Why, what's up?'

'Nuttin' …' Sweat beaded my forehead as I spoke, as I slipped my free hand under my knee and pressed it against the seat. 'I think I gotta go from here.'

'Go, why?' he said. 'You still at the hotel?'

So she was here; she was nearby.

'I think someone saw me,' I said, because that must be the worst thing either of them could think of, and something that was guaranteed to make Lisa run.

'What ya' mean, who?'

'Some old friend of Red's, he was here.'

'At the hotel?'

'Yes, at the hotel, I think he recognized me ... I gotta go!'

'Hold on.' I heard a noise, a scuffle, perhaps as he sat up, as he covered the phone with his hand to mask his words. 'You gotta wait for me, you know that ...'

'I'm scared, you gotta come, please!'

'Baby ... baby,' he said, his voice controlled and deliberately slow. 'You gotta hold it together, you gotta wait ...'

'Please!' I gasped.

'Baby, I can't leave until they say so, or it's gonna make me look guilty, you know that. Hell,' I heard the gust of breath as it caught in the phone, 'I weren't fixing on gettin' bust up like this, sure, but all you gotta do is hang tight, okay?' My heart was thudding so loud in my ears I was sure he'd hear it. I wanted to scream at him, spit at him, hurl the phone against the windshield, but somehow I managed to bring my breathing under control as I stared at the world outside the window. My silence worked. When he spoke again I could hear the concern in his voice. 'Baby? You still there? Don't you go freakin' out on me here. You know what we gotta do, and you need me, Baby, I lo—'

'Intersection three one one,' I said, unable to bear those words, cutting across him as if that might stuff them back down his throat.

'What?'

'There's a casino, a truck stop. I'm gonna go there, wait for you. You gotta come there, please, I need you!'

'How am I gonna ...'

'Oh, shit,' I said, pulling back from the phone. 'It's him again, he mustn't see me.'

'Lisa?' Paris's voice crackled from the cell.

'The place is called Stop Three Eleven, you got it? I'll be there, I'll wait for you I promise.' In a moment of inspiration I added, 'I got some money.'

'Lisa, you better …' But I hung up.

Did it matter if he came? No, but I knew he would; Lisa had money after all. I gripped the steering wheel and I forced myself to breathe out, the air juddering as it came. I glanced up and down the street and watched the people moving past the window; I saw them talking, walking, bodies rolling in and out of the world prescribed by the windshield's frame. I was still. For the first time in what seemed like forever, I felt I was alone, that there was no one here but me.

'Sorry to spoil the mood, doll,' Margarita said.

I flipped open the glovebox and took out the phone I'd retrieved from the wreck of the car. It was Monday, so I presumed that the state might finally find the time to haul it out of the reserve. Maybe not, seeing as they were unaware of any crime linked to it yet, other than reckless endangerment of a rock. And Paris had been sober when we'd crashed. The phone's battery was dead, but the nice man in the shop had found me a car charger that fitted it, so I plugged it in and pulled away.

A guilty man might give the 'other woman' a code name, probably a man's name as, he would reason, no woman's suspicions would be raised by a message from Bob or Geoff. That goes to show just how naive men can be when it comes to dealing with a wife with an unquiet mind; really, how less incriminating is a text from Geoff, when Geoff calls you honey, babe or sugar and indeed, texts you five times a day to ask how you're feeling? A smarter man would never have given the number a name at all, nor stored it on his phone. He'd also convince himself that he'd delete every text message after reading, but it would take a cold, hard genius not to get sloppy and keep the odd salacious message, or always remember about the call log. Even if he did all of that most of the time, there was going to be an occasion when he forgot, especially when he'd just crashed his car and was dialling out in panic.

There it was, that unidentified number, repeated just enough times to make it an easy guess. I couldn't access his voicemail and thought against trying, because if I heard her voice, I'd weaken. So I sent her a text. I looked at the words on the screen for a good while before I hit send.

'Got new phone, don't call me, not safe to talk.' That explained that, but what then? In the end I decided that all I could do was live my bluff to the fullest. 'M called from airport, left message.' I figured I'd let her ask.

Lisa and I had rarely talked on the phone. When she'd been with Red, it was always too risky, and even before then – after she'd committed the ultimate sin of her last and greatest escape – our parents had subtly forbidden me any contact with her. How much of what we do is habit we never question, until a stranger shows us our ugly?

Once she'd gone to Vegas, we'd texted, then she'd had to give up her phone, and it had always been emails after that, almost as if she were in league with our parents against herself, subconsciously submissive; still thinking there might be a way back if only she could finally behave as they wanted. Maybe there was a more sinister reason for that continuing, more than the fear she'd be discovered by Red or our parents; perhaps never speaking on the phone was all part of her plan. Just how far back had all this started? It was madness to go down that path; perhaps it was simply that if she'd heard my voice, she'd have weakened, just like me.

Then the phoned buzzed.

'Is he dead, is she okay?' Well, I was on the list, even if I was second.

'Yes, M fine, are you okay?' Another leap in the dark. 'Gotta change of plan – meet me at the casino at 311 intersection.' Then just to make sure, 'Not safe to talk – explain later. Got the money.' As soon as I sent it, I wished I hadn't added the last line, and I was right, her reply was almost instant.

'What money, what's going on why can't u call?' I waited. It would be too suspicious to write back and try and explain, silence was better. If there was a problem, if Paris was being interviewed by the police or hiding from Red and his Daddy, then he was less likely to be able to reply. If he was trying to run out on her with the money, then he'd reply as soon as he could to put her mind at rest, or so I thought. I think it worked, because there was a second message from her before I replied.

'Paris?' One word, one panic – good.

'Police,' I replied, wishing there was a way to give the word with Paris's customary pronunciation. '311 casino meet me there, 4, b-okay.' I wanted her to reply quickly, one word or two to say 'yes', to say 'okay', to say she would be there; or even to ask about the money again, but when the reply came it send a cold spike of anger and sorrow twisting into my belly.

'Do you love me?' Goddamn her. I threw the phone onto the seat next to me and pressed my hand over my eyes. No. Don't think, don't ask the question, move on. Count to ten, count to twenty-one, nothing's going to make it go away.

I picked up the phone again and illuminated the words. I wrote them, but when I sent them, I sent them from me, not Paris.

'Yes, I love you. Always.'

CHAPTER 28

WALKING INTO THE FOYER of the truck stop casino from the vindictive heat of the parking lot was an air-conditioned slap in the face. Beyond the foyer, the rest of the establishment tried to kiss and make up with its depressingly familiar aroma of spilled beer and grilled cheese, the ghost of tobacco and cheap carpet static. It was a gas-station-roses kind of sorry.

I sat at the bar. It was three thirty in the afternoon – just me and the hardened drinkers, all three of them. It was bright outside, dark inside, as though the dark needed someplace to hang until the sun went down. I pressed my phone to my ear, a notepad and pencil in front of me, and wrote. I had something I needed to write, and I wanted the rest of the world to think I was taking a long and tedious call from work. The woman behind the bar, all big tits and burgundy curls, even gave me one of those 'tell me about it, sister' faces as she brought me my iced tea. She was wasted on the joint, seemed too good for the place, the kind of good that made you wonder what the hell she was running from to have ended up there. Christ, she even started reading a book when she thought no one was looking, I mean an actual book, one without pictures.

After my phone calls to the hospital that morning, I'd gone into the beauty parlour and bought the wig I was wearing. It was a better quality than the one Paris had bought me: a glorious brazen red with a blond streak and heavy bangs. With a floral blouse and large, tinted glasses, when I looked in the mirror behind the rows of bottles, I was pretty well camouflaged. I could see all the lights on the fruit machines, flashing like they were sending out a message. If you focused on them for too long, you started to convince yourself you might understand it, if only you had a little more time and distance.

Lisa came in at about quarter to four. I knew her silhouette at the door without a second look, and forced myself not to react to the cold shivers that trickled under my skin. In the mirror I saw her gaze flick over and discount me as she walked through the bar. I waited. There were a few places to sit and talk, but none as inviting as the cluster of brown vinyl booths I'd turned my back on to sit at the bar. She disappeared to check out the rest of the place, before returning to the booths; she sat down where she could see the door.

I watched her in the mirror, how she placed her purse on the table, then her phone; how she rearranged them as she looked around her. She wasn't bad, shades, headscarf, trying to be anonymous, but she was giving it all away with her nervous, round shouldered stance and her fidgeting.

'Oh, she better be nervous,' Margarita muttered. The bar lady went over, taking her smile with her. Lisa waved her away, then changed her mind and ordered. I sprawled, leaning against the phone in my hand, being casual as anything, watching it all in the mirror. I tapped my pad with the pencil, and when Lisa was craning to see who it was when the door opened, I slipped from my stool and walked out of her line of sight. The booths were backed with an identical row of seats; I found the one behind hers and sat down, pressing my ear to the gap between my seat and the next.

I wasn't sure exactly when Paris came in, because to begin with they didn't speak, or they kept their voices too low for me to hear. I watched the seconds tick by, phone in hand, waiting.

'… Going on?' I heard Lisa say as her voice rose and Paris tried to hush her. Quiet. Then I heard her again. 'What money? You said you got money?'

'No, you said, baby?'

'You heard from her, what, she called you – was she okay?'

'She never called, what you sayin'?'

'You said she called, your text, you said she was at the airport?'

'I ain't seen her since she ran from the car.'

'But your text?'

'Shit, baby, what text?'

I walked as fast as I could to the exit without breaking into a run. Outside the sky was glass-hard, the light white and harsh. There were only a few cars parked near mine. Before them was the row of trucks to pass, high, wide backs turned on the world, heavy horses side by side in the starting gate. I turned right and ran to the head of the first truck, slipped round the front of it and counted along the row until I came to the penultimate. I ripped off the wig and shades, threw them under its wheel arch and ran down to its rear end.

I was just in time to see them come out of the door; Paris with his arm around Lisa, leaning to one side, both to cover her and because of his injuries. They were talking, more animated now they were outside. She broke away from his embrace, came to a halt and shouted at him.

I couldn't hear what she said, but he spread his hands out, patting the air as if to placate her as he glanced around. He tried to take her hand again but she jerked it from his grasp. Come on, I thought, come on.

'Closer, bitch,' Margarita hissed.

'For God's sake woman, we gotta go,' I heard Paris say as he got hold of her again. This time she went with him, plucking at her headscarf, feet working double time to keep up with his bow-legged stride. I drew my gun as they approached.

'Where your car at, you did …?' he asked, then a truck started up three away from mine and drowned out the rest of his words.

A second later I heard them '… the fuck was it, then?' Lisa was saying. 'How you know she's okay if you didn't see her, you said she was okay, you said …'

There were a lot of things I'd prepared to say, but when it came to it, I stepped from the shadow of the truck and said, 'Lisa.'

They both turned. I couldn't say how Paris reacted because I wasn't looking at him. Lisa's mouth dropped open; she staggered back as if I'd hit her. In a second she'd regained her balance, pulled away from Paris and came toward me. I backed off, and Paris snatched at her arm. 'Lisa! Wait, Lisa!'

'Oh my God,' Lisa said. She was crying, tears running down her face from behind her shades, expression stretched into fear, delight, panic.

'Baby,' Paris demanded, reluctant to enter the space between the vehicles. I took another step backwards.

'Come on, bitch!' Margarita urged, and I could feel her frustration boil inside me.

'It's alright,' Lisa said to Paris and she followed me, her smile breaking through her shock.

'Leave her,' I said and I aimed my gun at Paris. They both started and Paris darted forward as if to put his arm round her.

'What you doing?' Lisa said.

'What the hell you doing?' I asked her. 'What, so you ain't dead then?' Paris moved to catch my eye, hand out, fingers fanned towards me as he stepped between us.

'Shoog, you gotta relax here ... there's reason for all of this, but right now, right now you just gotta take it easy.'

'Don't you fuckin' speak to me.' I jabbed the gun at him but he didn't move. 'How could you ... how dare you even speak to me. I don't wanna speak to you, I want Lisa.'

She moved out from behind him. He tried to stop her but she brushed him off as he turned to me. 'I know you hate me.'

'Do I?'

She touched her hand to her mouth. 'There weren't no other way, you know ... you know what he did ...'

'You had to believe,' Paris said. 'I always told you that, an' you know it's true,' as if he were addressing an errant pupil. 'Sure, you' mad, but we can sort this. Come with us and we'll ...'

'Tell her you shot me, did you?' I flicked the gun at him again, and saw fear flash over his face. Lisa looked up at him.

'She were running away,' he said, 'I never meant it, was a' accident, I swear.'

'You said she was alright,' Lisa pulled away from him. 'You never said ...'

'He lied.' I backed away, drawing her to me. 'He's been lying to us both.'

'Please,' she said. 'Please, you don't understand, he ... he saved me,' and she came within reach.

She yelped as Margarita – or me – or both of us snatched a hank of her hair and dragged her face towards mine. Her glasses came off and clattered onto the floor, and I saw her eyes, so bright and blue and longed for.

'Don't!' but I forced the gun to her temple, just as I had to Red's in the shack. The space between the trucks closed down on me, on us, until all I could see was the black rod of the gun barrel and where it pressed against Lisa's skin, iron against ivory. We were half bent down together, folded one around the other, her going limp against me.

'Please,' I think she said, or 'no' or 'don't', but I couldn't hear her, not against the rushing of dark water in my ears, and Margarita's snarl.

'You lied to me. You used me.'

'I'm sorry, I'm sorry—'

'No,' and I yanked on her hair, and she yelped, and it felt so good to hear it, the fear in her. 'You don't get to say sorry, you' gonna know what you did, you' gonna understand—'

'Do it,' Margarita sneered, and her smile curled my lips.

'No,' I told her, but I so wanted to. Christ, I wanted to. The black rod of the gun burned against Lisa's skin, a line crossing her out. All the pain, the lies, it was her fault, all of this, her fault—

'No it's not—' I gasped. Through her tears and her pleading, Lisa frowned at me, trying to understand what the hell I was saying, knowing I wasn't talking to her.

'You going soft on me now, bitch? Look what the fuck she put you though, look what the—' my finger tightened on the trigger. Lisa sucked a great gulp of air into her lungs, and got hold of me, her hand squeezing my forearm. 'She's gotta know,' Margarita told me. 'She gotta know, doll, what she did. You know it.'

I'm not sure if it was Paris I heard first when he swore, when he jolted in surprise and took hold of Lisa to pull her away; or if it was the striking of a heavy foot on asphalt behind me.

'Now, ain't this sweet,' Red said.

I wrenched myself from Lisa and faced him, a rendered silhouette stood against the light. The tension in my arms burned to my fingers, and before I'd time to think, I reached behind and got hold of Lisa, and she let me, and she softened against me, and trusted me.

'No, oh, fuck, no—' she went to clutch at my hand, the hand that was holding the gun.

'You dead,' Paris yelled, his hand on Lisa's shoulder. 'You kill' him, I thought you killed him, girl?' He nearly went to put his hand on my shoulder too, big old Paris sheltering us both, keeping hold of his assets.

'Oh, she had a damn good try,' Red said. 'But boys like me don't go down easy.'

I grabbed Lisa's wrist behind my back, and pressed the gun into her hand.

'Take it,' I hissed, and I got between her and Red, shielding both from him. Red raised the shotgun he was carrying to his shoulder.

'Hate to crash the party here,' he said. 'But you weren't fixin' on leaving town without me, was you?'

'No, no …' Lisa sobbed, batting at my hand, not sure what I was trying to do. I turned for an instant, closed her fingers around the gun, then I raised my hands and faced Red.

'It's me you want,' I said.

'You reckon?' he raised an eyebrow. 'You so sure 'bout that?'

'I was the one, I killed you.' I stepped forward, ignoring the flaw in my reasoning.

'No!' Lisa grabbed for me but I shrugged her off.

'Make you feel good do it boy, hidin' behind a woman?' Red sneered.

'Hey, fuck you, I ain't scared of you,' Paris said, though he stayed behind me and Lisa, hiding behind the both of us.

'Let her go,' I said, watching the barrel of Red's gun follow me. 'You got me, you got me now, so you let them go.'

'Really?' Red lowered the gun.

'What you doin'?' Lisa sobbed behind me.

'It's alright,' I said, not looking round. 'Just you go an—' Red hit me with the butt of his gun, cracked it into my shoulder. I went down. Gravel bit into my arms and hands as I landed. Lisa screamed. I scrabbled in the dirt, groping to get my hands over my face, pressing them to my nose. I blinked up, face now oozing sticky redness, feeling it gushing over my lips. The slice of sky between the towering big rigs whirled and refracted above me; Red's form stark and black and cut out in rainbows. He pointed the shotgun down at me one-handed, the other slung nonchalantly in his jacket pocket.

'Don't think you gonna be enough, no more,' he said.

The shot cracked through the space between us. I twisted – but it wasn't me that was hit. Red spun away, impacted onto the flank of the truck and fell, the gun cartwheeling out of sight.

'Jesus Christ!' Paris bellowed. I heaved myself up, still on the ground and stared at Red's body. There was a gaping hole in the back of his jacket, mushy and blueberry dark.

'No,' Lisa sobbed, the gun she'd taken from me, the gun I'd given her and she'd fired, still in her hand, her white face melting into panic. As she began to scream, I grabbed at her legs, trying to embrace her, to hush her, but she kept on screaming.

'What the hell you done?' Paris demanded. 'Baby, what the hell you done?'

'Lisa, I never meant – Jesus fuck, Lisa!' I staggered to my feet.

Paris went to get hold of Lisa, then didn't, then gripped his hair with both hands. He was already backing away from us, checking his exits, up on his toes and ready to run. 'We gotta go, baby, we gotta go!'

'He was gonna kill her!' Lisa tried to say, but the words came out in a raw sob, 'gonna kill you an' her an'—'

'What the fuck you done?' I yelled in her face. 'How the fuck you think I'm gonna sort this?'

She tried to say she was sorry, tried to get hold of me, pleading and pleading. The gun fell from her grasp, then Paris tried to grab her.

'Come on,' he said, 'we gotta go, come on!'

'You want this? You fuckin' have her,' and I pushed Lisa toward him. She turned to him, and I saw him look at her. Then he looked at me with those eyes, those amazing dark blue eyes.

'Eyes are like birthdays, women always take more notice of them.'

Then he ripped Lisa's pocket book from her hand and began scrabbling through it.

'Paris—' Lisa seemed strung out between us, not knowing which of us to turn to. 'Paris?' I saw the flash of metal as he ripped car keys from her pocket book then slung it back at her. She made no move to catch it, and it hit the ground, landing with a dull, wet thud.

'This your mess,' he snarled.

Lisa grasped for him, but he slapped her hands back.

'Paris!' This time she got hold of him, dragging on his arm, one hand then the other, small fingers almost blue looking, an underwater creature trying to pull him back down with her. He pushed at her but she kept on clawing at him, saying his name over and over, 'Paris, Paris,' like the way it had buzzed about my head before I knew what it meant. 'Paris, I love you, I—' then he hit her.

'You think I love you? The pair of you crazy bitches go fuck you'self, you ain't worth this shit.'

I wondered if he might look at me again, but he didn't. He shrugged his shoulders as if brushing off a mosquito and reached the end of the trucks in three, loping strides. He slowed his pace just enough for it to count as a walk, until his nerve broke and he disappeared from sight across the parking lot at a run.

A sound hiccuped from Lisa, and she turned to me, mouth open. I knew she was trying to say my name.

'Oh, fuck it.' I grabbed her and pulled her towards me. With my arm around her shoulders, we stumbled away from Red. We made the end of the truck, then limped toward my silver car as I fought in my pocket for the keys.

Lisa was still shaking with sobs, scrubbing at her face with her hands. Her headscarf came loose and fluttered away across the parking lot. 'Oh fuck, oh fuck,' she was saying, 'Oh Jesus, you see him, you see him?' There was a screech of tyres and a car broke from the pack, heading for the exit. Its rear end swung side to side as Paris cornered too fast.

'You fucking bastard,' Lisa bellowed after him. 'You fucking two-faced bastard!' She pulled against my grasp as if she meant to start running after him, her face running with tears and spittle. 'You … I'm gonna—'

'Shut up!' I jerked her back round, made her look at me. 'Shut the fuck up. Right now everyone's looking at him, you want them to look at us?'

'But what we gonna do, we ain't even got a car, we ain't—' Lisa began, but I grabbed her wrist and started running, dragging her after me. 'Wait …' she fought me all the way to the silver car, 'I never meant to, oh fuck, I never—'

'Keep moving,' I yanked on her arm, and when I looked back, I saw people had come out of the casino, ants round the white sugar cube building, watching Paris cross the central reservation and head toward the freeway. He was at least making enough racket to draw their gaze for the moment. Lovers' tiff, I told myself, if any of them come over and ask, lovers' tiff, nothing more to see here.

And the bastard's stolen her car too, can you believe it? I clicked my car keys, opened its door and shoved Lisa inside.

'What … what's gonna happen, what we gonna do?' she asked, clinging to my arm as I tried to get her inside. She sat down, then at once tried to get up again. 'I'm so sorry,' she said, 'I never meant …' but the crying came again, too strong for her to finish. She was shaking, her face white and bruised black, both trying to fight me off and pull me closer. 'You gonna help me, you gotta, you …' So I hit her.

I punched her face, a good hit to the eye, one Ralph the personal trainer would have been really impressed with. It felt as good as hitting Red in the swamp, better even, because this time there wasn't a moment's doubt that she deserved it. She was almost too stunned to make a noise, just sucked back down a scream and clutched at her face with both hands, as if this was the first time she was really, truly scared. I wanted her to be scared, I wanted her to be more scared than when we were children. I reached down, grabbed the neck of her blouse and pulled her face up to mine.

'Shut the fuck up,' I said, and my voice was cold and hard and river-water black. 'Feel good, does it, now you got what you wanted?' She was shaking, pressing her lips together so as not to speak, hardly able to open her left eye where it was already swelling shut. 'That's what you wanted, right? Red dead, you bein' his wife an' all, his next of kin. How's it feel, Lisa, huh? Just how does it feel to kill someone, like for real, close up?'

She didn't answer. She was crying too hard, fighting for breath, crying like she'd never cried when we were children. I felt my grip loosen, my fingers numb with the effort of holding her. I let her drop back into the seat and stood up.

'I guess now you know, right?' I slammed the car door and clicked the central locking. 'Now I'm gonna clean up your mess.'

I made the shadow of the truck and, once I was out of Lisa's sight, leant my hand on it and drew breath, for what seemed like the first time in hours. The shock of it, of everything, crowded in on me, and the thought of what she had done, of what I'd done, made my legs weaken under me. I thought I was going to fall, sink down on my haunches and press my hands to my face, only Margarita mentally slapped me.

'Get up. We ain't done yet ... not unless you wanna go down for a crazy long time,' and she was right.

I skirted round the truck, glancing side to side. The people outside the casino were still there, watching Paris's vapour trail. In the alleyway between the trucks I headed toward Red's prostrate form. I slowed as I approached, and came to a stop beside him. I took a breath, knelt down and dipped my finger into the dark, sticky hole in the back of his jacket. Then, I licked it clean.

CHAPTER 29

THAT MORNING, I'd driven at dawn along the wide, wet, hot streets, waiting for their shoals of people. As I'd come through the empty, sidewalk-free suburbs, past low, lazy houses of clapboard and twine, I'd felt that the whole place was little more than a rainbow film of chicken grease, hair oil and heartbreak, glistening on the surface of a rock pool. What lay beneath was something other: alien and glorious.

I found Red's house, Carillon. It was far enough away from everywhere else to give the impression it was standing with its toes at the edge of that rock pool, hands extended yet not daring to dip a finger below the surface. All that might have swirled around it seemed to have left no mark; through war and rebellion, flood and famine it had remained aloof – a white death's head picked clean by time, with an expression of polite disdain. From where it sat you could just about see the dark fuzz of the city and, I imagined, when the river had finally broken free in the teeth of the hurricane, Carillon would have afforded a front row seat to all that had been done and undone by it.

I was not sure if I intended to climb the gates, presumably replacements for the ones Lisa had destroyed when she left, or ring the bell, or climb on the car and try and scale the wall, so I did none of these. I pulled up, got out and stood there.

I doubted Red would be out jogging, not with the mess I'd made of his leg, but habit fashions a man; and so I guessed he'd be up already, army life being what it was. Would he see me, as he stood at his bedroom window, the early morning sunlight catching on the windshield of my car? Or would he be on his veranda – because the place was sure to have one – with his morning coffee, the steam curling from the mug to join the damp air that promised heat? Probably not; it was most likely the two security cameras that slowly turned to look at me, that must have given away my arrival. No matter. Immodest thought though it was, I knew wherever he was, he would already have been thinking about me too. The wound on his leg would be enough to remind him, though the pain would until the scar was nothing more than a lopsided white smile, grinning up at him; years later it would still make him think of me, as I'd think of him. We'd cut deeper than flesh.

I'd tried to pretend Margarita was falling in love with Paris, but that was a lie. I'd thought I was thinking of nothing but Lisa, but that was wrong too. All the time I'd been thinking of Red. I couldn't call it love, but though I'd told myself I was doing everything to destroy him, all I'd done was pay him the greatest compliment of all, and given him my full attention. As I'd run through the dark evenings of my cold, northern-light-lit home town, I'd not been running from him, but to him.

The squawk box on the gatepost spluttered into life. 'What the hell you doing here?' it demanded. I put my hand on the gatepost and leaned into it.

'Breakfast,' I said. There was a long pause as the squawk box chewed things over. It considered turning me away, no doubt considered calling the cops, but in the end curiosity won out. The gates clicked and swung reluctantly open.

As I drove along the gravel drive, the house fluttered and rearranged itself; snapshot memories collaged into reality. Lisa had forgotten to mention the fountain at the front and the glorious colours in the borders that lined the drive; but the melancholy trees were just as she'd said, verdant widows bending their heads for the departed. And yes, there was a veranda. All in all, it felt as if I'd just driven up to a place I'd previously sketched in a dream diary.

I came to a stop at the foot of the steps and Red opened the door. I watched him limp down toward me, shirt hanging open, loose fitting cotton pants clinging to his legs, hinting at the bandages beneath. He came up and stooped to look in at my window.

'See you been shoppin' already,' he said, his gaze darting over the car. His lip was puffed up on one side, a stunning array of bruises complimenting it across his cheekbone. It suited him; he wore them well, like another man might wear a custom-made suit.

'I bought supplies,' I said. 'My mother's a terrible cook, and my father was a paedophile, so you'll have to take your chances.' Red looked down at me, elbow on the roof of the car as a sly, lazy grin dragged on his swollen mouth. 'Come on,' I said, 'I figure I owe you breakfast.'

'Breakfast?' He raised an eyebrow. 'You think that's what you owe me?'

'Sure, mind you ...' I shrugged. 'It was my food too last time, seeing as I'd stocked up the day before, but you cooked it, so fair's fair, I guess?'

He slapped the car and stood up, jamming his hands onto his hips and shaking his head. 'Girl,' he said, 'you sure is something of a charmer. You think that's enough to stop me shootin' you in the back of your head, an' dumpin' you out back?'

'No ... but you don't have a gun on you. That might,' I said.

Inside, the place was still as a saucer of milk. Red closed the door behind us and led the way, glancing back at me over his shoulder. I had a bag of groceries and Red, the gentleman he was, didn't offer to carry them for me. Our feet barely made a sound on the tiled floor of the hallway – his bare and mine in soft, slip-on shoes.

'Your Daddy home?' I asked.

'Nope.' He opened a door which led into a kitchen, with a high vaulted ceiling, squat black range and wide, white walls hung about with copper cookware. Only the microwave oven looked as if it were well used. 'Daddy was not best pleased, seein' his only son limpin' home with them bracelets on and no money. He's taken himself off to the capital, fundraising or some such prior engagement ...' He waved his hand.

It was a well-appointed kitchen, its long wall open to a sun-drenched conservatory curling with vines. It was the sort of place that needed a large family, couple of dogs, people calling in and taking tea, children's bare feet running in from the garden, something to show you, something to share. Sisters, perhaps, on an adventure?

'D'you mind if I take off my shoes?' I put the bag on the counter.

'Feet still botherin' you?'

'A little.' Bound in gauze as they were, the stone floor felt good under them.

'What you here for?' he said. He pulled out a high stool from the counter behind me but did not sit on it.

'To ask for help. You got a mixing bowl?'

'Darlin', you didn't need to put a gun to my head if that's all you wanted. Cupboard on your right.'

I glanced down. 'This one?' He came over. I ducked down and opened the cupboard. 'You sure?'

'I'm sure, darlin'.' I straightened up with the bowl in one hand, the other, with its bruises and pink nails, resting on the counter's edge. He reached round me and put his hand over mine. I looked down, watched as his thumb caressed my knuckles, then his strong, brown fingers closed round my wrist. The skin on my arm came alive under his touch, prickled as his fingertips grazed the inside of my elbow. He smelled good, like all the men your mother warned you about, like trouble, and that time when you should have known better. I could feel the warmth of him on my back, the inch of air between us barely there.

'Just how you fixin' on apologizing?' he said, mouth close to my ear. And I thought about it, for a good, long, hard second. Then I bit my lip and turned to face him.

'Oh please, Red, seriously? What sort of lame-ass novels d'you read? You think I'm gonna sleep with you to get your help?' I pulled my arm back and stepped away from him. 'Good God, you still wanna fuck? After I stuck your leg an' all … that really did it for you?'

He held his hands out to his sides. 'Don't go givin' yourself airs. I'm a man, an' a soldier I'd pretty much fuck a hog in high-tops if there weren't nothin' better.'

'Nice image. Thanks for that.'

'Well, I'm sorry, but we ain't exactly the types used to sipping tea together; we don't got that sorta relationship. I can fuck you or I can hit you, you just make your mind up which it's to be.' He ran his fingers through his hair.

'I got something else,' I said.

'Yeah?' Red slumped back onto his stool. 'You got fifty grand in that bag, 'long with the eggs n' all?'

'Just you sit and listen.'

I made him pancakes, just like my mother never did. A cloud

of white flour smoked from the bag into the warm, wet morning; the crack of eggs, then ripe apricot yolks dropping into the bowl. I poured in buttermilk and a box of jewel-black blueberries.

I told him everything and he listened, made himself another cup of coffee, got one for me, sat back down again. The light showed me the echo of his bare feet on the tiles, a whisper of heat before they were gone. His face gave nothing away, but I was grateful for the stillness in his gaze, his eyes watching the mouse-hole.

'You got a pan?' I asked. He sipped his coffee.

'Over by there.' He nodded his head. 'So, you think as how I'll help, now you've told me your story?'

'You don't have to,' I said as I took down the pan. 'But the way I see it, neither of us gonna go to the police. Even though you ain't really dead, despite my best efforts.'

'Sorry 'bout that.' He grinned.

'And I still don't think you want it getting round how you and your Daddy got took by a hooker and her pimp – not with your Daddy's stance on morality and firm, Christian values.'

'You read his campaign shit?' Red asked. 'That sure is dedication to the cause.'

'Well, way I see it, we've both been fucked royally.' I poured out some batter, watched it hiss into a circle then looked up at him. 'I mean sure, you got me, so if you wanna get on with fuckin' or hitting me, I guess there ain't much I can do about it.'

'I ain't mad at you no more,' he said. He tapped his finger on the rim of his mug. 'What you just told me, you lied 'bout any of it?'

'Not as far as I know.' I flipped the pancake.

'Darlin',' he said and the light made his eyes jade green and dangerous. 'Don't you remember how it is, between frogs and scorpions?'

'How is it, Red?'

'Your Daddy never told you that one?' He smirked. 'Scorpion asks a frog to take him across the stream, seein' as he can't swim. Frog says no, you might go sting me, but the scorpion says, hell, if I do that, we's both gonna drown.' He picked up his mug, watching me over the rim. 'Frog says all right then, yes, so off they go, but halfway across, scorpion goes right ahead and stings him. As the frog feels the poison creepin' through his legs, he says – what you go and do that for, now we both gonna drown? Hell, you even said as how you wouldn't sting me? Scorpion says, sure I did, but I never said I weren't a scorpion now, did I?' He drank. 'Guess you can't change your nature, when it come to it.'

'I get it.' I looked over at him. 'But you sure which one of us is the frog?' He chuckled, then his face cracked into a smile. I turned the pancake onto a plate and walked over to the refrigerator. There wasn't much inside, but there was some butter on a dish.

'You got any syrup, Red?'

'Not sure.' He picked up his fork.

'That's okay.' I went back to the counter and rolled down the grocery bag, revealing six plastic bottles. 'I bought my own.'

Standing between the trucks, standing over Red's prostrate body, I licked my finger. It was sweet as anything.

'You can stop being dead now,' I said.

Red rolled onto his side and grinned up at me. 'Hell, I'm all over molasses and grit. Daddy always said I was headed for a tar n' feather.'

'You better move, before the ants get wind of you.' I held out my hand and helped drag him to his feet. I saw the gun next to Lisa's spilled pocket book and went to retrieve it, but Red didn't let go of my hand.

'You sure?' he said. His t-shirt was stained, a great bloom of crimson dyed syrup soaked into the cloth. The air around us smelt like cotton candy and gasoline, just like a fairground. I could almost hear the music, the sound of flying horses, broken ponies, going round and round, all fixed grins and gilded candy-cane poles.

I pulled my hand away, reached into my jeans pocket and took out the pages I'd torn from the notepad. 'This is a list of all the people I remember Margarita and Paris conned.' Red looked but didn't respond. He pulled the remains of the blood pack detonator from his pocket and kicked it out of sight. 'Take it,' I said. 'One of them's bound to press charges.'

'That ain't what I meant,' he said.

'Please,' I said, and I held the list out to him. As his fingers closed around the papers, I put my other hand against the side of his face and I kissed him. He slipped his free arm round my waist and he kissed me too, his mouth hot and urgent as if we breathed through each other and might drown if parted. We clung together, suspended between this world and another, as the tick-tock of the universe slowed, as the horses came to a stop. I saw morning light spilling through the vines of the conservatory, with cool, grey tiles underfoot, its air still as a saucer of milk. I saw Carillon, and Red's smile thought the steam of morning coffee, and felt the finger curl of desire at the base of my spine. A big house, needing people to make it a home, needing better people than us. Our kiss tasted of sugar, and it made my teeth hurt.

'Stay,' Red said, as he held me, as I felt the sticky sweetness of his body seep into my clothes. I let my forehead rest against his cheek for a moment and closed my eyes. Then, I pulled away and looked at the mess I'd made of him.

'Oh Red, you said it yourself. I'm just a hog in high-tops.'

He winced, dragged his fingers through his hair and let his hand drop by his side. 'No you ain't, Margarita—' but the vision of Carillon faded. The water of the swamp flooded my mind and I tasted its salt black darkness again.

'That weren't nothing,' he said. 'That was just me being an asshole.' His fingers clashed against mine, then closed around my hand. I didn't stop him, but neither did I let his fingers relax into his. 'What you goin' back there for?'

'Red, it's not that, it's—'

'Well, what is it? Fuck me, I know we ain't normal or nothin', but tellin' me what you' going back to is better?'

'I'm not finished,' I told him. He frowned.

'Not finished? What the hell else d'you think you've got to do here?' I didn't answer, and saw the question building in his mind. 'What you not finished with? You don't mean to—' I pulled my hand away from his.

'This ain't real,' I said, and picked up Lisa's pocket book. 'This is just that old death and sex thing. You'll be all better with a shower and a good night's sleep.' He turned and struggled out of his jacket. Light flashed through the hole we'd shot in it earlier, a single eye watching me as he looked away.

'Don't do it,' he said.

'What, leave you?'

'Not that.'

I didn't answer. I walked away.

♂

Lisa flinched when I opened the car door. She was hunched down in her seat, clutching the water bottle under her chin. I had the keys ready in my hand, and fitted them into the ignition.

'I know you hate me—' she began, but I glared at her and snapped off her words with a look. It would be so easy, she was already dead after all so who would ever know? Hell, I wasn't even in the country, now was I? I let my gaze drop and as it did, I saw Mr Pooter where he lay in the glovebox. His little pearl buttons were bright against the blue of his velvet jacket and the light caught on the wet black bead of his eye as he regarded me steadily.

I flipped down the sun-shield and wiped the residue of red, the colour and the man, from my face. The taste in my mouth was one I remembered from childhood, sugar-spun and circus-sweet. I looked at Lisa hunched up in the passenger seat, waiting for me, trusting me even now, even after everything she'd done.

'I need a shower,' I said. I started the car and eased it from the parking lot. The rear-view showed me the front of the casino and, as we pulled away, Red. He stood between the trucks, shading his eyes with his hand, watching us go; a dark brush stroke against the hot shimmer of the asphalt. Tell me who you love, I thought, and I'll tell you who you are.

'There's something we gotta talk about,' I said. 'Face to face.'

'All right, Rita,' Lisa said. 'Whatever you want.'

I've always written and told stories, for as long as I can remember. My first self-published work at the age of seven, fully illustrated in felt pen and crayon. I continued with a series of insightful 'When I grow up I want to be an author' essays, and an attempt at a 'Bonk-buster' series of supernatural thrillers written from a position of utter ignorance on all topics, until I was distracted by Art college. A never ending, or never finished, fantasy epic kept me going through my twenties, but it was motherhood in my thirties which concentrated my mind enough to actually finish a novel. It's amazing what a bit of life experience and the sudden curtailing of your free time can do to concentrate the mind.

After that I began giving myself permission to take my writing seriously enough to spend time on it and listen to critiques. The writing festival in York proved invaluable, and time and disappointment got me to the point of producing something readable, which I was lucky enough to have read by Urbane Publications.

If you make or write anything, the number one question you get asked is 'where do you get your ideas from?' In answer to that question, it's an easy process which combines working on your craft every hour you can for as long as possible – hard graft – reading as much as you can of everyone else's work – stealing – and inspiration, which is just one of those things that just happens. The inspiration for 'Nemesister' comes from a dark episode of family history, and a moment from a dream; an image of a man standing in the doorway of what I knew was an abandoned shack, which was gone as soon as it came and yet lingered, the way some dreams do.

Urbane Publications is dedicated to
developing new author voices, and publishing
fiction and non-fiction that challenges, thrills and
fascinates.

From page-turning novels to innovative
reference books, our goal is to publish what
YOU want to read.

Find out more at
urbanepublications.com